THE DRAGONLORD'S HEIR

Alicia,
Happy reading!
Enjoy the book 😊
Sincerely,

THE ASCALON TRILOGY

BOOK ONE

THE DRAGONLORD'S HEIR

CHRISTINA KENWAY

• ENDLESS PAGE PUBLISHING •

CALIFORNIA

Copyright ©2014

Cover art designed by Corby Cupp

All rights reserved. Published by Endless Page Publishing. No part of this book may be reproduced or transmitted in any form or by any means, electronic or mechanical, including photocopying, recording, or by any information storage and retrieval system, without written permission from the publisher or author.

First paperback edition, 2014

Printed in the United States of America

ISBN 978-0-9914444-0-3 (pbk.)

*For you, my dear reader,
because you gave me the opportunity
to share my dream with you.*

CONTENTS

CHAPTER ONE
Thirteenth Birthday Surprise / 1

CHAPTER TWO
The Truth about William Lockwood / 15

CHAPTER THREE
The Scene at the Diner / 29

CHAPTER FOUR
The Second Nightmare / 44

CHAPTER FIVE
Grave Robbers / 58

CHAPTER SIX
The Second Trial / 84

CHAPTER SEVEN
Emma Kingsley / 100

CHAPTER EIGHT
Fire! / 125

CHAPTER NINE
The Final Piece / 140

CHAPTER TEN
Family Ties / 166

CHAPTER ELEVEN
Reunion / 186

CHAPTER TWELVE
The Awakening / 200

CHAPTER THIRTEEN
The Wolf Makes a Deal / 227

CHAPTER FOURTEEN
Cain's Last Proposition / 256

CHAPTER FIFTEEN
The Dragonlord's Bane / 273

CHAPTER SIXTEEN
The Vision / 289

CHAPTER SEVENTEEN
Saying Goodbye / 292

Dear Reader,

I used to think I was a normal kid, perhaps just like you. But boy, was I wrong. Very, very wrong.

You know those medieval stories about dragons attacking the villagers, and the brave, heroic knight in shining armor slaying the beast? Well, those stories are anything but fictional. In fact, I am part of those stories.

I just didn't know it until several nights ago.

I suppose that upon hearing this, I should have been excited, or at the very least, impressed with myself. After all, I'm a modern-day dragon slayer. If there were girls chasing after me, they'd be lined up around the block for days just to meet me.

Unfortunately, though, there are no girls chasing after me, and there are no perks of being a dragon slayer. I've spent the past few days avoiding being kidnapped or shot to death. I've been knocked unconscious more times than I care to acknowledge, and I didn't meet my father for the first time until a couple days ago.

Oh, yeah. And a madman named Cain Hunter wants me dead so he can resurrect a legendary dragon named Bolla.

You know, I always imagined that turning thirteen would be the time of my life. But this is the farthest thing from it.

You should be thankful that you are in your nice warm bed, or in a quiet library, or sitting in your English class reading this letter. Be thankful that you're nothing like me.

As the Order has taught me, being the Dragonlord is a duty that I cannot escape. Being the Dragonlord runs in my blood, as it did with my father, and his father before him. Be thankful that you are free of this burden.

You might have read those tales of dragons and dragon slayers and thought nothing of them. You might not even believe that dragons exist, that they're just part of a fairy tale told for the sake of entertaining children.

Well, after you hear my story, you'll change your mind.

The myths are real. Dragons do exist. In fact, I've fought one.

And now that I've survived the ordeal, I'm going to tell you all about it.

Sincerely,

Logan Lockwood

CHAPTER ONE

THIRTEENTH BIRTHDAY SURPRISE

BANG!

I bolted upright in my seat with a cry of, "DRAGONS!" I expected to find the big black beast with its fiery red eyes standing before me, ready to swallow me whole.

Instead, I found my math teacher, Mr. Blake, standing beside my desk with an amused smirk. All around me, the class was laughing.

"Are you awake now, Logan?" he asked in a rather condescending tone.

As my heart rate slowed down, my eyes went to the corner of my desk where a massive textbook sat. Being the jerk he was, Mr. Blake had awakened me from my terrible nap by dropping the enormous paper weight next to me.

He *could* have just shaken me awake, but that wasn't his style—and neither was allowing me to remain in class after my misbehavior, which he happily pointed out as he returned to the front of the classroom. "Since you find my lecture on algebraic expressions to be so boring," he said, "I thought it would be best for you to finish out this period in Mr. Smith's office."

My stomach sank. "Mr. Blake," I said, "I'm sorry. I didn't mean to—"

"It's too late for apologies, Logan. I've already written you up." He bent over his desk, ripped out a sheet of paper from his notepad, and offered it to me. The students around me snickered, eliciting a sharp warning from our teacher. "If you think it's so funny," he said to them, "perhaps you'd like to join Logan?"

The room fell silent immediately.

My hands shook as I collected my Batman binder and backpack. I rose to my feet and made the walk of shame down the aisles of desks and towards Mr. Blake. Then, I took the condemning piece of paper from his hands as a triumphant smile crossed his lips. "I'll see you next week," he said. "Enjoy the rest of fourth period."

Muffled chuckles broke out from some of the students in the back corner, but when Mr. Blake dramatically cleared his throat to get their attention, they fell silent. We didn't call him Commander Blake for no reason—he was notorious for putting even the smallest of crimes to justice.

Being one of the good kids, I had never ended up in the principal's office—ever. But for the first time (and on my birthday, of all days), I would have to battle my way through Mr. Smith's traumatizing interrogation.

I drew in a deep breath and headed towards the door. I could feel Mr. Blake's eyes following me until I left the classroom, and even after that. He could probably see through walls like a super-villain with x-ray vision.

Now, let me tell you what happened before Commander Blake has you thinking I'm some kind of delinquent. The night before, I didn't sleep very well—I'd spent the better part of the night dreaming the same strange, horrific nightmare that resurfaced every time I managed to fall asleep. So, as a result, I ended up going to school on little more than five hours of rest. I'm sure you can imagine how difficult it was to stay awake, especially during a boring math lecture.

To make matters worse, that same dream came back to me even during my nap in class. In my dream, a dragon was chasing me and a human shadow was holding a golden spear in his hand. As luck would often have it, no matter how fast or how far I ran, I could never seem to get away. The shadow man controlled the dragon, and for some reason, he had it out for me.

So, what's the usual way for a nightmare to end? Well, with near-death, of course.

Just before awakening, the dragon breathed a hot funnel of fire my way. The shadow man laughed—like my downfall brought him ultimate pleasure—and I was left on the ground, helpless and awaiting my inevitable death.

I probably would've slept right through it—you know, if the commander hadn't dropped the math book right next to my head.

But as much as I despised the man, I was thankful he had awakened me. Who knows what would've happened if he hadn't? The dream had felt so real, I wouldn't have been surprised if the dragon had actually killed me.

I stopped outside of the door labeled with the title of "Principal" across it. I drew in a deep breath, counted to three, and opened the door.

Mr. Smith was a short and stout older man with thinning hair, wire-framed glasses, and a potbelly. To be honest, he was nowhere near as scary as Commander Blake, but that didn't mean my heart wasn't thundering in my chest as I walked through the door. "You must be Logan," he said, "and this must be your first time in here. You look sick to your stomach."

I remained standing in the doorway, forcing my hands into the pockets of my sweater so he couldn't see me shaking. "I'm sorry, sir." I didn't know what else to say.

He gestured at the empty chair across from his desk. "Have a seat."

As I pulled up the chair, he removed a small pink notepad from inside his desk drawer and took the note from me that Mr. Blake had written. "So, Mr. Blake told me you fell asleep in class."

I nodded. "That's right, sir."

"Do you have anything to say for yourself?"

I wanted to say, "Commander Blake is a jerk, that's what I have to say for myself." But instead I responded with, "I didn't sleep very well last night—that's all."

He raised an eyebrow. "Do you think this excuse justifies your behavior?"

I hated when adults turned the question around like that. There was no way I could defend myself. "N-No, sir," I replied.

"You and I both know how Mr. Blake runs his class," he went on. "I would think you would've been more careful about misbehaving around him."

"It's not like I meant to, sir."

Mr. Smith sighed. "I should probably keep you in here for another grueling ten minutes, but I've got better things to do than harp on a sleepy thirteen-year-old—especially a first-timer like you."

I straightened up. "So, I'm *not* in trouble?"

"Oh, you're in trouble," he replied. "Mr. Blake would like me to give you a week of lunch detention—I'm only going to give you three days."

Either way was fine by me. It was better than sitting in the cafeteria with Brandon and Stephen, listening to them compare their mages on whatever new video game they'd started playing. Sure, they were nice kids, but at least in detention, I could get my homework done and read my comic books.

Mr. Smith retrieved a pen with his pudgy fingers and scribbled across the brown lines of his pink notepad. "You're in seventh grade, right, Logan?" he asked without looking up at me. "It's always a surprise when a fresh face comes in towards the middle or end of the year. You must be one of the good ones if you've lasted this long."

"Thank you, sir." I said it because nothing else would really be better.

"That being said," he continued, "I suggest you watch yourself. Today is a warning—next time, you'll find yourself a little deeper in trouble." He tore the pink detention slip from his notepad and extended it towards me.

"I will, sir. I promise it won't happen again." I braced myself to run.

He leaned back in his chair and waved a hand at me. "You're excused," he said. "Enjoy the rest of your day. And *stay awake.*"

I rose from the seat and practically ran out of his office. As soon as I was in the hall with the door closed behind me, I released one big, relieved sigh.

Students emerged from classrooms all around me as the bell rang, casually making their way towards the cafeteria or the picnic tables outside. I was the only student moving into the oncoming wave of hungry kids, heading down the hall towards the Responsibility Center.

Once my lunch detention passed, all I had to do was survive two more classes. Then, I would be home-free. There really was nothing better than having your birthday on a Friday—I would be free for two long, amazing days, eating nothing but cake and pizza, and playing video games nonstop.

But, before any of that could happen, I had to survive the festivities at home first.

I made my way down the hallway, past the lockers on my left and the tall, stretching glass windows on my right. I stopped walking, however, when I spotted the man parked in front of the school, staring my way.

His eyes searched back and forth in the direction of the school, as if he was looking for someone. Then, his gaze landed on me, and he stopped searching. A tiny smile crept over his face.

My heart skipped a beat as I watched satisfaction flood his features.

Then, he turned away, climbed into his car, and drove off.

A small, hopeful thought arose in my mind: *Could it be him?* But I doubted the father I'd never met would be so sketchy—something told me this man was not my estranged parent.

Whoever he was, though, he had left. So, I continued on the path towards detention, pushing the image of his face to the back of my mind, and hoping that it hadn't meant anything.

"HAPPY BIRTHDAY!"

My mother's screaming startled me as I opened the front door to our house, but I forced myself to smile anyway.

My mother was always more excited about my birthday than I was. I tried not to be bitter, but birthdays and holidays were the times during the year when I wanted to fall into a deep, uninterrupted sleep. Every event was celebrated by me and my mother alone. No grandparents, no siblings, and certainly no father.

You see, my mother's family lived on the other side of the country in Pennsylvania. For whatever reason, my mother had moved to the west coast in her early twenties, which was when she supposedly met my father. I didn't know much about their relationship—she never spoke more than two sentences at a time about him, and she hated when I brought up the subject.

Unlike my mother, though, I didn't even know what the man looked like. He was a ghost to me, and I feared he always would be.

I didn't know why they split up—I only knew that it had happened shortly before I was born. My mother dismissed the subject in the same way she would if someone brought up work or politics at the dinner table. I tried not to get angry about it—she had her reasons, whatever they were—but I deserved to know the truth about myself and where I'd come from.

In spite of every birthday and holiday beginning and ending with just the two of us, she always went through great trouble to make things as enjoyable as possible. When I came home, I found the dining room flooded in birthday decorations. Our small table was draped with a bright red tablecloth and doused in birthday confetti. Streamers hung along the ceiling, stretching from the entryway through the dining room, and meeting at both ends of a banner that read, "HAPPY 13TH BIRTHDAY!"

My mother hovered over the table, which had been arranged with one of those massive pop-up birthday cards and a shoebox-sized gift wrapped in shiny green paper, topped with an enormous golden bow. She gestured excitedly at the birthday spread. "What do you think?"

I smiled at her. "It looks awesome, Mom."

She yanked a chair out from under the table and ushered me into the seat. Then, she hustled towards the oven and removed my traditional homemade birthday cake: chocolate with chocolate frosting, cut into the most perfect circle you've ever seen. Neatly scrawled on top in white frosting were the words, "Happy 13th Birthday, Logan!" but the thirteen red candles planted across the chocolate-y surface obscured most of the lettering.

I knew they were trick candles—like they were every year—but I pretended otherwise. My mother had to know I hadn't forgotten.

She placed the cake in the center of the table and lit each of the candles. Then, she dimmed the lights and stepped back, eagerly clasping her hands together and eyeing me with a gleaming smile. "Go on!" she said. "Make a wish!"

I dropped my backpack to the floor and stared down at the cake. Then, I drew in a deep breath and closed my eyes, grinning mostly to appease my mother.

I made the same hopeless and half-hearted wish I'd made since I was a child: *I wish to meet my father.* Then, I blew a deep breath across the flickering flames and opened my eyes.

The flames were still there, just as I had predicted.

"Trick candles, Mom?" I asked, forcing a chuckle. "I think I'm a little too old for that now."

My mother laughed and picked a handful of candles out of the cake, moving towards the sink to extinguish the flames under running water. "You're never too old for trick candles," she returned.

Yes, I am, I thought, but I would never say so.

After all, I *had* just turned thirteen. I was officially a man—well, almost. In just three years, I could get my driver's license and go out cruising the streets (in my mother's car, since I definitely wouldn't have one by then). And two years after that, I could vote in the presidential election, or buy lottery tickets. I could even serve jury duty—not that I *wanted* to. But knowing it was possible made me feel that much older.

The real problem was convincing my mother that I wasn't a kid anymore. Unfortunately, she would still see me as her little boy and nothing more. When I turned fourteen, fifteen, and even beyond that, she'd still make me a chocolate cake with trick candles.

My mother returned to the table with two small plates and a serving knife. She sliced two wide pieces so large that nearly half of the cake disappeared. Then, she placed a slice before me and offered me a fork with a smile.

I took the fork from her. "Whoa, Mom," I said. "Dessert before dinner? Are you sure you want to break your own rules?"

She shrugged and seated herself opposite to me at the table, scooping a bite of the chocolate cake into her mouth. "It's not every day you turn thirteen."

I grinned. *This* was a first-time occurrence. And it was a nice one, at that. I shoved a fork-full of chocolate cake into my mouth and ate it before it could disappear.

"So, how was school?" my mother asked, watching as I inhaled my food.

I slowly stopped eating and stared down at the table. "It was…" I couldn't lie to my mother, but I also couldn't bring myself to admit that I'd gotten a week of detention, *and* on my birthday.

She lowered the fork in her hand and frowned at me. "That doesn't sound good."

I sighed and started poking at my cake. "Don't be mad, but I, uh...I got detention."

She rolled her eyes. "Logan, what happened?"

"It's not like I did it on purpose. I just kind of fell asleep in math class."

"You *fell asleep*?" she asked, raising an eyebrow.

"Last night was rough," I said, shrugging. "I kept having nightmares."

I thought maybe she'd tell me to get over it and get my act together, but she seemed interested—and a little worried, which concerned me.

"What kind of nightmares?" she asked.

I told her all about the shadow man, the golden spear, and the dragon. Again, I expected her to scold me for my behavior—or lack thereof—but when I finished, she seemed even more troubled.

I watched her try to keep her cool, but clearly something was bothering her. "What is it, Mom?" I asked. "You aren't mad."

She managed a grin. "Do you want me to be mad?"

"I'd rather you be mad than scared, like you seem to be."

She put her fork down and drew in a deep breath. Several moments passed before she met my gaze. "I'm not mad, Logan," she said. "And I'm not scared. But I *am* concerned. There's…there's something we need to talk about."

I frowned and my stomach turned. "Am I grounded?"

She shook her head. "It's not like that. It's something entirely different."

She remained silent for quite a while before summoning another deep, preparatory breath. With each second that passed, I became more and more nervous. "We need to talk," she said, "about your father."

My stomach did a flip. I wasn't sure if I was nervous or excited, but either way, I remained silent and waited patiently. I'd been waiting for this moment for years, and I wouldn't risk losing it by saying the wrong thing at the wrong time.

"You've been asking about him since you were a child," she continued, "as is natural for someone who grew up without a parent. But there is so much that I don't know how to explain, and for good reason, I waited until today to tell you. And for *other* reasons, too."

I still didn't say anything.

"I should have told you about this day years ago," she said, "but it wouldn't have been appropriate. It would have been too much for you to handle. I made a promise to your father to explain it on your thirteenth birthday, when you were old enough to understand and old enough to handle it."

"To explain *what* to me?" I asked in a small voice.

She looked up at me with heavy eyes and her mouth set in a firm line. "You're the Dragonlord, Logan."

I could only stare at her. She was talking like a crazy person. Just what in the heck was a Dragonlord, and why was she calling *me* that?

"What is a...*Dragonlord*?" I asked.

She sighed for the umpteenth time and rose from the table, collecting both of our plates. I would have protested—my slice of cake wasn't even halfway gone—but my nerves were racing and my stomach was turning. She dumped the leftovers into the trash and rinsed off the plates and utensils. When she was done, she turned and faced me.

"Mom," I said, "you're freaking me out."

She paced her way towards the table, deep in thought. "Logan, your father isn't a...*normal*...person."

"What do you mean?"

She opened her mouth to speak just as the doorbell rang, interrupting our conversation like all great inconveniences did.

My mother and I exchanged inquisitive glances before she headed towards the front hall. She peered through the peep-hole for a moment before a gasp escaped her mouth. Stepping back, she covered her mouth with her hand, her eyes wide with fright.

"Mom, what's—?"

"Shh," she hushed me, pushing me away from the door. "Go into the other room."

"Why? What's going on?"

"Just do as I say."

I started to back away, but my curiosity got the better of me, and I lingered behind to see just what had irked my mother so much. She muttered curses under her breath and paced the foyer, lost in thought. I had never seen her so unsettled.

Finally, she stopped moving and shook her head to clear her mind. She drew in a deep breath and faced the door as the bell chimed once more. "I'm coming," she called irritably. I pulled myself into the hallway, peeking around the corner to watch the scene unfold.

My mother rested her hand on the knob, hesitated for just a moment, and opened the door. Our guest was not the mailman dropping off a package or a junior high kid selling chocolate bars to raise money for a school trip. My heart skipped a beat when I recognized the stranger standing on our porch: he was the man whom I had seen outside my school watching me.

"You," I said, stepping into the entryway.

My mother wheeled on her foot. "Logan, I told you to—"

"This guy was at my school today," I said, stepping protectively to my mother's side.

She jerked her head towards him. "*What?*"

His gaze drifted between me and my mother before he chuckled and shook his head. "What a way to greet each other after thirteen years," he said. "Let's start over."

Taking a step towards our doorway, he dipped his head in greeting towards my mother, who had gone still as a statue. "Good evening, Laura. I'm here for your son."

CHAPTER TWO

THE TRUTH ABOUT WILLIAM LOCKWOOD

My mother remained frozen in the doorway, her entranced gaze fixed upon the stranger. It was as if she hadn't heard anything he'd just said. "Marcus," she breathed. "What are you *doing* here?"

He approached us and his eyes immediately fell upon me, looking me over and cutting me down to size. My hands became sweaty, and I no longer felt comfortable. I wanted to leave. I wanted to say something. I wanted to do *anything* to divert this guy's attention.

Finally, he met my eyes and grinned. "So, you must be Logan," he said, extending a gloved hand. "My name is Wolf."

I reached forward and shook his hand. "Nice to meet you…I think."

He grinned again, and dimples formed in the sides of his cheeks. I guessed that he was somewhere in his late thirties, but he looked pretty good for his age. He removed his gloves and shoved them into the pocket of his blazer. Then, he ran a hand through his hair, which was an attractive dark gray color that, as my mother might say, made him look like he would continue to age well.

There was something about his eyes, though, that made me anxious. It was the shifty way they surveyed me, as if searching for some kind of secret about me that even I didn't know. It made the hair on the back of my neck stand on edge.

"You didn't answer my question," my mother said, looking him in the eye.

He turned his attention towards her and grinned. "Do you mind letting me inside so I can explain? It might take a while."

She glared at him before stepped aside and allowing him to enter. The stranger stepped into the warmth of our house, his eyes darting in every direction like he was looking for something.

"Marcus," my mother began, facing him, "I didn't think…well, I didn't know—" She shook her head to clear her mind. Then, she cried, "What are you doing here?"

"I don't expect that you're happy to see me," he said. "I wish I could've warned you that I was coming, but"—his suspicious gaze fell over me once more, and my mother seemed to understand something that wasn't obvious to me—"I think you can understand why I didn't."

When neither my mother nor the man spoke after several long moments, I couldn't take it anymore. "So, your name is Wolf?" I blurted out. "That's a weird name."

"It's a nickname, kid," he said, chuckling. "My real name is Marcus, Marcus Wilson. I'm a friend of your father's."

I blinked several times before staggering backwards into a nearby chair. My mother, of course, was at my side in an instant, ready to catch me in the unlikely event that I passed out from shock.

"You all right, kid?" Wolf asked, standing over me. "You look a little sick."

"I-I'm fine," I insisted. "You said you know my father?"

"I work with him," Wolf replied. "I've known him all my life."

My mother rose to full height. "Marcus, please. He doesn't know yet. I haven't had the chance to tell him."

Wolf stared her down with firm, cold eyes. "You know that it can't be kept a secret any longer, Laura."

She shook her head as her face paled. "I just don't understand," she breathed. "How did you…I mean, *when* did you—?"

"When did I find out that you and William Lockwood had a child together?" he asked dryly. "Only a couple days ago." He shoved a hand into his blazer and removed a folded slip of paper, extending it towards my mother. "William left a letter for the Order so that we would know where to find his kid."

She snatched it from his hands and turned away from him, her eyes skimming over the page. I heard her muttering the words aloud to herself, but I was only able to catch snippets of information like, "in terrible trouble," "must inform the Order," and, "leave Logan in their care."

She lowered the letter in her hands and faced Wolf again with sorrow in her eyes. "I must admit," he continued, "it was quite a risky little trick you two tried to pull against the Order. Julianna is upset, to say the least."

My mother glared at him, all traces of sadness gone. "We don't owe you an explanation, Marcus," she said. "We don't owe the Order, or even Julianna, an explanation. I think you can understand why."

Wolf glanced at me once more, his eyes darting up and down. "Yes, I think I can." He returned his gaze to my mother. "Nonetheless, it's no excuse."

Finally, I said, "Is anyone going to tell me what's going on? What is this all about?"

"This is about who your father is," Wolf replied, "and about who you are." He glanced up at my mother, daring her to protest as he divulged information to me, but she only continued to glare at him. He drew in a deep breath and met my eyes once more. "Your father has been captured."

I looked up at my mother, whose hardened expression had finally melted to one of utter shock. "What are you saying?" she asked.

"Captured by who?" I added.

"By a man named Cain Hunter," Wolf replied. "The Order has been searching for him for the past thirteen years."

My head bobbled between my mother and Wolf. "The Order? What is that?"

Wolf glanced at my mother. "It might be a better idea if we talked about this elsewhere."

"No," my mother said. "It's not your place to tell him."

"Please, Laura," Wolf begged. "You've had thirteen years to tell the kid! It's your own fault that it's happening this way."

"I made a promise to William to tell him on his thirteenth birthday, which is *today*. But thanks to you, now I—"

"Thanks to *me*? Had you and William informed the Order of the next Dragonlord *thirteen years ago*, we would have been able to protect him. Because of your poor choices—"

My mother waved a hand to silence him. "Had we informed the Order, Cain would have pursued him, and you know it." Her blue eyes sizzled with passionate rage, daring Wolf to accuse her again. "As I said before, we didn't owe anyone an explanation."

My blood was boiling, and I could not wait another second. "WILL SOMEONE PLEASE TELL ME WHAT IS GOING ON?!"

Thankfully, my shouting distracted them—they both looked away from each other and turned their attention towards me. "Let's have a talk, Logan," Wolf said.

"No," my mother denied. "I will tell him. You can wait here."

Wolf sighed, clearly displeased with the verdict. "Fine. You've got ten minutes."

She glared at Wolf one last time, then faced me and forced a sympathetic smile. "Let's go upstairs and talk, honey."

I rose to my feet and followed my mother to the second floor. Wolf's gaze lingered over me until I disappeared up the stairs and out of sight. I shuddered with relief as soon as I was out of his range of vision.

My mother opened the door to her room and

gestured for me to enter. I seated myself at the edge of her bed, watching as she sealed and locked the door behind her. She sat down at the computer chair next to the desk and clasped her hands together, staring at the white carpet with concerned eyes. Her dark brown hair hung in a curtain around her face, shielding me from the view of her dismay.

Finally, I asked, "Who exactly is that guy, Mom?"

She drew in a deep breath and looked up at me. "He works with your father, like he said."

"What kind of work do they do together?"

She stared past me at the wall, twisting her hands. "You're going to think I'm crazy," she said. She met my gaze once more. "I should have told you about your father a long time ago, but you have to understand that I kept him a secret for your own safety. The whole reason we had to leave each other in the first place was for your safety."

I scowled. "Stop avoiding my question."

She sighed and remained silent for several moments. "He works for a secret society," she said, "called the Order of Ascalon."

A burst of laughter escaped me. "I know you're trying to let me down easily, but you don't have to lie."

"Didn't I tell you that you'd think I was crazy?" she said. "It's true, Logan. He has served the Order since he was a child. He was born into it, as was his father before him. You remember your grandfather, Silas, don't you?"

"No, I don't," I responded. "You're as secretive about my father's family as you are about my father himself."

"There are reasons for that, Logan," she returned heatedly. "I know you're upset with me, but you don't need to be rude."

I sighed and stared down at the floor. "Yes, ma'am."

After shooting me one of those unpleasant looks of warning that only a mother can give, she continued. "Your grandfather was involved in the Order's affairs, too."

I decided to suspend disbelief for just a second. "All right. Let's say I believe you. This Order thing—what do they do?"

My mother glanced at the door. "They protect the Dragonlord."

I raised my eyebrows. "There's that 'Dragonlord' word again. What does it mean?"

"He is the person responsible for keeping the great dragons of legend entombed, so that they can never rise again."

"Like a dragon slayer?"

"Something like that." She drew in a silent breath and slowly rose to her feet, locking eyes with me. "*You* are the Dragonlord, Logan."

I blinked. "What?" She had already told me once, but it hadn't fully hit me until that moment—until I actually knew what a Dragonlord was. It had taken Wolf's arrival and the truth about my father to confirm its importance.

She sighed and paced the floor in a small circle. "If I had told you the truth when you were younger, you wouldn't have been able to handle it," she said. "That's why your father and I decided to wait until you were thirteen to tell you. It's not something to be taken lightly, and we couldn't chance you letting the truth slip to anyone. We wanted you to have a normal life."

I shook my head, feeling rather dizzy. "I-I don't understand. This can't be true. This has to be a joke."

"I wish it was," she muttered.

I stared at her, waiting for her to burst out laughing and tell me this was all part of a terrible birthday prank. There stood my mother, the most grounded, reasonable, and clear-headed person I'd ever known, and she was calling me a "Dragonlord." And the worst part was that she seemed totally serious about it.

Her face had gone completely pale, as if the stomach flu had unexpectedly overtaken her. Since I had told her about my dream, her winter blue eyes had begun to shine with edgy, suspicious panic, like she expected the house might burst into flames at any moment. Along with Wolf's arrival had come a past that she thought she would never have to face again: my father himself.

"Me," I breathed, jumping to my feet. "What are you *talking* about? This is ridiculous!"

"It's true, Logan," she replied miserably. "The Dragonlord's powers are passed onto him upon his thirteenth birthday, handed down from his parent before him. Your father *was* the Dragonlord before you, but as of today, you are the new Dragonlord. That's probably why you're having that strange nightmare—it must be some sort of sign." She made a frustrated sound, like she was angry with herself. "Your father could explain it much better than I can. He'd have all the answers you need."

I shook my head. "No. This is absolutely ridiculous. This kind of stuff only happens in books and movies."

My mother placed firm hands on my shoulders. "Honey, please. I know this is a big pill to swallow, but I need you to be strong."

I shook myself out of her grasp. "After *that* nonsense, I'm supposed to be strong?"

She covered her face and muttered into her hands. "This is why I waited so long to tell you. If you can't handle it now, there's no way you could've handled it before." She uncovered her face and exhaled. "You want to know about your father, right?"

I stared at her for a long, silent moment, trying to decide if this woman was still my mother or some kind of space alien who had taken over her body when my back had been turned. Finally, I said, "Yes."

My mother paced the room, staring down at the floor as she spoke. "A little over thirteen years ago," she began, "we found out that I was pregnant with you. Naturally, we would have told the Order about this, and they would have protected you when the time came. But a man named Cain Hunter was set on destroying your father. In order to protect you, your father and I had to part ways.

"To prevent Cain from finding out that William's identity as the Dragonlord would cease to exist on your thirteenth birthday—to prevent him from finding out about *you*—I left. To this day, Cain still believes that William is the Dragonlord, and that he has no heir to succeed him."

She spoke the words quickly, as if from memory. As if they were part of a speech she'd written thirteen years ago and had barely gotten around to delivering.

My head was spinning. This *couldn't* be true. Dragons were myths, were made-up stories from medieval times and even before that. And dragon slayers were equally fictional. This story couldn't be true. There was no way in this world or the next that it was.

But in spite of such thoughts, a tugging in my gut told me that all of it was true, and I needed to know more. "If he still thinks my father is the Dragonlord," I said, "then what is Wolf doing here?"

"If your father truly has been taken by Cain Hunter," my mother replied, "then the Order must make sure you're under an extremely watchful eye. They'll want you within their reach." She swallowed and averted her eyes. "Marcus is here to take you with him."

"You want me to go with *that* guy?"

"I don't *want* you to go anywhere," she replied. "But this is the Order's job. They must protect the Dragonlord, and your life depends on them." She closed her eyes and dropped her head in shame. "I'm afraid Marcus is right: your father and I should have told the Order as soon as we found out that I was pregnant with you. They could have protected you, and we could have avoided this entire mess."

My stomach turned with guilt in spite of my anger, and I immediately felt sorry for being so hard on my mother. "Don't believe that guy, Mom," I said. "You did what you thought was right. You did it for me."

She lifted her head and smiled at me as tears ran down her cheeks. She ran a hand through my messy brown hair and looked me over, memorizing my face and features. How long would I be away from her?

"I made my peace with your father when we left each other," she said. "We both knew it had to happen. But I can't make my peace with this. You're still my son, after all."

Then, she pulled me into her and embraced me, softly crying as she held me in a tight, warm hug. I was almost the same height as her, but it made no difference. I returned the embrace and closed my eyes. No matter how upset I was with her for hiding such a life-changing secret from me, I could not imagine being without her. I had spent every second of my life with her, and now, I would have to leave her.

A gentle rapping on the door interrupted our moment. My mother sighed irritably and unlocked the door to find Wolf hovering in the hallway with an impatient look across his face. "I hate to rush this," he said (although I suspected he didn't mean it), "but every second Logan spends here puts him one step closer to being tracked down by Cain. We need to get going."

My mother narrowed her eyes. "As far as

Cain knows, he doesn't exist."

"Yes, well, let's not risk that by wasting time." He smirked at her. Clearly, there was some bad blood between the two of them that went beyond my parents' secrets.

My mother glared at him before facing me and forcing a smile in spite of her wet eyes. She drew in a deep breath, moistened her lips, and placed a gentle hand on my shoulder. "You should get your things together. You'll be gone for...several days." She choked on the last two words.

"You mean, you don't know how long I'll be gone?" I asked.

"You will be gone as long as it takes for us to track down Cain and lock him up," Wolf said. "It could be days. It could be weeks."

I nodded, staring down at the floor. I heard my mother and Wolf talking, but I could not make out the words. Everything seemed distant and drowned out.

I dragged myself down the hallway and into my room. I watched my hands retrieve various articles of clothing and shove them into a duffel bag and my school backpack. I felt the cold spring breeze drift across my room from the open window and bite the back of my neck. Amidst all of the small movements and distractions, I was terrified. I was worried. I was angry. I was too numb to actually *feel* anything going on around me.

It wasn't until after I'd zipped the duffel bag shut and slung it over my shoulder along with my backpack that I realized I wouldn't see my room again for a while. I surveyed the mess, miserably remembering that I had never gotten around to playing my new video game or even making my bed.

My mother entered my room, clutching a small white envelope in her hands. She opened her mouth to speak, but no words came out. With a defeated sigh, she extended the envelope towards me.

I took it from her hands and removed an old, wrinkled photograph of a young man and woman. The woman had long, dark hair and smiling sky blue eyes, but she looked nothing like my mother. If my mother had had a daughter, this was her. My mother's younger self must've been somewhere around eighteen or nineteen years old in the photograph.

My mother's arm was wrapped around a young man with short, dark hair and a relaxed grin. He smiled back at the camera, matching the genuine happiness that my mother exhibited. He looked exactly like me, from his dark hair to his sapphire eyes. The only difference was the facial hair.

The people in the photograph were my parents, but they were as foreign to me as Wolf. I'd lived with my mother my entire life, had shadowed her footsteps as a child and had made her my best friend as I grew up. But I realized that I didn't actually *know* her. The life she had led with my father was an entirely different life altogether. It was a life that I did not feel like I belonged in.

"Are you giving this to me?" I asked.

My mother nodded. "That way you'll

recognize him when you see him."

    I stared down at the photo until I had memorized both my mother's and father's faces. Then, I pocketed the snapshot into the front pouch of my duffel. I rose to full height and drew in a deep breath, standing as tall as I could. I had to be strong for my mother if she couldn't be strong for herself. I had to be brave.

    She turned away towards the door and wiped at her face, but as soon as she did, her cheeks were wet again. "Wolf is waiting for you downstairs," she said. "I think it's time to go."

CHAPTER THREE

THE SCENE AT THE DINER

"You hungry, kid?" Wolf asked as we drove down Interstate 5 through Redding, California.

I stared out the window of Wolf's old red pick-up truck. My entire body bounced with every small bump that we drove over, and the engine sounded as if it would explode at any second. I pulled my duffel bag closer for warmth and turned up the collar of my coat. "I could eat," I said, shivering.

Truthfully, I was starved. I hadn't eaten since lunch, and we had been on the road for the past two hours. In my haste to leave with the wolf, I hadn't thought to bring any snacks, or even a bottle of water. My stomach grumbled as the image of a cheeseburger popped into my mind.

"Good," Wolf replied. "Because I can, too." He flicked on his blinker and pulled onto the nearest off-ramp. The road made a half-circle and dumped us onto an empty main street. It was only nine o'clock in the evening, but most of the small shops lining either side of the street seemed to have already closed for the night. One sign remained lit at the end of the street above a small diner called "Glenda's." Wolf pulled the truck into one of the empty spaces in front of the restaurant and parked.

I climbed out of the truck as fast as I could.

The air outside was colder than inside the vehicle, but even the dead silence around us was better than being stuck with Wolf. Since we had left my home in Ashland, we'd hardly exchanged three sentences of dialogue.

Unfortunately, when we entered the diner, it wasn't any livelier.

Wolf seated himself in one of the empty booths near the front window and waved down the waitress at the far end of the restaurant. She glanced up and nodded as she wiped down one of the tables, then headed towards us. I seated myself opposite to Wolf and pulled out two twenty-dollar bills that my mom had given me before leaving Ashland.

"Put that away," Wolf insisted, removing his wallet. "Dinner is on me."

"Are you sure?" I asked, feeling a bit embarrassed for some reason.

"I'm sure. Keep your money."

Guilt sank over me as I pocketed my cash. There the man was, protecting me with his life and even buying my dinner, and all I could think about was getting away from him—and how I half-suspected him to be in the mob.

The waitress appeared at the edge of our table in black slacks and a white button-up shirt. She whipped out a notepad from her apron and looked upon Wolf expectantly. He glanced at the menu for the briefest moment, folded it up, and said, "Cheeseburger, no onions. Seasoned fries. And I'll drink water." Then, he gestured at me.

I fumbled with the menu in my hands, trying to skim over all three pages in a quick instant. I would have taken my time, but since Wolf was paying, I closed the menu and said, "I'll have the same."

The waitress took the menus and smiled. "It'll be up in twenty minutes," she said. Then, she moved down the walkway, rounded the corner, and disappeared.

Wolf folded his hands together and peered across the table at me. He studied me once more in that creepy, suspicious way of his, and my skin tingled. I cleared my throat and folded my hands into my lap. "So, are you from around here?" I asked. What was I supposed to say to a wolf?

Wolf grinned, amused by my attempt at small talk. "No," he said. "I'm from Seattle."

"How long have you lived there?"

"About ten years," he replied.

"What do you do there?"

"I'm a criminal defense attorney. I own my own firm."

He definitely looked like a lawyer by the way he dressed, with his nice blazer and crimson-colored button down shirt. "Are you married?" I asked.

"I don't have time to be married."

"Any kids?"

"No kids," he answered. Then, he chuckled. "What's with the interrogation?"

I shrugged and sank into my seat, rather embarrassed. "Just thought I'd fill the air," I said. "So, you traveled eight hours from Seattle to get to Ashland?"

Wolf shrugged. "I've been on the road since

dawn. I had to reach you in time, didn't I?"

"Since dawn," I repeated. "So, that would mean that my father was taken…?"

"Yesterday," Wolf replied. "Well, some time in the night, actually. Between yesterday evening and dawn this morning. Julianna informed me of his disappearance and sent me out to find you immediately."

"Who is Julianna?"

"The head of the Order." He frowned. "How much did your mother tell you?"

"Not much," I said with a shrug. "Just a little about my father, and even less about the Dragonlord."

Wolf sighed. "For the tantrum she threw, I figured she would have told you more."

I glared at him. "Well, she was pressed for time. I suppose you'll have to catch me up."

Wolf seemed unperturbed by my comment. "I suppose I will." He glanced up as the waitress returned with our glasses of water. When she left and the coast was clear, he continued. "*You* are the Dragonlord, Logan. As of today, your father's powers were handed down to you."

"I still don't understand exactly what the Dragonlord is," I said.

Wolf drew in a deep breath. "Have you ever heard of Saint George of Lydda?"

I shook my head. "No."

"He was an officer in the Roman army some time between the Second and Third Centuries. Some hundreds of years before the Crusades took place, Saint George was said to have rescued an entire town from a dragon that had been living there. He used his lance, Ascalon, to slay the beast, and since then, word of his encounter with the dragon has traveled down through history." He leaned closer to me and glanced behind him, making sure no one was around. "What people don't know is *how* he was able to defeat the dragon. He possessed supernatural powers that allowed him to do so."

I frowned. "And where did *his* powers come from?"

"Therein lies the true mystery," he said with a grin. "See, long ago, Saint George erected a great, underground library somewhere in Israel—that's where Lydda is, before it became what is known today as the city of Lod—dedicated to everything he knew about himself, his powers, and the Dragonlords. Unfortunately for us"—he sighed sadly—"we have no knowledge of that library's whereabouts. It was lost some hundreds of years ago after it caved in on itself. A real shame, if you ask me. It's probably got some great secrets buried within it."

"No one has tried to find it?" I asked.

He shrugged helplessly. "We hardly know where to begin looking. It's a bit of a project, if you know what I mean."

I stroked my chin and stared down at the table, thinking. "So, Saint George is some great-great-great ancestor of mine?"

Wolf nodded. "*He* was the first Dragonlord. All of his descendants to follow him carried on his powers, slaying dragon after dragon throughout history."

"All of his descendants to follow him," I echoed. "I don't know much about dragons, or even about legendary dragon slayers. Care to elaborate?"

"*Beowulf*," he immediately replied. "Ever read it? It's an old epic poem. In the story, Beowulf slays a dragon. How much do you want to bet that the tale was inspired by actual events?"

I cracked an amused grin. "Go on."

"Haymo, the Austrian giant," he continued. "Lesser known than someone like Beowulf, but equally impressive. He cut off a dragon's tongue and brought it back to the village as proof of his slaying."

"And?" I persisted.

"Merlin, the great wizard. Although, he was a little more indirect with his methods. He released a pair of dragons living beneath a castle. Then, they turned around and fought each other to the death." He grinned at me. "Convinced yet?"

"And they all used Ascalon to slay the dragons?"

He scrunched his eyebrows and frowned. "We don't know that for sure. But we *can* confidently say that these tales are anything but mythical. After all, if there is some truth to Saint George's story, why couldn't there be some truth to the rest?" He paused, narrowing his eyes in thought. "Or maybe, there are more Dragonlords out there, descended from these other slayers. We've definitely considered it as a possibility, but we haven't found any leads to prove it true." He hesitated again, like the very idea had taken over his mind.

Then, he exhaled and turned his gaze upon me again. "Needless to say, these stories are anything but legends."

I sighed in defeat. I had no choice but to accept it, after all. "So, my father and I are descendants of Saint George, the first Dragonlord?"

Wolf nodded. "You carry the powers to slay the beast."

"Well, that would be interesting," I said, "if there were dragons to slay."

Wolf grinned at me. "So, you don't believe in dragons?"

I shrugged. "Have we seen any around here at all?"

"You have a point," Wolf said, nodding, "but that doesn't mean they don't exist. In fact, there have been a few incidents in the past couple centuries that the Order has managed to keep quiet. There hasn't been a dragon sighting in about 150 years, since the American Civil War."

I straightened up excitedly. "Do tell."

"Well, during the Civil War, infamous renegade militias went around murdering and pillaging anyone who was for the other side. During one particular incident, two villages were destroyed—*not* by renegades, but by a great dragon called Coca. From what I've been told, it took the Order quite a bit of effort to subdue Coca."

"Talk about scary," I muttered.

He shrugged. "Scary, maybe. But certainly incredible." I thought it strange that he said that, but I guess he had a point.

"So, back to my original point," he continued. "Like you said, if no one has actually *seen* a dragon, then why *wouldn't* they deny its existence? People think dragons were exaggerated tales of large serpents, or even crocodiles or winged dinosaurs, but this is just a twist on the truth. Dragons *do* exist, Logan. And it's *your* job as Dragonlord to make sure they remain entombed."

"Entombed where?" I asked.

"We know the tomb locations of some of the great dragons," Wolf said, "but not all of them. Since the power of the Dragonlord descends from Saint George, we have most to worry about on Saint George's Day: April 23rd. The power of the great dragons always seems to stir around that time, and that's when the Dragonlord's powers are most needed. It's also when he is the most powerful." He cracked a grin. "Invincible, in fact."

"Invincible?"

"To anything and everything except the great dragons. Believe me, we had some fun times testing *that* out."

I suppose that fact alone should have intrigued me, but it still felt like a great big joke.

I opened my mouth to speak, but the bell over the front door rang, signaling an entering guest and startling me. Both Wolf and I glanced up as a young girl entered, removing the furry hood of her thick green parka. She yanked the beanie off of her head and ran a hand through her messy blonde hair. Then, she seated herself at a booth in the back of the restaurant and unraveled her scarf. Even across the restaurant, I could see the pink in her cheeks from the cold outside.

She didn't look like she could have been any older than I was, but she had come into the restaurant alone, which was rather suspicious, especially since the waitress didn't seem to recognize her. If she wasn't a regular, then she must have come off the road from traveling. I glanced out the window, but no other cars had been parked. Had she traveled on foot?

The girl removed her jacket and settled into the corner of the booth. She lifted her head, searching every square-inch of the restaurant. Then, her gaze fell upon me, and my stomach dropped.

It wasn't the first time a girl had caught me staring open-mouthed at her. But it wasn't my fault that she was beautiful, either.

I instantly looked away and shifted in my seat, attempting to play off the awkward moment, but I could still feel her eyes lingering upon me.

"So, what does the Order want with *me*?" I asked, trying to resume the conversation.

Wolf's eyes darted across the restaurant to the blonde girl, and a small grin spread across his mouth. "To protect you from Cain, of course," he continued, sparing me the embarrassment of commenting on my sudden anxiety, "and to stop Cain from resurrecting Bolla."

I frowned. "Bolla?"

"One of the great dragons," Wolf replied. "Her body rests somewhere in southern California, and Cain has supposedly discovered it. If that's true, then killing you will be his first priority."

I shuddered. "What does he want with me?"

Wolf sighed irritably. "Have you not been listening? As the Dragonlord, *you* are the one responsible for protecting the tombs of the great dragons, and for preventing anyone from going near them."

"But how could he possibly know how to resurrect a dragon?"

Wolf sighed again and leaned back in his seat, staring down at the table. "We don't know," he said. "But he's been set on this for the past thirteen years, so he obviously thinks he knows a way. It's why he went after your father in the first place. If he still believes that William is the Dragonlord—why else would he have taken him?—then he is the only thing standing in Cain's way. Rather, *you* are the only thing standing in Cain's way. As long as the Dragonlord lives, the great dragons remain conquerable."

"But if the Dragonlord is gone," I said, "and if Cain can't control the dragon like he thinks he can, then who will stop him?"

Wolf narrowed his eyes at me and grinned, evidently pleased with my reasoning. "That's the exact reason why the Order—*and* the Dragonlord—must find him and stop him. We can't risk his recklessness."

Wolf glanced up as the waitress rounded the corner with our food. My stomach grumbled upon the sight of my meal. I dove into my cheeseburger as if I hadn't eaten in days.

My meal was halfway gone before I noticed that another guest had entered the diner. I would have paid no attention if it hadn't been for Wolf, who dropped his burger and stared across the restaurant with wide eyes. "What is it?" I asked through a mouthful of food.

"No time to finish dinner, kid," he said, rising to his feet. He yanked me out of the seat by my arm and plowed down the aisle towards the back of the restaurant.

"Hey!" I protested, but Wolf did not release his firm grip, and made no indication that he had even heard me. I glanced back for the briefest moment, wondering what had irked Wolf so, but all I saw was an older gentleman waiting near the counter at the front of the diner. He carried a folded newspaper in one hand and had his other hand tucked into the pocket of his slacks. With his thin, graying hair and wire-framed glasses, he looked as harmless as a father out for a cup of coffee at night. Apparently, though, Wolf was concerned.

"Where do you think you're going?" a woman demanded, and I slammed into Wolf's back as he halted. The waitress blocked the aisle with her hands on her hips and an angry glare in her eyes. "You have to pay for those meals, you know!"

I glanced backwards, hoping the pretty blonde girl in the back booth and the man hadn't noticed the scene, but the girl was no longer seated at the table. As for the man, he had taken interest in our dine-and-dash attempt, staring both of us down with beady, suspicious eyes.

The girl moved up the aisle towards the front of the restaurant with a Styrofoam cup in one hand and her head down. Perhaps she had also taken the opportunity to flee without paying for her drink while the waitress was preoccupied with Wolf. She suddenly collided with the man near the door, spilling the entire cup of hot coffee down the front of his shirt.

The girl gasped and the man cried out, leaping backwards. Both Wolf and the waitress turned their attention to the scene at the front of the restaurant.

The man stared down at his yellow-brown shirt with angry eyes. "I'm so sorry, sir!" the girl exclaimed. "I wasn't paying attention to where I was going, and I have to get home before my parents—"

The man forced an amused chuckle and dabbed the front of his shirt with his newspaper. "It's quite all right, young lady," he said, although he was clearly irritated. The girl continued to express her apologies, but the man paid her no attention. He glanced up in our direction, glaring at us as if it had been our fault.

Suddenly, Wolf shoved the waitress aside into the adjacent booth. She cried out, banging her elbow on the edge of the table. I stared on with horrified eyes, but in the next moment, Wolf was dragging me down the aisle again.

We hastened towards the back of the restaurant and into the kitchen. As we shoved our way through the swinging door, I glimpsed the man coming our way—or, at least trying to. The girl continued to plead with him and offer ways to pay him back, stopping him from pursuing us.

The cooks looked up at us like we were insane, but Wolf paid them no attention. He pushed open the back door, and we found ourselves welcomed by the cold night's air once again.

Finally, Wolf released my arm, and together we sprinted down the alley and to the front of the building. "Get into the car!" Wolf cried. We threw open our doors and climbed inside the truck in record time.

Wolf quickly turned over the ignition and shifted into gear. He peeled out of the driveway in reverse, nearly colliding with a parked car on the opposite side of the street. By the time he shifted into Drive, the man from the diner was rushing out through the front door, waving his hand.

Wolf floored the gas pedal and the tires squealed. Then, the truck took off down the road. I glanced behind, trying to glimpse the man one more time. When I did, though, a sharp banging noise filled my ears. If I didn't know better, I'd say someone had thrown a large rock at the back window.

Then, I realized we'd been shot at. The bullet must've hit the side of the truck.

"What was that?" I demanded.

"Don't worry," Wolf muttered. "He missed."

"He missed *what*? Us?"

"Yes, I mean 'us.'"

"That guy had a *gun*!" I cried. "And you're acting like it's no big deal!"

"What did you expect, kid? Have you already forgotten that Cain wants you *dead*?" He drew in a slow, deep breath and leaned back into his seat, trying to remain calm. "Thankfully, that girl in there bought us a few seconds. If she hadn't distracted him, we might be dead right now."

I exhaled and leaned back in my seat. I closed my eyes, struggling to slow my racing heart by taking deep, steady breaths. I counted to ten, then I counted to twenty. My eyes remained shut until my fingers no longer tingled and I didn't feel like I would pass out.

Finally, I opened my eyes and looked up at Wolf. "So, who was he?"

Wolf glanced in the rear-view mirror. I couldn't help envying how calm he had remained after such a brief, terrifying moment. "That man works with Cain," he explained. "His name is Ridley Bancroft. When Cain was kicked out of the Order thirteen years ago, Ridley joined him. So did a woman named Arianne. I haven't seen them since then."

I glanced suspiciously at him. "You almost sound like you miss them."

Wolf didn't seem bothered by my unsubtle accusation. "The Order is like a family," he replied evenly. "And what Cain did was unspeakable. So, yes, you might say that I'm somewhat upset over all that has happened in the past two decades."

I stared out the window at the rolling hills in the distance. "Sorry," I muttered.

Wolf didn't even glance my way. "I hope you don't get carsick, because I'm going to be driving this thing like crazy for the next couple hours."

"Where are we going?"

"Carson City, Nevada. We're going to meet

up with David Underhill. He's another member of the Order."

My stomach turned with anxiety, fear, and even sadness. I forced myself to focus on the hills in the distance once more to keep from losing it.

Redding alone was already so far away from my home in Ashland, where I had spent my entire life. The farthest I'd gone away from home had been to Vancouver when I was a child, and even then, I had been with my mother. With every mile that we sped away from Ashland, I grew smaller and smaller, and my resolve continued to disappear.

I wished I could be stone-cold like Wolf, who seemed neither afraid nor uncollected in any situation. I wished I could be like my mother, who had been strong enough to let her only son go.

I wished I could be brave, but I felt like the farthest thing from it.

CHAPTER FOUR

THE SECOND NIGHTMARE

Tap, tap, tap.

I shivered and blinked my eyes open. The air was filled with a bone-biting chill so cold that my fingertips had gone numb. I looked out through the side window of Wolf's pick-up truck and found him standing outside, tapping on the window.

"Come on, kid," he called. "We're here."

I clutched my duffel bag and climbed out of the truck, thankful that I had been spared from my recurring nightmare during my short nap.

Up ahead on the dirt path sat a two-story cabin. Tall trees flanked its sides, shielding it from the light of the hanging moon. A stone path led from the dirt road to the front door, where a single light flickered through the curtains downstairs. I followed Wolf up the path, to where he rapped twice on the door.

"What does this David guy do?" I asked.

"He's in construction," Wolf replied. "A construction manager, actually, if it makes a difference. He built this cabin himself."

"So, the members of the Order are normal people, too."

"As normal as members of an ancient, dragon-slaying Order can be," Wolf said with a chuckle. "We *do* have lives outside of our Order-related duties."

We heard approaching footsteps, then the door opened a few inches. A man stood on the opposite side, looking Wolf up and down. Then, his eyes darted towards me. After a few hesitant moments, he opened the door completely.

"Sorry we're so late," Wolf said to the man. "We had some trouble in Redding."

The man gestured for us to enter. "Understandable," he replied. His voice was strong, yet comforting and reassuring in an odd way. "Come inside."

I instantly warmed up once I entered the cabin. A fire blazed in the fireplace on the back wall, keeping away the springtime chill that lingered outside. The man sealed the door shut as we entered, and I caught a glimpse of him settling a nine-millimeter Glock on the nearby coffee table. He fastened three deadbolts across the top of the door once we were inside. I swallowed the lump in my throat, fearing whatever it was that required a gun and three locks on the door for safety.

Once our security was assured, he exhaled and faced his guests. He was a tall, well-built man with light brown hair and facial stubble, dark brown eyes, and a sharp jaw. If it was at all possible, he looked even more intimidating than Wolf did.

"So," he said, grinning. "You're our Dragonlord."

I stood as tall as I could and nodded. "Yes, sir."

"You look like your father, you know."

"Thanks," I said, blushing just a bit. It was

the first time I had ever been told that.

The man extended a firm handshake, stronger than Wolf's had been, but less overwhelming. "I'm David Underhill."

"Logan," I returned.

David grinned at me before turning his attention to Wolf. He stood tall, folding his arms over his chest. "Any word from Julianna?"

Wolf shook his head. "Not since William's disappearance. I've been on the road since."

David nodded, pacing the living room until he stood before the fire. "You said you had trouble in Redding. What happened?"

Wolf locked eyes with him. "Ridley tracked us down. I don't know how, but he did."

David nodded towards me. "Did he see Logan's face?"

"Unfortunately, yes," Wolf sighed. "I did what I could, but we didn't get out of there quickly enough."

David nodded, but a million thoughts seemed to be racing through his mind. Finally, he said, "Ridley won't be able to find us here. We'll be safe for the evening." He turned and headed towards the stairs near the front door. "I'll bring down some blankets. There's a spare bedroom upstairs if one of you wants to—"

Wolf grabbed him by the arm and stopped him as he passed by. David looked down at Wolf's hand and then up at Wolf, narrowing his eyes like he didn't appreciate Wolf touching him. After all, I wouldn't either.

"The piece?" Wolf asked quietly.

David's eyes darted towards me. Then, he shook his arm out of Wolf's grasp and continued up the stairs. "You don't need to worry about that, Wolf," he called as he ascended to the second floor. "That's for Logan's eyes only."

Wolf quietly huffed, clearly displeased with the results of his inquiry. Then, he turned and faced me, looking me up and down in that suspicious way of his. "You want the spare bedroom or the couch?" he asked.

Anywhere away from Wolf was fine. "I'll take the couch," I said. During the cold night, I'd be thankful for the warmth of the fire downstairs.

Wolf nodded. "Fine," he said, and he turned towards the stairwell. "Get some rest, then. We'll see you in the morning. Tomorrow we're headed for Lake Tahoe." Then, he trudged up the stairs and disappeared into the darkness of the upstairs corridor.

I exhaled, relieved to finally be out of the wolf's watch. I dropped my duffel bag next to the couch and turned towards the fireplace, seating myself on the brick step in front of the iron grating. I extended my hands towards the flames, warming my cold fingers.

Footsteps creaked along the stairs as David returned with an armload of blankets and pillows. He dropped them onto the couch and smiled at me. "Well, have a good night, then."

"Wait," I called, rising to my feet. David stopped at the base of the stairs and faced me. "What was Wolf talking about earlier? About 'the piece'?"

David glanced up the stairs, as if checking to see if Wolf was hovering at the edge of the landing. "He was talking about one of the three pieces of Ascalon," he replied.

"That's the lance, right?"

David narrowed his eyes. "How much did he tell you?"

"Not much," I said with a shrug. "A little bit about being a Dragonlord, about Cain, and about Bolla."

David sighed irritably, but he didn't say anything. Instead, he headed into the kitchen, filled two mugs with hot tea from the kettle on the stove, and seated himself in the rocking chair near the fire. He offered one of the glasses to me and nursed his own, watching as the flames danced in the pit. "He shouldn't have said anything," David said. "It wasn't his place to tell you. But I guess you'll have to find out eventually."

I stared on expectantly, hoping for more information to be shared. After almost a minute of silence, David glanced at me and grinned. "All right, I'll tell you."

I shrugged innocently, suppressing a grin. "Tell me what?"

David chuckled as he leaned forward and placed his mug down near his feet. "Well, I wouldn't want to be left in the dark, either." He hesitated and glanced towards the stairs again. "Between you and me, Wolf and I don't exactly see eye-to-eye. He's certainly good at what he does, but—"

"He's sketchy," I finished. "Trust me, I get

it."

David grinned before continuing. "The truth is, only the protectors of the pieces are allowed to know where they've been hidden. Julianna, your father, and I know where to find the three pieces, but Wolf doesn't, and neither did Arianne, Ridley, or Cain when they'd been members of the Order. It's for security purposes, really. It won't matter if anyone else knows where they were hidden *after* they've been retrieved, but until that point, we keep it secret."

"So, what piece do you protect?" I asked.

"I protect the vamplate," he replied. "It's the iron funnel attached to the bottom of the shaft, used to protect your hand. It was hidden not too far away from here. We'll pick it up tomorrow before we head to Tahoe."

I nodded and remained silent, waiting for him to offer more information.

"Julianna has another piece of the lance: the spearhead," he continued. "And your father protected the shaft, the final piece. We'll have to pick that up, too, at some point. Hopefully, it was hidden somewhere where Cain would never chance finding it."

I swallowed. "This Cain guy—how afraid of him should I be?"

David stared thoughtfully down at the floor. "You shouldn't be afraid," he said. "But you *should* be on your guard. Cain is cunning and clever, more brains than brawn. That's why he uses people like Ridley and Arianne for his muscle while he hides in shadows."

I scoffed. "Ridley? He's an old man! He looks like he doesn't go ten miles over the speed limit."

"He was a weapons specialist in the military when he was in his twenties," David said, "and he's deadly. Don't underestimate Cain or any of his accomplices. They will take your life in a second if it's of benefit to them, which it most certainly is."

I nodded, trying not to panic after hearing this. It was something I had already realized, but hadn't yet come to terms with—even after being shot at.

I groaned and flopped down on the couch. "I should've known today would be weird," I muttered. "It all started with that dream."

I mostly meant to say it to myself, but David seemed interested in my complaint. He leaned forward and raised his eyebrows. "Dream?"

I nodded. "It's nothing important. It's just that—"

"Tell me about it," he insisted. "I want to hear."

So, I did. I told him about the black dragon, about the shadow man, and about the golden spear. By the way his expressions changed, he seemed to be so enveloped in my nightmare.

"Every time I've managed to fall asleep since last night, I've had that same nightmare," I explained. "My mother thinks it's some kind of sign, since today was the day I became the Dragonlord."

He studied me for a moment, although not in the creepy way that Wolf often would. He looked at me like he was trying to solve a puzzle written on my face. It made me want to know more about this Dragonlord business.

Finally, he sighed and leaned back in the chair, retrieving his cup of tea for another sip. "Interesting."

I raised an eyebrow. "Interesting? That's it?"

He shrugged. "What do you want me to say?"

"I don't know. Tell me it doesn't mean anything. Tell me I'm overreacting."

"You aren't."

I stared at him for a long moment. "What do you mean?"

"That man is Cain," he said matter-of-factly, "and the dragon is Bolla. The golden spear is actually Ascalon. You're probably having these dreams because Saint George's Day is right around the corner, and that's when your powers and the powers of the great dragons are most active. This dream is a manifestation of your greatest fear that you have yet to face. That, and a foresight of what is to come."

My stomach did a flip. "You mean, that's going to happen to me?"

"I can't say for sure," he replied, staring down at his coffee mug. "But this is part of who you are, Logan. You can't outrun it."

Maybe not, but facing off against a dragon the size of an office building wasn't exactly my idea of fun.

"You know," I grumbled, "this seems a little

unfair. I mean, none of the other Dragonlords had to actually slay a dragon in the past hundred years. Now, all of a sudden, it's my turn. And I think I'm the most ill-equipped person for the job."

He smiled at me. "You're afraid."

I drew back. "N-No, I'm not afraid."

He gave me a pleading look.

"Fine," I sighed. "I'm afraid, okay? After all, I just found out about this stuff a couple hours ago. And in a few days, if I don't move fast enough, some guy I've never met will unleash a dragon to kill me. How *should* I feel?"

"Well," he sighed, "you're not alone, Logan. That's why the Order of Ascalon exists: to protect and aid the Dragonlord."

"Sure," I muttered, "but *I* am the one who has to bring the beast down in the end. Only me. And if I don't, well…" I shrugged helplessly. "What, then?"

David rose from his chair and made his way towards the kitchen, washing out his empty mug. "Don't think about it that way," he called over the sound of the running water. "It will drive you crazy. We've suspected this would happen at some point, although we prayed it wouldn't. But it's not something we're unprepared for." He shut the water off and leaned against the counter, studying me. "The power of the Dragonlord runs through your veins, Logan," he said. "So, if anyone can do it, *you* certainly can."

I guess he had a point. After all, I was the heir of Saint George, the only person on the planet who bore the supernatural powers required to slay a dragon. If I couldn't do it, who could?

David trudged wearily towards the stairs. "Now, get some sleep," he insisted. "We need to be up early in the morning to get the vamplate. After that, we're off to Lake Tahoe to meet with Julianna. *She* is the one you need to be afraid of—not Cain." He laughed at his own joke, but it only made me more nervous.

Who was this Julianna lady? And why did everyone speak of her like she was some kind of evil queen we ought to fear?

David switched off the light at the top of the stairs, and the house fell into darkness with the exception of the flickering flames in the fireplace. I crawled into a mess of blankets on the couch and faced the fire, watching it die down.

A thousands thoughts and fears raced through my mind, but I tried to ignore them so I could sleep. I missed my mother already, although I was more worried about her than about myself. I hoped she wasn't sitting on the couch crying through the night. I hoped she was sound asleep, knowing that I was in safe hands.

But I couldn't admit any of my fears or concerns to Wolf or David—what would they think of their great Dragonlord, then, if he couldn't be away from his mother for more than a few hours? What would they think if they knew I was so afraid?

I pulled the blankets over my head and immersed myself in darkness and warmth, praying that I would sleep long enough to shake myself free of my fears. *You've got to toughen up, Logan,* I told myself. *You're a dragon slayer. You can't be afraid of everything.*

Unfortunately, being fearless was easier said than done.

As it turned out, sleep was easy to come by, though not peaceful at all. Another terrible nightmare racked my brain—perhaps worse than the first.

In my dream, I lay on my back on cold, hard ground. My eyes remained closed, but that didn't block out the terrors around me. A chilling voice whispered somewhere in the distance: *Come, Dragonlord. This way...*

My eyes flickered open, and I stared up at the ceiling. Walls around me reached so high that I couldn't see where they ended, and the ceiling above me stretched into darkness.

Awaken, Dragonlord, the voice continued to call. *Come to me...*

I sat up and rubbed my eyes, observing my surroundings. I was trapped in a large circular room with no doors or windows. The only discernible escape was through the massive black pit in the center of the room, although that hardly seemed like the right way to go.

I rose to my feet and peered down into the pit. A sudden gust of wind blew by—where it came from, I had no idea—and nearly knocked me down into the unending hole, as if whatever beast lay down there was trying to draw me in.

I couldn't see anything, but I knew something was down there. The whispers had to be coming from within.

I am your only escape…

Then, the shadow man appeared on the opposite side of the pit, materializing in a vapor of black clouds. He crept towards the edge of the pit, and I could feel his empty features staring upon me. He outstretched his arms over the massive hole. The shadows engulfing his body swirled towards the pit before him, becoming one with the darkness. He began to fade away.

A shudder ran down my spine as I focused on his empty face, on the hollow sockets that should have held human eyes. "This is who you are, Dragonlord," a chilling voice whispered in my ear. He was on the opposite side of the room, but I knew it was his voice, and it was as near as if he had spoken it into my ear. It made the hair on my arms stand on edge. "This is what you are to become."

I tried to reach towards him or call out to him, but despite my efforts, I found myself cemented to the ground, found my lips sealed shut and my vocal cords frozen. Didn't he realize he could die?

Then, the shadow man dissolved completely, and I was alone in the room once more. With him gone, I found my limbs mobile again. I scrambled forward on my hands and knees to the edge of the pit and peered down, hoping I would catch a glimpse of him, but I still couldn't see anything.

Suddenly, a terrible quaking shook the ground. If I had remained standing, I would have certainly tumbled to the ground—or worse, into the pit. I crawled backwards until my back pressed up against the wall. The ceiling above me began to crumble, as if it were being sucked into the pit by a massive vacuum.

The walls followed next, disintegrating inch by inch until a tornado was blowing over my head. I had first thought that maybe I could escape the room, but as the wall came down, I found that only a gray void existed outside. I had only two choices, neither of which seemed very appealing: I could fade into the nothingness outside of the room, or disappear into the pit.

Just when I thought I would be sucked away and vanish forever, something appeared in my hand. I stared down at the glowing golden rod and felt the weight of its power in my hands. A sudden surge of strength overtook me and I rose to my feet, no longer afraid of the pit below.

NOOO! a shrill voice cried from within the pit. It was sharp and ear-splitting, but a dark, deep voice echoed behind it, like two people speaking in unison. *We must destroy the lance! We cannot withstand its strength!*

I cocked my arm back and aimed the spear towards the pit, waiting for something to happen. The walls continued to disintegrate until they were no longer standing. The bricks that had formed the walls swirled in a tornado around me and the pit, like an audience cheering us on. The ground beneath my feet began to crumble as well, until the bricks upon which I stood were sucked into the twister spinning around me. I needed to make a decision immediately.

My grip on the spear tightened, and beads of sweat trickled down my neck. My platform was narrowing by the second, and I had only a few feet of space to stand upon.

I drew in a deep breath and dove forward into the pit, falling into darkness.

A piercing scream filled my ears. *DON'T LET HIM DESTROY US!* the shrill voice cried.

I continued to fall into the pit, closing my eyes as I descended further into emptiness.

CHAPTER FIVE

GRAVE ROBBERS

Footsteps awakened me from what felt like a very bad nap. I doubted that I'd gotten more than five hours of sleep, since the sun was barely rising outside and we'd been awake past midnight.

My thoughts immediately turned towards my latest nightmare. This one felt stranger than the other had—it was darker and more powerful, and it felt as real as being hunted down by Ridley had felt. I wanted to tell David about it, but I wasn't so sure that would be a good idea. For some reason, I felt guilty about my new dream, and I didn't know why.

My body ached as I sat up in my makeshift bed on David's couch, pushing aside the thoughts of my troubling nightmares. Wolf trudged down the steps fully dressed with a mug of coffee at hand. He grinned at me. "Finally awake, eh?"

I rubbed my eyes and groaned. "Not really."

"Well, you're gonna have to be," he said. "We've got to hit the road soon."

Thanks, Wolf. But I hadn't forgotten.

The longer I spent in my warm cocoon of blankets, though, the longer it would take me to reckon with my early awakening. So, I tossed the blankets aside and stepped out into the chill.

"Do I get to shower, at least?" I mumbled.

"No time," Wolf replied. "When we get to Julianna's, you can get comfortable. But until then, we're still on the run from Ridley."

I frowned. "But that was hours ago."

"Don't put anything past Cain or one of his guys," Wolf warned.

I sighed and seated myself on the couch once more, running my hands through my greasy hair. Whatever feelings of anxiety I'd had the night before immediately returned when I thought about Ridley chasing us out of the diner with a gun at hand.

People wanted me dead. It was something I was going to have to get used to.

Another round of footsteps sounded as David came down the stairs, dressed warmly for the day with a duffel bag slung over his shoulder. "You might want to hit the road soon, Wolf," he suggested.

"You're right," Wolf sighed. "The sooner we get to base, the sooner we can relax."

I frowned, glancing between David and Wolf. "He's leaving?"

"We have to get the vamplate," David replied, "and if we split up, Cain is less likely to track us down."

I was utterly thankful. Anywhere away from Wolf would be great, even if the trade-off was Ridley chasing us down in a fighter jet with mounted rockets.

I tried to suppress my smile of sheer delight. Knowing Wolf would be away gave me newfound energy. I gathered up my things and set them aside on the couch, barely realizing that I had slept in the same clothes I'd worn the day before.

Wolf retrieved his keys from the counter. He

saluted me and headed towards the door, donning his blazer. "See you in Tahoe," he said. Then, he opened the door, stepped out into the chilly spring morning, and disappeared.

I exhaled in relief. Why did I feel so uneasy whenever Wolf was around? He had saved my life twice, after all.

But it was that look he gave me that set me on edge. I couldn't stand it.

David dropped his duffel bag to the ground and poured a thermos full of coffee. He looked at me and held the thermos up. "One for the road?"

I'd tried the stuff once and didn't like it, but it had helped me stay up to watch the ball drop on New Year's Eve. So, I thought I'd have some. "Sounds good."

He poured a thermos of coffee for me and switched off the coffee pot. Then, he collected his things and headed for the door. We were ready to go.

David stepped outside and warily glanced around, as if he expected Ridley to jump out of the bushes at any moment. He reached his hand inside his jacket—I guessed he'd hidden a gun inside of it, which should have reassured me, but instead made me nervous.

Finally, he opened the door to his truck and gestured for me to get in. After climbing into the driver's seat, he turned over the ignition, backed out of the driveway, and we were on our way.

I had only known David for a few hours, but I already felt much safer and more comfortable with him than I did with Wolf. And, unlike Wolf, he had a more reassuring way of pointing out the truth without making me feel like all roads would end in an inevitable death.

The road merged onto the main highway, and tall green trees surrounded us on both sides, blocking out almost all of the approaching morning sunlight. David fiddled with the knobs in the truck, and a blast of cold air hit me in the face. "It will warm up soon enough," he said, stretching a hand over the vent.

"I don't mind," I said. "I'm just glad to be with you instead of Wolf. The guy is a creep."

David chuckled. "I don't blame you."

I shifted in my seat and cleared my throat. "So, this Julianna lady—who is she, exactly?"

"She's the head of the Order," David replied. "She's got eyes and ears everywhere."

"That's a joke, right?"

He glanced at me with a grin. "Sort of."

"Well, why is she in charge?"

"Because she's best suited for the job," he answered. "Trust me, you'll be thankful for her in the end. She knows what she's doing."

"I'm sure I will be," I said, although I didn't know if that was true. "So, how come Marcus calls himself 'Wolf'?"

I thought I saw David roll his eyes. "'Weasel' would have been more fitting," he mumbled. Then, he sighed and shrugged. "I don't know, Logan. The guy thinks he's a secret agent or something. Don't get me wrong—he's good at what he does. He earned the nickname when he hunted Cain down thirteen years ago. Found him plotting to kill your father and stopped him. Unfortunately, Cain escaped, as you know by now."

I almost laughed. It was a ridiculous explanation, but quite fitting. I didn't doubt that Marcus Wilson could hunt like a wolf, and I wouldn't put anything past him. Not to mention the fact that *he* had been the one to stop Cain from murdering my father was rather surprising. I probably should have given him more credit for what he'd done.

We drove for another twenty minutes until the canopy of trees blocked out all of the sunlight. "Here we are," David said. He pulled off the main highway onto a narrow dirt road hidden beneath the tree branches. The truck rumbled and bounced across the uneven surface, and hanging branches smacked at the windows. Eventually, the cluster of trees thinned out, and the dirt road dissolved into a grassy pasture.

David pulled the truck to a halt and shifted into Park. I stared forward at the endless rows of headstone lining the grassy meadow. "Why are we at a cemetery?" I asked hesitantly.

"The vamplate is hidden here," David replied. Clearly, he wasn't uncomfortable with being in a graveyard, surrounded by dead bodies.

I pulled my backpack over my shoulders—just in case I needed it—and climbed out of the truck, stepping into the squishy grass dampened by the recent rainfall. David tucked his hands into his pockets and walked past the rows of headstones, heading towards the back of the cemetery. I followed after him, reading each name on the headstones, memorizing them and reciting them in my mind. I hoped I might find some significance and solve the puzzle before David pointed the answer out.

But I didn't. He stopped in front of a mausoleum and stared at it with an affection of familiarity. The mausoleum looked like a small house you might see used for scenery on a miniature golf course. It was the same size and height as one of those decorative houses, although it looked a lot less fun and a lot more…well, dark. And dead.

A tall pillar stretched from the top and pointed to the sky, like a hand reaching to the heavens for salvation. The door looked old-fashioned and medieval—the metal clasps were painted black, although they were rusting and the color was fading. An iron pull was situated on the right side of the door, so that one could walk in with ease—although, I didn't know who would want to.

Apparently David did. He ascended the two painted white steps and stopped at the door, brushing his hand over a dusty nameplate positioned above it. He glanced back at me and gestured for me to approach. "*This* is where it's hidden?" I asked.

He stepped back and pointed at the nameplate. "Take a look."

I climbed the narrow stairs and peered up at the rusty metal nameplate:

BLESSED SAINT GEORGE OF LYDDA

I grinned. "It's clever, but I don't think you're fooling anyone."

David rolled his eyes, but he grinned in spite of himself. "That's not exactly the point, is it? It's simply to revere your ancestor." He took hold of the iron pull and looked at me "Do you mind? I need muscles to get this thing open."

"Then you've come to the right person," I said, approaching his side. Together, we yanked on the iron pull and opened the door. Dust stirred and met my face, eliciting a vicious cough.

"Reverence, eh?" I managed in the midst of choking.

David shrugged. "It's not like he's actually here. He won't mind."

He stepped back and gestured for me to enter, which I did with great caution. The inside of the mausoleum was pitch black, sending a shudder up my spine. The air was cold and stale, and I suspected that no one had entered inside in at least ten years, maybe more.

A moaning creak echoed behind us as the door slid closed, and the narrow crack of sunlight faded until we were enshrouded in absolute darkness. Then, I heard a *click*, and the beam of a flashlight danced in the corner across from me.

"Here," David said, handing the flashlight to me. A moment later, another beam of light illuminated the room as he switched on a second flashlight.

In the middle of the room lay a stone coffin. I didn't want to know if it was empty or not, so I looked away, shining my light into the corners. The ceiling was only two feet above David's head, and the entire mausoleum wasn't much larger than a closet.

"What now?" I asked.

David didn't reply. Instead, he bent down near the coffin and ran a finger along the edge of the stone, his eyes fixated on something that I couldn't see.

I moved and stood behind him, observing the intricate carvings and markings upon the coffin that intrigued him. They looked like Egyptian hieroglyphs fused with the Greek alphabet. I didn't recognize them at all.

David ran his finger along the crease until he reached the left end of the coffin. Then, he brushed his hand against the glyph, pushing it in like an elevator button. He ran his hand along the stone to the right, stopping again to push in another glyph. Then, another, and finally, one more at the end of the coffin.

He rose to his feet, and a gentle rumbling followed. I jerked the light towards the ceiling, half-expecting the roof to cave in, but the rumbling had come from the coffin. A moment later, the top of the coffin unhinged like the jar of a lid popping open. Dust stirred in its wake.

David slid the heavy lid of the coffin towards the floor. It crashed against the brick wall with a loud thud. "The Order would probably disapprove of me accompanying you during the trial," he said, shining his light inside of the coffin, "but what they don't know won't hurt them, so I'll go with you. After that, though, you're on your own."

"On my own? Why?"

"Because the trials are to test *you* and you alone," he replied. Then, he drew in a deep breath and looked up at me, gesturing towards the emptiness within the coffin. "Well, after you."

"In *there*?" I asked.

"Don't worry. There aren't any dead bodies. Maybe rats and spiders, but no bodies."

I snorted. "I think I prefer the dead bodies." But I climbed into the coffin anyway. On the south end of the coffin nearest the door to the mausoleum, a set of narrow stone stairs descended into the darkness. I followed the stairwell down, guiding my hand against the wall to steady myself.

David followed behind me, shining his light ahead of us and illuminating the seemingly endless set of stairs. The further down we went, the more tightly my stomach curled. I couldn't help feeling like we were walking into the arms of some kind of sewer monster—or something worse—straight out of a bad horror movie.

Finally, we found flat ground. We followed the widening path forward for several feet until we heard a sharp, crunching noise up ahead. We shined the light before us and stared in horror at our blocked path.

About one hundred feet ahead of us stood a tall stone door stretching at least fifteen feet high, but in order to reach it, we had to get through the swords—that's right, *swords*—keeping us from going forward.

The ground and walls between us and the

door were punctured with holes from which the swords sprang forth every few seconds. Four rows of scimitars shot out from the ground, one row at a time. And since there were blades shooting out from the wall, too, there was absolutely no way around it.

"David," I said, "what is *that*?"

David stepped towards the first row of blades, watching as they emerged. "This," he replied, "would be part of your first trial. We'll have to go one at a time." He looked at me and grinned. "Ready?"

"Me first?" I asked, taking a nervous step back.

"It's safer that way," he said. "Come on, then. I won't let you get chopped up into little pieces."

I glared at him. "You're so funny."

He gestured me forward, still grinning. "Let's get this over with."

I drew in a deep breath and stepped alongside him, inching as close to the blades as I could get. "Is there any strategy to this?"

"Well, firstly, don't get killed," he said. "Secondly, pace yourself. After each set of blades retracts, stop before the next one. Then, continue forward."

I nodded, swallowed hard, and watched as the rows retracted one-by-one. The row directly before me sprang forward, stretching high above me, and remained that way until the fourth row of blades—the ones farthest back—emerged. Then, they were sucked back into the earth, and I rushed forward.

Each row was separated by about twenty feet of space, but in those vacant areas, the blades from the wall shot towards me, trapping me in a tiny cocoon of space—and by tiny, I mean that there were only inches between me and the blades on either side of me. They retracted into the wall every ten seconds or so, then came towards me once more.

I waited for the next round, and once the second set of blades emerged, I darted forward to the second empty space. The blades on my sides reminded me to watch my footing. I was halfway through.

"I'm following behind you, Logan," David called. "Keep moving."

"Okay," I returned. "Good luck. Don't get yourself chopped up into little pieces."

The third row shot towards the ceiling, waited, and then sank into the ground. Again, I raced forward, stopping just before the final row of blades. I glanced behind me as the swords from the walls shot towards me. David was two rows behind me, still very much alive and unharmed.

One more to go, I thought, my heart pounding. Behind me, each row of blades retracted into the ground. I listened for the first, then the second, and finally the third, bracing myself as the path before me was clear. I leapt across the open space and into the safety of the stone path before me, where there were no more swords reaching for me and trying to kill me.

Behind me, David emerged safely, glancing behind him with a careless shrug. "Well, that was nothing," he said.

"Let's hope that was the worst of it," I added.

Finally we made it towards the door. On its left side, another stone door stood, although it was much simpler in appearance. The same glyphs that I'd seen on the coffin decorated the outside of the main door. However, I didn't see any visible form of entry through either of the doors—they lacked any kind of handles, and I doubted we could simply push either one open.

David ran his hand along the face of the main door and glanced behind him, below him, and above him. Then, a grin spread across his face. "Bingo," he said.

Off to the side, a rope was tied to a hook in the shadows. David tugged at it twice, then pulled down in one strong yank. In the darkness above us, a bell rang, a loud *dong* that gently shook the earth around us.

The door opened, and once the earth stood still again, we moved forward. The path continued ahead for another few feet, dissolving into a platform that overlooked the crypt beneath us.

Two tall pillars stood on both our sides, stretching from the ground twenty feet below to the ceiling ten feet above. They had been ornamentally carved with disturbing depictions of crying faces. The indentation near the bottom of the pillar stretched into an arc, like a wailing mouth, and the eyes slanted like the face was bawling.

On the ground floor near the base of the pillars sat two furnaces with dancing flames already lit. A copper chandelier hung overhead, burning flames as well. "How are those fires lit?" I asked, frowning.

David shrugged, not nearly as concerned as I was. "Probably magic."

I looked pleadingly at him. "Seriously."

"I *am* being serious," he replied. "Some hundreds of years ago, a great, underground library contained all the information we ever needed to know about the Dragonlords and the wonder behind their kind. But after some time, the structure collapsed, and all the literature was buried with it. Supposedly, those books and scrolls explained the phenomena behind these crypts."

"Wolf mentioned that to me last night," I said. "But…if the library was buried, how could the Order possibly know about it?"

"Please, Logan," he said. "You don't think our ancestors would have carelessly forgotten to mention it, do you?"

"Well, no."

"Of course they preserved their memory of the library," he went on. "Don't you think the absurdities of these crypts and the Dragonlords have crossed our minds as well?"

"Well, until now, I was beginning to think I was the only one. You and Wolf act like these creepy, underground crypts are as normal as shopping malls."

He raised an eyebrow. "Don't tell me you're scared."

I straightened myself up and narrowed my eyes. "Of course not. I *am* the Dragonlord, after all."

He grinned at me before returning his attention to the scene before us. Two sets of narrow stairs descended towards the ground floor on the sides of the pillars, dropping off in front of an ornamental stone box centered in the middle of the floor. David pointed at it. "That's where the vamplate is," he said.

I craned my neck, still taking in the sights of the crypt. "So, you just happened to find this underground crypt and thought, 'Hey, here's a good place to hide the vamplate'?"

David scowled at me. "It doesn't work that way. Before Saint George passed away, he had Ascalon dismantled into three pieces which he then entrusted to three of his closest confidantes. To keep prying eyes away from the pieces of Ascalon, they built and destroyed the trials every century."

"But the New World hadn't been discovered yet," I said.

"Not yet," David replied. "Eventually, though, they made their way to the Americas, then to the west in the late 1800s. They then built the trials that *you*, young Dragonlord, will be facing. They hid the pieces in three separate locations—not too far apart, but not too close either. These puzzle chambers were built with their bare hands."

"And how did you guys figure out where they were hidden?"

"Well, Saint George couldn't risk his descendants losing track of the weapon," David replied. "So, he left his secrets with the same people who hid the pieces away. They passed down the hiding places to their descendants, so that the weapon would never be lost if the time came to reclaim it." Then, he grinned. "And we members of the Order are the descendants of said confidantes. *That's* how we know where the pieces are hidden."

I stared down at the crypt, thinking that somehow a guardian angel had guided the Order to this place. "Probably magic," I muttered, echoing David's earlier suggestion. "It definitely seems that way."

"Like I said, you learn to stop asking questions eventually. After all, you *are* a dragon slayer—if you can accept something as farfetched as *that*, the rest will come along with it."

It would probably take me a little longer than it had taken the others to accept things without much question, but I nodded anyway.

"Well, let's go," David said.

I drew in a deep breath, and we descended the stairs to the floor. Once we reached the ground, I glimpsed a hallway behind us, stretching into darkness beneath the platform above. I swallowed my fear and returned my attention to the stone dais.

David gestured towards it. "Go for it."

"Me?" I asked.

"The pieces can only be retrieved by the Dragonlord. Think of yourself as King Arthur, and Ascalon as Excalibur."

Comparing me to King Arthur should have boosted my morale, but I still felt uncertain.

I reached a tentative hand towards the ornamental box, unsure of what I was supposed to do. A symbol was carved into the top of the box, with four parallel wavy lines that curled into swirls at the right end. It almost looked like a childish drawing of an ocean wave.

I went with my gut instincts and carefully pressed my hand over the top of the box, centering my palm over the symbol of the wave. The symbol pushed into the top of the box like a button, and two small doors opened from the front.

Inside sat a small iron funnel, narrow and open on one end, and wide on the opposite. Dainty swirls and lines carved the edges in an antique fashion, contradicting the harsh glyphs on the outside of the box.

I reached inside and carefully retrieved the vamplate, which was much heavier than I had expected. I stepped away from the box, and the small doors slowly sealed shut on their own accord.

I glanced at David with a grin and held up the vamplate for him to see. "That wasn't so hard."

But he didn't seem pleased. He was frowning, observing the crypt with a curious glare. "No, it wasn't," he muttered.

I frowned, and my stomach curled. "What's wrong?"

"That was surprisingly easy. *That's* what's wrong."

"Be thankful," I said, mostly to ease my own nerves. "And...well, let's get out of here."

I took one step towards the stairs, and as soon as I did, a great rumbling noise followed. David and I both jerked our heads towards the door at the top of the platform, watching in horror as it sealed shut.

"Oh," I said stupidly.

Then, something even worse followed: the flames in the furnaces and the hanging chandeliers extinguished like God himself had blown them out in one quick breath.

The crypt fell into complete darkness. The stone pillars with the crying faces began to spout water from the corners of their eyes and mouths. The water rushed forward, pouring out of the statues in small waterfalls. In the few short moments it took us to collect ourselves and get our flashlights out again, the entire crypt had filled with water up to our ankles.

"There's got to be a way out of here," I said. "There's always a way out!"

David craned his neck left and right, hoping the answer would appear. Then, his gaze focused upon the dark hallway beneath the platform. "There," he said, and he took off running.

I sprinted after him, shoving the vamplate into my backpack. We ran into the darkness, splashing in the shallow pool of water and hoping the shadows would save us. Unfortunately, we slammed into a dead end against the stone wall. We frantically grasped against the stone, searching for an optical illusion of escape as the waterline met our knees. The water was bone-chilling cold, but the adrenaline pumping in my veins helped me ignore it.

"You didn't see this coming, did you?" I asked David irritably.

He ignored me and continued to search for an answer or an escape. He stared up at the ceiling—rather, at the unending darkness that should have been a ceiling.

Should have been a ceiling.

"There's a tunnel above us," David said, speaking my thoughts. "So, that means—"

"We have to wait for the waterline to rise," I finished. "And the water will take us up through the shaft."

"And right back to the entrance," he added, "through the second door outside of the crypt."

The image of the second stone door standing aside the main door of the crypt appeared in my mind. That was our ticket out.

Unfortunately, waiting in the freezing water wasn't going to be fun. The waterline was rising quickly, and every creeping inch sent a stabbing pain across my skin. I began to shiver—my teeth chattered and my limbs cramped.

Minutes passed, and the waterline rose to our chests. We floated on the surface as the water pressed us higher. The ceiling stretched only fifteen feet above us as we continued towards the top. The faint trace of the stone door was carved on the outside wall, although there was no visible way of escape.

David and I paddled against the rising waterline as it continued to press us higher and higher, until only one foot of airspace remained above us. The door was almost fully submerged in water.

"We don't have much time," David said, struggling to keep his head above the surface. The water had reached his bottom lip. "You have to be the one to open the door."

"How?" I asked.

"I don't know, Logan," he said, spitting out water as it filled his mouth. "But do it quickly!"

I paddled forward. My brain had almost forgotten how to function under the pressure of the cold water and the urgency of the matter. I drew in a deep breath and submerged myself entirely.

I had never experienced a cold so terrible in my life, so sharp and painful that I wanted to cry. It made it almost difficult to hold my breath, but I ignored it and pressed forward. I opened my eyes underwater and brushed my hand against the empty face of the door.

A bright, glowing glyph appeared upon contact, and I pressed my hand against it. The white light shifted to hues of neon green and blue as the breath in my lungs continued to deplete. I needed air.

Then, a rumbling noise followed. The door retracted into the ceiling and revealed the path outside as my throat and lungs tightened. If it had taken ten seconds longer, we might have drowned.

The water rushed forward and spilled us onto the stone pathway. David and I crumpled to the ground, choking on water and coughing up our lungs. Our breaths escaped in a fog as we shivered against the bone-biting chill. Unfortunately, we'd gone from the ice box to the freezer.

David rose to his feet, soaked to the bone. "Let's go," he said, his teeth chattering. He reached a hand out and helped me to my feet. My body protested, aching from the cold, but I grit my teeth and rose alongside of him.

Our flashlights had obviously stopped working, but we no longer needed them anyway. The blade trap had been disabled, and the path ahead was clear for us to make our way out. We set forward towards the entrance of the mausoleum, running our hands along the walls until our feet met the base of the stairs. Then, we trudged forward and emerged from Saint George's empty tomb.

"That was close," I breathed. I faced David and scowled. "You didn't say it would be that crazy."

He shrugged. "I had no idea it would be. I didn't put the vamplate here."

It made sense, though—the Order could never risk leaving the pieces in a place where they might easily be discovered.

I reached my hand out to the side and followed the wall to the door of the mausoleum. With a creak, David opened the door, exposing us to the faint sunlight outside and the drifting breeze that made us shiver even more.

We descended the steps and emerged from the mausoleum, thankful to be out of that death-trap. But what awaited us outside was the last thing I'd expected, and probably worse than almost drowning inside the crypt.

Ridley Bancroft stood before us with a subtle smile on his face and his hands folded before him. He looked harmless, except for the eerie way his wide eyes watched me. With that creepy smile and those unblinking eyes, he looked insane.

"Hello, David," he said politely. "It's good

to see you again."

David stepped before me and outstretched an arm, gesturing for me to stay back.

Ridley's mouth twitched as he suppressed a smile. "May I ask what you're doing in this part of town so early in the morning?"

"Oh, you know," David replied with a shrug. "Taking a stroll and visiting some of our deceased relatives."

Ridley raised an eyebrow. "'Our'?"

He nodded towards me. "My nephew."

I swallowed the lump in my throat as Ridley looked upon me once more. I hoped he couldn't see through our lies.

But if he could, he made no mention of it. "Ah, yes," Ridley said as his curious smile returned. "He was with Marcus at the diner last night. It's a shame you two have caught him up in your troubles, David."

"You're alone, I take it?" David asked, ignoring his comments.

"I am," he confirmed. "Though don't take it lightly." He opened the left flap of his jacket and revealed a shiny 40-caliber pistol cradled in a shoulder holster. His faint smile returned for a brief moment.

David narrowed his eyes and smiled darkly. He opened the left side of his blazer, too. "I guess it's a standoff," he said, revealing his own weapon.

Ridley smiled, as if having his life threatened only excited him more. "Well, I hate to say this, David, but I'm afraid I can't let you leave. You and your nephew will have to come with me."

David laughed. "You don't honestly expect me to go along with that, do you?"

"Well, I hoped you wouldn't be difficult."

With a bitter grin, David said, "How about we make a deal?"

Ridley narrowed his eyes at David. "What do you have in mind?"

"The boy goes free," David answered, "and you can take me with you."

"What?" I demanded. "David, you can't—"

"After all," David interrupted, ignoring me, "this has nothing to do with him."

Ridley stared at him for a good minute before a dark grin crossed his face. "It's a deal." Then, he turned his attention towards me. "You're free to go, young man."

I faced my guardian. "David, I'm not leaving you."

David placed a hand on my shoulder and squeezed tightly. "The keys are in the ignition," he said very slowly. "Get yourself out of here."

I thought I saw the smallest grin tug at the corners of his mouth, paired with desperation in his eyes. *The keys are in the ignition.* There was some hidden meaning behind that. He wanted me to act.

Finally, he released me and stepped back, lacing his fingers behind his head like a captured criminal. I sprinted away from the scene and towards the truck, my heart thumping wildly in my chest. Ridley's eyes followed me until I climbed into the passenger's seat.

The keys were still in the ignition. Did David want me to run Ridley over? Or had I been imagining that he was trying to communicate something with me in that tiny moment before I'd abandoned him? I didn't think we would have come this far just for David to be taken away and me to be left alone. After all, I couldn't get very far on my own.

In the distance, Ridley had forced David to his knees. He fished out a pair of handcuffs from his blazer and clamped one of the cuffs over David's left wrist.

My gaze darted between David, Ridley, and the keys. Quickly, I placed my backpack on the seat. I crawled over to the driver's side, my eyes glued upon the scene before me. My frozen hands reached for the key.

Ridley had almost closed the second cuff around David's right wrist when I flicked over the ignition. The truck rumbled to life, distracting them for the briefest moment.

David and Ridley jerked their heads in my direction. I fumbled with the gear stick, shifting into Drive. Then, I floored the gas pedal. The truck lurched forward with a terrible jolt, knocking my head to the back of the seat. I gripped the steering wheel with both hands and stared forward at Ridley, driving the truck in his direction.

His eyes grew wide as the truck sped towards him. He remained rooted to the earth, uncertain if I would actually run him over. I might not have, but the adrenaline pumping through my veins told me to do otherwise.

With Ridley distracted, David leapt to his feet, elbowed Ridley across the face, and push-kicked him until he fell onto his back. I slammed on the brakes at the last minute and yanked the wheel to the left. The truck came to a halt and David dived out of the way, snatching up the gun that Ridley had dropped during his fall.

David sprinted towards the truck and threw the driver's side door open, gesturing wildly for me to move over. I scrambled out of the seat and to the other side of the truck. He jumped into the moving vehicle, pulling the door closed behind him.

On my side of the truck, Ridley was climbing to his feet. He scrambled for the gun lying in the grass that he had taken from David. His face was beet red with anger, and his eyes raged with hatred. He locked his gaze upon me and raised his weapon. My instincts commanded me to hit the deck.

David floored the gas pedal, and as soon as he did, a bullet shattered the back window. David dipped his head down, ducking just long enough to avoid the waterfall of glass shards sprinkling onto our seats and into our hair. Another gunshot echoed somewhere behind us, thankfully missing its target.

I kept my head down and closed my eyes, waiting until I no longer heard gunshots firing. After what felt like minutes, I craned my neck and peered up at David. "Are we safe yet?"

He glanced at me. "We're safe. You can sit up now."

With a relieved sigh, I straightened up and carefully brushed bits of glass out of my hair and off my jacket. With the back window destroyed, the truck had quickly become an ice box.

David gripped the steering wheel with one hand and removed a gray blanket from behind the passenger's seat with the other, handing it to me. "It's not much," he said, "but it will do for now."

I wrapped the blanket around me as David fired up the heater in the truck. His hands shook, frozen to the bone, but he didn't complain. Then, he leaned back in his seat and stared forward at the road, exhaling with relief. "Well," he said, "that was fun."

"It was…something," I said. "I don't know if 'fun' is the word."

"I'm sorry, Logan," he said. "I hope you're not permanently damaged after all that's happened in the past two days."

"If I'm not yet," I said, "I'm sure I will be eventually."

He chuckled. "You'll be just fine."

"You weren't seriously going to leave me on my own, were you?" I demanded.

"Of course not. Don't you think I'm smarter than that?"

"Well, if it hadn't been for me, you would have—"

"Exactly," he said. "If it hadn't been for *you*. I knew you'd figure something out. The only way I could have been clearer about the truck was if I'd screamed it."

I raised an eyebrow. "So, you risked your life in hopes of *me* saving you?"

"Well, if I can't trust my Dragonlord to save me, then who can I trust?" But he said it with a humorous tone, like he knew I was bigger than I thought I was.

I couldn't help laughing. There we were, driving away from Ridley for the second time, narrowly avoiding death. Relief sank over me like the sun's warming rays, and for the briefest moment, I forgot how cold I was.

But then, a thought crossed my mind, and a chill ran over me once more. "How did Ridley find us?"

He shrugged. "He's probably been trailing us since last night, when he found you and Wolf at that diner."

"Then why didn't he come after us during the night?"

He narrowed his eyes, seemingly disturbed by my suggestion. But after a long moment, he said, "I don't know, Logan, but I wouldn't worry too much about it. Once we get to Julianna's, we'll be safe. That place is like a fortress." He glanced at me and saw the concern in my eyes. "Really. Don't worry."

I nodded, recognizing the hint to drop the subject. Silence settled over us.

David turned the radio on low enough to give us company, but not loud enough to distract us. I leaned back in my seat and wrapped the blanket around my shoulders, staring out at the highway that lay before us. My skin tingled as the adrenaline rushing through my veins slowly faded, and I smiled to myself. For whatever reason, I couldn't help feeling like David was right.

That *was* fun.

CHAPTER SIX

THE SECOND TRIAL

The more I heard about Julianna Thorne, the more I expected her to be an old witch or an evil queen. But when we got to Lake Tahoe and I finally met the head of the Order herself, she was nothing like I had imagined.

That's not to say she wasn't scary, but in ways different than I had expected.

Around noon later that day, we pulled into the driveway of the nicest house I'd ever seen in my life. Once Wolf had told me we were traveling to Lake Tahoe, I expected to see cabins like the ones I'd stayed in at elementary school camps. Julianna's home, however, wasn't anything like that.

A balcony wrapped around the entire exterior of the house, which was three stories high. A massive window with long drawn curtains shielded my view from what I assumed to be the living room. The front door was at least eight feet tall, with iron pulls instead of doorknobs. Three thick, cobblestone fireplaces reached high above the roof, wide enough for Santa and his entire sleigh to fit through. Unlike David's home in Carson City—let alone, my house—this cabin looked more like a celebrity's getaway.

Wolf's red pick-up truck was already parked in the driveway, blocking part of the entrance to the three-car garage. David pulled his truck in behind Wolf's, and we climbed out into the cool afternoon.

Our clothes were still a bit damp, but we had gotten used to the chill in the past hour. David promised that Julianna would have spare clothes for us.

I stared up at the house with my mouth hanging open. "She lives *here*?" I asked.

David grinned. "You'd think she ought to be less conspicuous, but I'd be more afraid for anyone who tries to mess with *her*."

I shuddered at that remark, and the image of a spell-casting witch returned to my mind. "What does she do for a living?"

"She's an art director," he said. "There's good money in that, I hear."

"Does she have any kids?"

"No," David replied. "Her life is dedicated to the Order."

"Well, what about you? Why don't *you* have kids?"

"That's a bit of a loaded question, isn't it?" he asked, but he was grinning.

"Sorry," I said, shrugging. "I guess I just thought the members of the Order were sworn to remain childless for the sake of keeping their families safe, or something like that."

"That may be true to some extent," he replied, "although we're not *sworn* to it. I guess you could say life simply hasn't brought forth the opportunity for a family yet."

"So, you *do* want kids."

He chuckled and clapped a hand on my shoulder. "Let's go inside."

And the conversation ended there.

I really liked David. He seemed like he

would be a good father—but then again, what would I know? I'd never had anything even close to a father figure in my life.

I followed David up the driveway and to the front door, where he entered without knocking. The interior of the house was even more impressive than the outside. The ceiling stretched two stories high, where planks of dark wood crisscrossed into an artistic pattern. A large gold chandelier hung directly above the center of the room, its small lights flickering and dancing off of the sand-colored walls. Loveseats, armchairs, and sofas were arranged around the floor, and a piano sat in the back corner. Not the piano your kid uses to practice for the school musical—it was a grand piano, the kind that makes you feel like Mozart himself if you even dare to touch it.

Antique sculptures lined the walls on expensive display stands, and massive oil paintings of Venice, of a duke in formal attire, and of a woman on stage at the opera hung on three of the walls. On both of the far walls, two fires blazed in the pits. The window I'd seen from the outside reached forward like a San Francisco bay window, and a couch lined the bottom sill. The glossy wood floors were covered by expensive burgundy rugs embroidered with golden flowers and vines.

I was already overwhelmed by the house itself—what would I do when I finally met Julianna?

I never thought I would be happy to see Wolf, but I was thankful to find a face I recognized. He rose from a loveseat near one of the fireplaces and headed towards us, frowning. "What took you two so long to get here? Carson City is only an hour away." Then, he looked us over, scrunching his eyebrows. "And...why are you wet?"

David and I exchanged glances. "It's a long story," he replied with a sigh. "We had some trouble."

Wolf hesitated. "Trouble?"

"Ridley."

He shook his head and drew in a slow breath. "Julianna won't be happy." he said. "But I'm glad you two are safe, anyway. Did you manage to get the piece?"

"Yes, we did," David said, and that ended it, much to Wolf's dismay.

I heard the clicking of a woman's heels coming from one of the adjacent hallways, and a tall woman in a nice pair of black pants and heeled boots entered the room. Her long, honey-colored hair hung in neat waves around her shoulders, and her wintry blue eyes instantly fell upon me. A pleased grin crossed her lips, and she headed towards us.

She stopped before me and looked me over, as if inspecting me for flaws or determining if I was an imposter. Then, she offered me a smile. "You must be Logan," she said. Her voice was soft and delicate, like skating on thin ice. But as with skating on thin ice, I imagined her cool demeanor could shatter in an instant. There was a reason she was the head of the Order.

If anyone could keep me safe, if anyone knew what they were doing, it was Julianna.

"That's me," I said. "In the flesh."

I immediately felt stupid. What did that even mean? I'd heard a character say that in a movie, and it had sounded cool then. When I said it, though, it sounded ridiculous.

But she didn't seem to notice. "I can't tell you how pleased I am to finally meet you," she said, extending a hand. "My name is Julianna."

I stood up straight and grasped her thin, bony hand. I suddenly became aware of how messy my hair was and how bad I must have smelled beneath my soaked clothes. I had always considered my mother to be the most beautiful person in the world, but this woman certainly held her own, and I found myself wanting to impress her. "Nice to meet you," I said.

She glanced at David. "The vamplate?"

"It is with our Dragonlord," he replied.

She smiled, pleased. "As it should be." Then, she faced me. "Grab yourself a jacket and come with me, Logan. We're going to take a walk."

I looked desperately at Wolf and David, hoping they would rescue me, but they were in no position to argue against Julianna Thorne. Wolf shrugged off his thick blazer and handed it over to me, which I gratefully took. I pulled it over my shoulders and followed after Julianna, my gut twisting with uncertainty.

We exited the house through the front door and headed down a steep descending path that led towards the lake far below in the distance. The path formed into a jagged set of roughly carved stairs. Splintery ropes guided the walkway down the side of the mountain, stretching all the way to shore of the lake down below.

I followed Julianna down the stairs, using the ropes as my guide. As we neared the lake down below, the air became even chillier, which did nothing to help me. I thought to ask if I could go back and take a moment to change clothes, or at least warm up by one of the fires in the castle, but I didn't want to speak out of turn around Julianna.

Julianna waited at the base of the stairs for me. Once I reached the ground, she continued ahead towards a small boathouse in the distance. "How was the first trial?" she asked.

Speaking of the trial made me shiver even more—the mere thought of that icy water sent chills across my skin. "It was an underground crypt that locked me inside after I found the vamplate," I said. "It was a lot of fun."

She grinned at me. "Well, did you think the trials were meant to be easy? The Order can't risk just anyone finding the pieces."

"But David said they can only be retrieved by the Dragonlord. So, what does it matter if they're hidden well or not?"

"Do you think the Order would take such a chance?" she asked, raising an eyebrow. "Ascalon is a weapon that bears the power to slay the mightiest beast ever known to man. Would you want to leave something like that lying around for any passer-by to find?"

"Well…no."

She studied me for a moment, as if contemplating whether or not I was worthy of my inherited title. "I imagine that it won't take Cain long to discover that your father is no longer the Dragonlord," she said. "He will try to force your father to retrieve the pieces, but when Cain finds that he can't, he will know that there is a new heir. I don't know how long it will take him to realize this—that is, if he hasn't already."

"Then what was that Ridley guy doing, chasing us?"

"If we're lucky, he did not know who you are, and was only after David and Marcus," she answered. "Cain will have undoubtedly sent them after us. We are the only things standing in his way. Us, and you."

We approached the boathouse, and Julianna reached into her pocket for a ring of keys. She fished through each one individually until she came to a small silver key. Then, she unlocked the door to the boathouse. It creaked open, revealing a small living space with a wide, stretching window on the opposite wall and another door that led out to the dock. A rickety wooden desk was positioned in the back corner.

Waves lapped gently against the beams beneath the house as we entered. Julianna crouched down to the ground and ran her fingers along the creases of the wood paneling. She tapped her knuckles in various spots, stopping only when a hollow echo answered. Then, she glanced around the room and pointed to the desk. "Bring me that crowbar."

I retrieved the metal bar and handed it to her, nearly tripping over my feet with the eagerness to obey.

She pried at the wood paneling until a loud groan erupted and the panel opened on some invisible hinge. Cobwebs stretched across the blackness below, and a musty smell of cold air met my nose. I leaned back and covered my mouth, avoiding the dust and stale odor.

Julianna didn't seem bothered. She rose to her feet and stepped back, gesturing towards the cavernous depths below. "And this is where you go on alone," she said.

I leapt to my feet. "*Alone*? But..." I almost told her that David had gone with me into the crypt, but I remembered him saying it was forbidden, so I closed my mouth. "Well, are you sure you can't come?"

"I'm sure, Logan," she replied. "I promise you will be fine."

I glanced down the dark shaft, trying to be brave—especially in front of Julianna—but I didn't know what lay beyond the darkness. That thought alone made my stomach turn.

But I stood tall and drew in a deep breath, facing Julianna. It wasn't the time to be a coward. "All right. I'll go down there."

Julianna reached into her blazer and removed a small flashlight about six inches in length. I didn't think it would brighten my path very much, but I took it anyway. "I'll wait for you here," she said.

I nodded and faced the shaft. The edges of a ladder protruded near the lip. I carefully lowered myself, gripping the cold bars and descending into the darkness. The shadows enveloped me, and within several moments, I could not see five feet in front of me.

"Good luck, Logan," Julianna called from above. Then, she slammed the ceiling panel shut, and I was alone.

I can't say that the second trial was any better or worse than the first. What *was* worse, though, was being alone. I tried to convince myself that Saint George's confidantes wouldn't have built the trial in a way that could *really* kill me—right?

Then, I remembered that the trials were made in an effort to keep out the uninvited.

Although I was the Dragonlord, as Julianna had pointed out, the Order wouldn't have taken such a risk. My life was on the line in a way I did not yet understand.

The tiny flashlight didn't do much to help me as I crept through the dark tunnel, other than to show me that the course was unending and straight. The option to turn or stray from the beaten path did not exist.

I continued ahead for what felt like an hour until I finally saw the faint, orange glow of a light in the distance, flickering off the walls. My pace quickened, and I found myself standing outside of a gate.

Shiny, brass bars extended towards the ceiling, but there was no visible indication of how to go beyond them. There was no lock or handle, and they certainly weren't separated enough for me to slip through.

Lit torches hung on both my sides on the far walls, but they were not bright enough for me to see what lay beyond the bars. I took a cautious step towards the bars and felt myself drop a few inches into the ground. I looked down and found myself standing on a square panel with the same intricate carvings and designs upon it that I had seen at the crypt.

Then, the bars rumbled and retracted into the ceiling above, allowing me to move beyond. What followed next, though, made me question whether I really wanted to go on.

As soon as the bars disappeared and made way for me to continue, a loud crunching noise echoed beyond, like a gear being jammed into place to start a machine. A repetitive *clunk-clunk-clunk* followed without cease. One by one, torches ignited on the walls in the cavern before me, revealing the dangerous task at hand.

The cavern beyond the bars was massive and deep. The ceiling stretched for at least fifty feet, and the ground below was equally far. The darkness prevented me from seeing where the ceiling ended and where the ground began.

Scattered throughout the room were pillars of various heights, some too high for me to even imagine reaching, and others low enough and near enough for me to jump to. To make matters worse, the pillars were rotating, which was probably the cause of the clanking noise.

On the opposite side of the cavern, I could see a long, stretching balcony. It was narrow—

probably enough that I could easily fall off and plummet to the endless earth below—but it was my goal. An ornamental box on a stone dais was positioned in the center of the balcony, identical to the one I'd seen in the crypt. Somehow, I was going to have to make my way across the room—across those rotating pillars—and get to the other side. Alive.

The very idea was ludicrous. What other thirteen-year-olds could say they had to do something like that in their life?

I swallowed the lump in my throat and moved forward, stepping onto the stone platform that jutted out towards the lowest pillar before me. I surveyed the room, hoping I'd missed some kind of staircase that would take me to the other side without having to face the death-trap, but of course, there was nothing.

Then, the gate behind me rattled towards the ground, its spiked ends meeting the earth once more. I wheeled on my feet and threw myself at my only escape, but I was too late. The gate was sealed. My only way out involved moving forward. Hopefully, reaching the piece on the other side would cause the gate to reopen and give way to my escape. Hopefully.

I drew in a deep breath and walked towards the edge of the platform, staring down at the rotating pillar before me. Beyond it, about ten feet up and to the left, there was a shorter pillar.

In the distance, there was a much taller pillar, taller by at least ten feet. I could have easily jumped between the first two, but not the second and third.

The fourth pillar was a bit shorter than the previous, and the final pillar—though it was a decent height—rotated so quickly, I thought I would lose my balance and fall to the earth below if I could even make it that far.

So, in summary: I had only one chance—*one chance*—to get across the rotating pillars of death and make it to the other side to retrieve the second piece of Ascalon. *And* I had to make it back the way I came.

I tried to calm my shaking nerves as I tiptoed to the edge of the platform, closing as much distance between myself and the first pillar as I could.

No time to think about it, I told myself, *you just have to move.* I clenched my fists, drew in a deep breath, and bent my knees. Then, I leapt forward, landing on top of the first pillar just five feet below me. I crumpled to my hands and knees to slow my momentum.

Well, that wasn't so bad.

Then, the unpredictable happened. The pillar began to descend into the darkness below, triggered by my weight. My head jerked this way and that, searching for some source of rescue. My only means of escape was through returning to the platform from where I had come, or continuing on down the line of pillars.

Drawing in a deep breath, I threw myself across the space towards the second pillar as it became more distant. My fingernails scratched against the stone, flailing for a grasp on the edge of the pillar. I gripped the edges tightly and pulled myself up. Unfortunately, my relief didn't last long.

The second pillar began to rise. I didn't doubt that the column would ascend towards the ceiling and crush me flat. I had to get off of there. I scrambled to my feet and braced myself, facing the third pillar as I continued to rise. I prayed a quick prayer and threw myself across the distance, barely landing atop the third pillar with a heavy thud.

But I was nowhere near out of the woods. The second and first pillars had returned to their original heights, and fortunately the third had not risen or descended. It was the closest I would come to a break before reaching the piece on the balcony.

But when I looked back at the previous pillars, I saw that they had begun to spout fire from the top, preventing me from returning the way I came. I stood on top of the third pillar with a stupid look on my face. How the heck was I supposed to get back?

I would have to worry about it later. First, I needed to reach the second piece.

I drew in a deep breath and took advantage of the long break I had between the third and fourth pillars. Then, I threw myself across the way towards the next pillar.

The fourth pillar rotated too quickly for me to gain a steady balance, but I remained on my feet anyway. I kept my focus on the final pillar, trying to figure out how I would reach it without falling into the pit below.

But I had no time to ponder it. I wasn't getting anywhere by just standing there. I braced myself, and when I rotated to face the final pillar, I threw myself across the open space. Somehow, by an unforeseen miracle—or, more likely, triggered by my weight—the final pillar came to a complete halt. I almost tumbled over the edge of the pillar with excitement, and I clawed for my grasp once more. Perhaps whoever had designed the trial thought that if someone could reach the final pillar *alive,* he deserved a lucky break.

My limbs ached and shook as I collapsed on my back, heaving deep breaths and thanking God for my survival. After I recollected myself, I crawled to my hands and knees. I was so worn out and high with adrenaline that dropping to the balcony below was nothing.

Solid earth had never been such a blessing. I turned and faced the death-trap behind me, watching as fire danced atop the pillars. I still had no idea how I was going to get back, and the very thought alone exhausted me further.

I made my way across the narrow balcony towards the stone dais, examining the box and the markings upon it. The symbol on the top of the box was different—instead of a wave, there was a circle with a flame inside of it. It was appropriate, of course, but I hated it all the same.

I pressed the button in and the doors of the box swung open, revealing a shiny obsidian spearhead a few inches longer and wider than my hand. My eyes feasted upon the weapon as I retrieved it from its shelter.

The stone was smooth and glassy, but the edges and the point were sharp and rigid. I carefully pressed my finger against the tip, in awe of the fact that such a small weapon had slain countless dragons in the past, that it now belonged to me to carry out the same task.

My admiration was cut short when a great quaking shook the earth around me. I collapsed to my hands and knees and looked up to see the pillars coming to a startling halt. A screeching, crunching noise followed, as if the gears operating the rotating pillars had been jammed, or perhaps destroyed altogether.

I didn't need to be told twice to get up and make a run for it. The flames had extinguished completely, but the pillars were collapsing and crumbling, falling into the void of darkness below. On the opposite side of the cavern, I could see that the gate had opened up once again.

I grit my teeth together, shoved the spearhead into my sweater, and bolted forward, crying out loud like a wild man as I jumped across the space to the crumbling pillar before me.

I nearly lost my footing as the pillar fell towards the earth below. I took advantage of the slope and leapt across the open space, using my momentum to propel forward.

I waited until each pillar had begun to crumble before continuing ahead. Once the columns before me had crumbled enough for me to reach their height, I powered through. I almost slipped and fell into the shadows below on several occasions, but some powerful will inside of me kept me going.

I leapt from the final pillar to the balcony,

landing with a heavy thud on my shoulder. The spearhead poked me sharply in the side through my sweater, but the pain wasn't enough to catch my attention.

I crawled onto my knees and stared at the scene before me, watching as the pillars continued to disappear. The cavern fell into darkness as the roaring quakes continued. The torches lining the walls of the cavern extinguished. Within a moment, I couldn't see anything but the balcony upon which I stood, illuminated only by the torches on the walls that had remained lit.

And then, the cavern fell into complete silence. The pillars had collapsed completely, leaving only an empty space of darkness between the balconies. Clearly, whoever had built these chambers never meant for them to be used again.

I rose to my feet, my limbs aching and my head pounding. Since the task was complete, I finally had time to acknowledge my pain, and there was a lot of it.

As I headed down the dark tunnel to return to Julianna, guided only by the light of my small flashlight, one thought sprang to my mind: I didn't need to dry off for *that*. There had been enough fire to do the job.

I cracked a smile and continued forward.

CHAPTER SEVEN

EMMA KINGSLEY

After the second death-trap, I was finally allowed to rest and relax. A warm shower had never felt so good.

Somehow, Julianna had figured out my size in shirts, jeans, socks, and (embarrassingly enough), boxers. Five sets of clothes awaited me in the room I had chosen for the evening. Although I had brought my own clothes with me, I couldn't help choosing my new wardrobe over the old. I had never owned such expensive clothing before, and I wanted to find out if it actually *felt* different than my usual wardrobe.

I headed down the stairs after I was cleaned up and made my way to the dining room. A long oak table stretched from one end of the room to the other. Carved ham, mashed potatoes, various fruits and vegetables, and three casserole dishes were settled on the center of the table.

But even *that* wasn't as impressive as the maid and butler moving between the dining room and the kitchen, bringing refills whenever necessary and standing watch nearby if anyone should need anything. Julianna really was like a queen living in a castle.

Wolf, David, and Julianna had already dug into plates full of food, talking over their meals like visiting relatives. They glanced up when I entered the room.

"Ah," Julianna said, setting down her glass of water. "You found your new wardrobe, then."

I nodded and looked myself over. "Thanks," I said. "Uh…how did you know my sizes?"

She smiled at me, a look that was both beautiful and convicting. "It's my job to know."

And that settled it. Julianna gestured over the spread of food before her. "Come. Sit down and eat. You must be starving."

I didn't need to be told twice. Seating myself on David's side, I filled an empty plate with food. I felt like I was having an early Thanksgiving. They watched me with amused grins as I inhaled my meal.

"So, what was the second trial like?" David asked.

I shrugged. "It wasn't too bad. I really liked the part where the rotating pillars collapsed."

He grinned at me.

"You still have the third trial," Julianna reminded me. "I imagine it won't be any less complicated or dangerous."

"But we're two-for-three now," I said. "Almost out of the woods."

"Almost," she agreed. "But retrieving the pieces of Ascalon is only our first task."

I raised my eyebrows. "And the tasks that follow?"

She took a dainty sip of her water and returned the glass to the table. "Stopping Cain Hunter."

I already knew the answer, but hearing her voice it only made me dread it more.

I shuffled through the contents on my plate with my fork, suddenly no longer hungry. "Can you promise that my father is alive?" I asked.

They exchanged glances with each other. Wolf and David returned their attention to their food, and Julianna's eyes drifted towards the floor. "The only thing keeping your father alive is Cain's ignorance," she replied. "So long as he doesn't learn of *your* existence, William Lockwood is safe. If we move quickly enough, we can stay his execution."

Her words were sharp, yet truthful. I wished she would soften the blow, but she really couldn't do anything to help me. I suppose I shouldn't have been so bothered—I had never met the man, after all—but he *was* still my father. He was in captivity, on the brink of death, because of me.

I leaned back in my chair and fixed my gaze upon her. "Then we'll just have to move more quickly."

"We can only move so quickly, Logan," she said. "We can't control Cain's next move anymore than we can control time."

I stared down at the lumps of my food and nodded, wishing to change the subject. "So, this Ridley guy," I said. "Who exactly is he?"

Her features softened. I guessed she was relieved to be off the subject of my father. "He was once a member of the Order, as well," Julianna replied. "He spent his entire life by our sides. Then, when Cain turned on us, he joined him. The man was always like a father to Cain, but Cain never took advantage of his affections."

"And not of Arianne's either," David added

with a chuckle. "The woman is madly in love with him, but he'll never give her the time of day."

"The Order was divided upon Cain's betrayal," Julianna continued. "And as you can imagine, we don't want the truth about the Dragonlord and the great dragons to be leaked to the world. So long as Cain roams free carrying the knowledge he possesses, we are not safe."

I nodded slowly, feeling ten times smaller than I had moments ago. The more I heard about Cain, the less safe I felt. I could only pretend to be brave for so long before the nagging itch in the back of my brain reminded me that the odds weren't exactly in my favor.

I pushed back in my chair and rose to my feet. "If you'll excuse me," I said, "I think I'm going to go up to my room for a bit."

Julianna nodded. "If you need anything, let us know."

She, David, and Wolf continued to chat amongst themselves, immersed in a conversation about the woodwork of Julianna's house that bored me to near-death. They paid me little attention as I headed down the hall, admiring the art lining the adjacent hallways.

I glanced back at them, pretending to be captivated by a bust of a Roman soldier, and snuck into the shadows. Then, I slipped out the front door of the house.

I stood on the porch, alone except for the sound of a car door slamming nearby. I guessed it was the neighbors—although, if I'd thought harder about it then, I would've realized Julianna didn't *have* any neighbors. I breathed in the fresh scent of the trees and the mountain air, thankful for the short time I would have to myself for the rest of the evening. For the briefest moment, I felt like I was home in Ashland again. My heart ached, and I thought of my mother.

I tried to push those thoughts aside and set forward down the dirt path towards the trees in the distance. I figured a walk on my own would do me good.

The path led away from the house to a descending cluster of trees. I followed it for about fifteen minutes until it narrowed and disappeared through the forest, walking until the house was no longer visible when glancing backwards. Crickets chirped on my sides, and owls hooted in the distance. I found myself relaxing, longing for the solitude of nature. I had gone far enough inland that I couldn't hear any cars or voices. I was completely alone, and I loved it.

Deeper into the woods, the trees flanked my left side and a narrow cliff jutted out on my right. Far below in the distance, the lake glistened beneath the moonlight. The wind blew past me, carrying me towards the body of water below. I smiled inside, thinking that after things were over, my mother and I ought to visit Tahoe for a vacation. A long, healthy vacation.

Then, I heard a rustling in the bushes nearby, and I suddenly realized how stupid it was for me to have left the house on my own. There were people who wanted me dead, after all. How could I be so careless?

I glanced behind me, trying to convince myself it was just the wind, but then I heard a twig snap. There was something hiding in the darkness, watching me, waiting for the right moment to strike. And there I stood at the edge of a cliff, unarmed and alone. If Ridley Bancroft was sitting in the bushes with a gun, I'd be dead in seconds.

I had two choices: I could run. Or I could fight.

Well, I hadn't been in many fights in my life—for the most part, I avoided them at all costs. But I was the Dragonlord, and I didn't want to be known for running away from a confrontation like a scared child.

I kept my eyes trained on the bushes in the distance and slowly bent down to scoop up the sharp rock near my foot. I cocked my arm back, preparing to launch it.

The bushes rustled again, and from out of the shrubs leapt a big brown mountain lion, roaring as it sprang into my path. I stumbled backwards with the rock at hand, too paralyzed with fear to actually attack the creature. It crouched before me with its soft yellow eyes locked on me. It bared its ivory fangs and growled low in its throat.

At home in Ashland, we had been taught at a young age how to react if a mountain lion approached us. I knew better than to run, because if I ran, it would think I was prey and chase me down—and besides, there was no way I could outrun a mountain lion. But if I stayed where I was, it would still attack. What choice did I have?

Why the heck did I leave the house in the first place?

The mountain lion arched its back, preparing to leap towards me. I staggered backwards and tripped over a tree root jutting out of the ground, landing flat on my back.

For a moment, my heart stopped beating. Time stood still as I waited for the mountain lion to crush me and make me into its next meal—but the attack never came.

The beast continued to growl as I peeked at it from the corner of my eye, but its attention was directed elsewhere. I carefully sat up to find a hooded figure standing before the wildcat with a bow and arrow drawn back. The mountain lion snarled angrily and swatted a paw in warning in my rescuer's direction. I glimpsed its sharp claws, and my throat tightened with fear.

My savior was a lot braver than I, thankfully. Instead of panicking, he shot the arrow at the mountain lion's feet. The cat snarled and leapt backwards. He fired another arrow, and the mountain lion backed away further.

Then, he advanced on the beast and let out a loud, "*HA!*" But it wasn't a *he*—I was surprised to find that my savior was a girl. She waved her arms and continued to hoot at the cat, making herself look a little crazy.

Another thing they had taught us back in Ashland: make yourself appear bigger, and the beast is likely to back down.

The cat backed away and growled, flattening its ears against its head. Its tail flicked back and forth as it watched the girl, as if trying to decide whether or not she was worth the kill. After an extremely long minute, it turned away with one last angry growl and trudged off into the woods. The girl kept her arrow trained on the mountain lion's trail for almost a minute until he was gone for good.

Finally, she turned towards me. As she approached, she removed the hood of her dark sweater. "You shouldn't be out here, you know," she said. "Cain and his followers are like ghosts. They appear out of nowhere and are impossible to get rid of."

"Well, after *that*," I replied, "I'm not exactly worried about Cain Hunter. I'm more worried about mountain lions and woodland beasts."

"And you should be," she said. "We got lucky. That thing could've torn out your neck."

I reached a hand to my throat and swallowed. "Thanks for putting it in such graphic terms."

"It may have left," she said, "but it could still come back. Let's get out of here." She slung her bow over her shoulder and offered me her hand.

I recognized her instantly once she stepped into the moonlight. She was the girl who had spilled the coffee on Ridley at the diner in Redding. Her long blonde hair was pulled back into a low ponytail, and her aqua-green eyes locked firmly with mine.

"Who are you?" I asked as she pulled me to my feet.

"My name is Emma Kingsley."

I removed my hand from hers, trying to ignore the warmth of her skin. "But...*who* are you?"

"I'll explain on the way back to the house," she said. And she was off.

I picked up the pace and chased after her. "So, you're my guardian angel? Is that who you are?"

"You should be so lucky," she shot back. "My father is a friend of your father's." Her eyes darted to the ground, and she slowed her pace just a bit. "Well...he *was* a friend of your father's."

I frowned. "What do you mean?"

She didn't respond for several moments, leaving only the sound of our footsteps as we trekked the path towards Julianna's house. "Never mind. Where is your father? I need to speak with him."

"He's...not here," I said. "He's missing."

She stopped walking and her eyes widened. "*Missing*? No, that can't be."

"Well, it's true. That's the whole reason I'm here. I'm going to find him."

She sighed irritably and continued down the path.

"And just *where* do you think you're going?" I demanded, following after her once more.

"I need to speak with the Order."

"Are you sure that's a good idea?" I asked. "They're not too welcoming of strangers."

"I'm no stranger."

"Then who are you? I mean, you know who Cain is. You know what the Order is. Just how much do you know about all of this?"

"I probably know more than you do, Dragon Boy."

I scoffed. "Dragon Boy?"

"Do you prefer 'Your Highness, the Great and Magnificent Dragonlord, Logan Lockwood'?"

"I prefer Logan, actually," I muttered.

"Fine," she said. "Logan, it is, then."

I slowed my walk, frowning. "And how do you know my name?"

She glanced at me, raising an eyebrow. "You'd be surprised how much I know about you."

I grinned mischievously. "Oh, yeah?"

"Don't flatter yourself," she shot back. "The only reason I know so much about you is because it's my job to know so much about you."

"Well, once you *really* get to know me, I'm sure you'll love me."

She rolled her eyes. "My father never told me you'd be so arrogant."

"I'm not arrogant," I argued. "I just find it interesting that I'm your personal project."

She shook her head disapprovingly and did not respond.

We ascended the hill, and the light from Julianna's home came into view. I should have considered myself lucky that the only things I'd found in the woods—or the only things that had found *me*—were the mountain lion and Emma, but my stomach turned as we continued towards the house.

The girl wouldn't take "no" for an answer, and I wasn't so sure the Order would be happy to see her.

"So, how did you find me?" I asked.

She shot me a pleading look. "I saw you leave and wander into the forest just as we pulled up to Julianna's house."

"We?"

"My aunt dropped me off," she explained. "At first, I didn't think you'd be dumb enough to wander into the woods alone, but you proved me wrong."

"Well, we can't all be outdoors experts like you, lugging around bows and arrows," I said, glancing at the quiver of arrows hanging across her back. "Why do you have that silly thing, anyway? Why not a gun, or at the very least, a knife?"

She glared at me. "These were specially designed and made by my father. Besides, I'm not trying to kill anyone. I'm just trying to stop them."

"Stop them from what?"

Without looking at me, she replied, "From killing you."

I was both offended and impressed. Offended, because this girl, who had to be about my age, thought I needed *her* to protect me. As if I didn't already have the Order to watch over me, too.

Impressed, because for one who seemed to dislike me so much, her main focus was to keep me alive. Her main focus at the diner had been to keep me alive, as well, which was why she'd so clumsily spilled a cup of hot coffee all over Ridley Bancroft.

Then, it occurred to me that she'd been following us since Redding, perhaps even longer than that. Whoever she was, this objective to keep me alive was no joke. She was a huntress, and the bow and arrow suited her.

But I couldn't let her know I admired her. So, I said, "Well, it's just a little too Robin Hood for my taste."

She yanked on the iron pull and pounded on the front door before shooting me a glare. "And what's your taste? Running scared and letting everyone else protect you?"

Unfortunately, she was right, and I had no retort. I was thankful that Julianna opened the door a second later. But in the moment that followed, I wanted to run.

Julianna's eyes lit with fire as she stared down at Emma. "Who are you?" she demanded. Then, she glanced at me. "And *what* are you doing out here, Logan?"

"I…uh, went for a walk," I replied.

"A walk," she repeated.

I nodded until my head felt like it would fall off. "You know…for fresh air."

Julianna stepped aside, opening the door all the way. "Come inside, please."

I trudged past her into the marble hallway. Wolf and David were in the grand foyer on their feet, reaching into their jackets for what could only be guns. I felt guilty for giving each of them a miniature heart attack.

"And *you*," Julianna said to Emma, "are to leave. *Now*. This is private property."

She started to close the door, but Emma wedged her arm into the crack and cried, "Wait! Please!"

Julianna hesitated and glared at her.

Emma drew in a deep breath. Even she faltered underneath Julianna's convicting glare. "I need your help," she said. "My father is Edward Kingsley. I think you've heard of him?"

Julianna stared down at her with narrowed eyes, still as a statue. "Yes, I know who he is."

Emma lowered her eyes to the floor. "He…he was killed three days ago by one of Cain's friends. Except for the help of some people he sent me to, I've been on my own since then."

Julianna narrowed her eyes, but she seemed to be listening. "So, what do you want?" she asked. It was more of a curious inquiry than a rude demand.

Emma rustled through her pants pocket and removed a folded piece of paper, extending it towards Julianna, who took it with hesitation. "He sent me to find William Lockwood. He told me the Order would help me."

Julianna unfolded the note and skimmed over the words. After only a few brief moments, she folded it and looked upon Emma once again. "I don't know how your father expected us to help you," she said. "These are life-or-death circumstances. The Order of Ascalon only exists to protect the Dragonlord. We're not babysitters."

Emma stood tall and drew in a deep breath. "We can help each other," she said. "I know everything there is to know about the Order, and about Cain. Even about the Dragonlord."

Julianna glared at her. "I asked you to leave. Don't make me call the police."

"You won't," Emma replied, returning Julianna's cold expression. "The last thing you want is for anyone to know where you are. And the police showing up on your doorstep would put you on Cain's map faster than if you'd announced it yourself."

I expected Julianna to slap her, or at the very least, scream at her. But to my surprise, she chuckled. "A Kingsley, indeed. Like your father, you don't seem to know when to walk away." She sighed and stepped aside. "For the next few minutes, at least, you're welcome inside. But don't get comfortable."

I exhaled in relief, even though I hadn't noticed that I'd been holding my breath. Perhaps I felt sorry for the girl—*I* would have buckled under Julianna's icy gaze. But she had held her own, and for that, she deserved a medal.

Emma climbed the steps and entered the hallway of the house, and Julianna sealed the door shut behind her. "We have a guest," Julianna proclaimed as she returned to the grand foyer. David and Wolf kept their eyes on Emma, as if they expected her to whip out her arrows and kill us all. Wolf's suspicious glare fell over her, which surprisingly made me even more uncomfortable than if he had been watching me instead. "You're the girl from the diner," he declared.

Emma nodded. "I was in the right place at the right time, it seems."

A grin spread across his face. "Yes, so it seems."

"She's a Kingsley," Julianna announced.

"Edward's daughter." She removed the letter Emma had given her and handed it over to David, who read it over more thoroughly than Julianna had. His features slowly contorted, and curiosity became sympathy. Once he reached the end of the letter, he looked up at Emma. "When did he pass?"

"Three nights ago," Emma said quietly. "Arianne Harper was there when it happened."

He paused, allowing for a brief moment of silence. "How did it happen?"

She swallowed, and her eyes filled with tears. She stared down at the floor. "It was just another night," she began in a shaky voice. "We were having dinner, and someone came to the door. My father got up to see who it was, then he came back in a panic and told me I needed to leave, to get as far away from home as I could and head for my aunt's house a few miles away. He gave me the letter before I left and told me to seek out the Order. I snuck out through the backyard and got about a half-mile away when…" She paused and drew in a breath to collect herself. "The house exploded. And I saw a woman leaving the scene of the crime. It couldn't be anyone but Arianne Harper."

"What makes you so sure it was her?" Wolf asked, arms crossed and eyebrows raised in disbelief.

"A few weeks ago," Emma said, "he'd become so jumpy, like he thought someone was watching him or following him. His letter only confirms his suspicions."

"That doesn't prove it was Arianne."

Emma glared at him. "I *saw* her leaving our

house."

"It could've been anyone."

"Who else would have been after my father? And what other answer could there be to *this*?" She held up the letter. "It was her. I have no doubt about it."

Wolf smirked at her, like he thought she was an incompetent fool. Ignoring him, she turned to David once more, finished with her horrific tale. He nodded understandingly and lowered his gaze. "I'm sorry," he said.

"And what are you doing here?" Wolf asked, invading the air of sympathy.

Emma drew herself upright, like a soldier standing tall. "I've come to seek out the Order, so that I might be appointed as a member."

Wolf released a hearty chuckle, but when no one else laughed—especially not Emma—he settled down, offering her a pleading look. "You're serious?"

"What's so funny?" she demanded. "As far as I understand, there are no conditions to be met when it comes to being appointed."

"Actually, there are," Wolf argued arrogantly. "It's a duty handed down from our fathers before us, descendants of Saint George's personal confidants. Just because your father stuck his nose into things that didn't concern him and *happened* to learn the truth doesn't mean you're welcome here."

"Half of my father's life was devoted to the secrets he knew about the Order and the Dragonlord," Emma fired back. "I think it's time for a change in tradition."

"And you're entitled to make that decision?"

"Maybe not," she replied, glancing suggestively at Julianna. "But what else are you going to do with me? I already know who you are, and I know where you're headed. If I were you, I'd be concerned about what would happen if I became a flight risk. You wouldn't want such precious information to fall into the wrong hands, would you? Perhaps into Cain's hands?"

Wolf glared at her. "I remember your father. He never knew when to keep quiet, and it seems that neither do you."

"She has a point," I spoke up. Everyone looked at me like they'd forgotten I was present. Emma narrowed her eyes, as if challenging me to open my mouth and say *anything*. I had the feeling that she wished I would shut up altogether, but I was the Dragonlord after all. I had a right to speak up. "I mean, she just saved my life, after all."

Wolf raised an eyebrow. "What are you talking about?"

My stomach sank. "Oh, yeah," I muttered. "When I went out for a walk, I kind of got chased down by a mountain lion."

The exclamations overlapped each other as David, Julianna, and Wolf expressed their disappointment in me.

"What in the *world* were you thinking?"

"You should've been smart enough not to wander out into the woods *alone*."

"Logan, you have *got* to be more careful."

I cringed until silence ensued. Then, I straightened up and sighed. "I'm sorry," I said. "I know it was stupid. I won't be making that mistake again. But if it weren't for Emma, I'd be dead. And after all, what's the harm in letting her team up with us?"

"The Order doesn't welcome outsiders," Wolf declared. "We don't know that we can trust her."

The question had actually been directed towards the more reasonable people, David and Julianna. "Well, everyone apparently knew her father, and you trusted him."

"His discovery of the Order was thanks to his dumb luck," Wolf argued. "And also thanks to your father."

I glared at him. "What does that mean?"

"That William has a history of making bad decision after bad decision."

Sure, I didn't know my father, but the guy was still my father after all, and I wasn't too thrilled hearing Wolf speak about him that way. "Besides that," I continued, ignoring him, "I think we ought to reconsider. After all, she's on her own."

Emma's expression softened. I don't know if it was because I had defended her or because of the cold, blatant truth in the statement. Either way, I was pleased that she wasn't giving me anymore death glares.

I looked to Julianna, but I could not interpret her expression. She had not taken her eyes off of Emma the entire time we'd been arguing. She didn't creep me out the way Wolf did when he looked at people, but I wasn't so sure I liked her face either. I felt as if she was deciding Emma's sentence in her mind, as if she hadn't heard a single word any of us had said.

"I don't think we have to decide this tonight," David spoke up, much to my relief. "It's late anyway, and the girl *is* on her own. The least we can do is offer her a place to sleep for the evening. If we decide against her accompaniment, we'll send her on her way at dawn. If not, well…" He shrugged, surrendering. "Then, we can always use another friendly face."

Julianna still did not move, and her gaze did not waver. I considered that maybe she could read minds—which wouldn't surprise me at all.

Then, she looked away. "A place to sleep for the evening," she echoed. "I agree. There is plenty of room here." I figured none of us would ever know what thoughts had been processing in Julianna's mind for the past several minutes.

"Are you sure about this?" Wolf asked. "The girl has practically come in off the street! Do you think—?"

"She's a girl, Marcus," Julianna said. "And we are trained members of an ancient Order. Honestly, what harm can she do?"

I had to hide my grin of sheer delight. Julianna was the only person whom Wolf would listen to, and watching her shut him down like that was an early Christmas present.

Wolf stood in place, clearly irritated. Julianna merely smiled at him, then faced Emma. "Have your pick of the spare bedrooms on the second floor."

Emma nodded. "Thank you," she said, and she turned away and headed towards the staircase down the hall.

I wanted to know more about Emma, but I figured that if I chased her down as she headed for her room, she'd think I was crazy. So, I faked a big yawn and said, "I think I'm gonna get to bed, too, actually. It's been a long day."

I turned on my heel, but David said, "Logan, wait." He approached me and glanced backwards at Wolf and Julianna, who had quietly resumed their argument over Emma's presence. He handed Emma's letter over to me. "Why are you giving this to me?" I asked.

"You're part of the Order, too," he said. And then he turned away and resumed his position on the couch by the fire.

I stared down at the piece of paper in my hand. Then, I shoved the letter into my pocket and headed towards my room upstairs.

Emma had settled into the empty room down the hall from mine. The door was cracked open, and I could hear her rummaging beyond. I wasn't sure, but I thought I heard her sniffling and crying, too.

I thought about speaking to her, but what would I say? And what would she say that the letter wouldn't already explain? I figured that if there was any chance of getting her to like me—or at least, tolerate me—it would be best if I left her alone.

Besides that, if she really was crying, she probably wanted her privacy. So, I turned away and headed for my own room, sealing myself inside.

    I lay across my bed and removed the letter, carefully unfolding it. It was worn-out and dirtied, as if it had been passed across a dozen pairs of hands. The ink was smudged in various places, and the creases from being repeatedly folded and unfolded had begun to tear.

    I read over the letter, absorbing each word so that I might not miss anything:

To the Order of Ascalon:

    I send you cordial greetings. You may have heard of me, or you may know me personally. I have been a friend of William Lockwood's for over two decades, and, by my own fortunate chance, I discovered the legend of the Order, and of the great Dragonlord.

    Let me assure you immediately: your secret is safe with me. I would never do anything to put the Order or its members in harm's way. It has always been my sincerest wish to join the Order and assist in protecting the Dragonlord, but as I understand, tradition dictates otherwise.

    If you've received this letter, I am no longer alive. Cain has long since been hunting down the Dragonlord. As he eventually became aware of our friendship and affiliation, he pursued me and my family in an effort to gain what secrets and information he could. I've repeatedly considered sending my only daughter your way for safety and protection, but I could not bear the idea of being without her.

Unfortunately, if you are reading this letter, this passing consideration must regretfully become an imperative demand. Cain has finally discovered my whereabouts and my connection to the Dragonlord, and I have neither the strength nor the resources to defend myself against him. I suppose I could only evade death for so long, and my time has come to an end. I will gladly give up my life to protect the Order.

My only request is that you look after my daughter, Emma. She does not know it, but I have been preparing her for the Order since her birth. She may be a child, and she may not fulfill the conditions of the Order's traditions, but she was born to fight. I humbly and respectfully appeal to you: please protect her.

My daughter knows only what is necessary to keep her alive. The true secrets of the Order remain yours and yours alone. It is at your discretion that you reveal to her what you will. Otherwise, your secrets die with me.

Humbly yours,

Edward Kingsley

I lowered the letter and stared across the room at the taupe-colored walls.

Emma was completely alone.

I could never imagine being alone in the world. Sure, I'd grown up without my father, but growing up without my mother, too, would have been a totally different story. And Emma's father had been killed only days ago. How had she remained so strong in the midst of his recent passing?

I felt somewhat guilty for having given her a hard time earlier—I mean, she kind of deserved it—but I suppose it was her way of shutting herself out from the pain of losing her father. I couldn't blame her for being the way she was.

I folded the letter once more and tucked it into the front of my duffel, along with the photo of my mother and father. I climbed underneath the blankets and enveloped myself in warmth.

My eyes drifted shut as I listened to the chirping crickets outside, but what was really on my mind was Emma. I thought about her until I drifted off to sleep.

Then, my sleep became consumed in dread and another horrible nightmare.

I lay on my back in wet grass with my eyes closed. A light breeze drifted across the stormy sky, and I heard the sound of crashing waves somewhere in the distance.

Thunder rumbled overhead. The storm had yet to break, but the chill warned of its approach. I opened my eyes, and the world around me sat in the dull light of an afternoon without the sun's warming rays. From the corner of my eye, I saw a repetitive flash of light coming in and out every few seconds.

I sat up in the grass and looked to the

distance on my left, searching out the source of the light. A tall white lighthouse stood on the cliff's edge, overlooking the sea below. The lens of the lighthouse flickered every five to ten seconds, rotating like clockwork. Its beam stretched across the ocean until it faded against the misty backdrop and was no longer visible.

I would have thought nothing of the nightmare at that point, if it hadn't been for the drifting storm waiting to unveil itself. Except for the thunderheads and the occasional bolts of lighting, everything was rather peaceful.

I rose to my feet and noticed something in my hands for the first time. In my left hand was a wooden rod, jagged at the top edge as if it had been snapped in half. Fastened only half an inch beneath the broken edge was the vamplate. In my right hand was a finely-carved spearhead with a sharp point. Somehow, Ascalon had been damaged.

Then, I heard a mighty, earth-shaking roar. It was so loud that I considered it had been thunder, but as the sky instantly darkened, the massive figure of a black dragon rose over the cliff's edge. Its red eyes locked upon me with a hungry desire for human flesh.

My heart began to race. I told myself to run, but my feet remained in place, as if I had stepped into cement and had been settled in the same place for eternity.

I heard a loud, maniacal laugh, and I jerked my head towards the lighthouse in the distance. The shadow man stood on the balcony at the top of the lighthouse, peering down as the dragon hovered in the air, his eyes focused only upon me.

Then, the man evaporated in a mist of shadows. "Are you afraid, Dragonlord?" a chilling voice whispered in my ear, as if it had been carried by the drifting breeze. I swung the spearhead in my hand, trying to combat the invisible force that taunted me, but nothing appeared, and my feet still wouldn't budge. I was trapped.

The dragon flapped it wings, hovering before me with a snarl on its face that almost looked human. I froze in place, stricken by fear. The spearhead dropped from my hands and fell to the ground. The dragon swooped down, and I closed my eyes.

Death was coming for me.

CHAPTER EIGHT

FIRE!

We were on the road again by dawn the next day, leaving Julianna's castle in our wake. The sun had barely begun to rise, and the air was as chilly as ever.

Overnight, I suppose, Julianna had decided to allow Emma to join us on the journey. I didn't know what had made her change her mind, or what thoughts had run through her mind since Emma's appearance and that morning, but I found myself thankful anyway.

The five of us had crammed into Julianna's minivan, which was a stark contrast to her personality. I figured she would have driven a Hummer or a tank—but a minivan? I almost laughed. Almost. Then, I remembered who Julianna was, so I kept quiet.

"Where to now?" I spoke up from the row of seats farthest back.

Julianna peeked at me through her sunglasses in the rear-view mirror before returning her attention to the road. "Ontario," she replied. "It's an eight-hour drive."

I groaned and sank into my seat. Eight hours. Eight long hours. I could barely last eight minutes cooped up in the car.

I glanced to my side at Emma, who sat cross-legged and immersed in a book. I read the cover: *Pride and Prejudice.*

"So, are you a book nerd?" I asked. What a stupid way to start a conversation.

She raised her eyebrows, barely glancing at me. "If you're asking if I like to read, then the answer is yes. I don't think that makes me a nerd."

"Well, what's that one about?"

She practically slammed the book down in her lap and gave me a pleading look. "You *really* don't know about *Pride and Prejudice*?"

I shrugged. "No. Should I?" Actually, I'd never even heard of it. The cover had a picture of a woman in some kind of old-fashioned, eighteenth century dress. What was a thirteen-year-old girl like Emma doing reading a book like *that*?

She rolled her eyes and shook her head disapprovingly. Then, she lifted her book and started reading again. "It's a story about love," she replied. "It's about other things, too, of course, but it's mostly about love."

I wanted to laugh. I didn't know Emma very well, but I couldn't picture *her* reading a romance novel. She seemed better suited for something with swords and mythical battles. Or something with dragons and medieval castles.

Then again, like us, she *lived* in that world. Why would she want to read about it?

"Oh," I said, nodding. "That's…cool."

"You don't read." It wasn't a question.

"Of course I do," I replied. "Not for fun, though."

She rolled her eyes again. "Then what *do* you do in your free time, besides slay dragons?"

"I..." Man, she was making me feel unintelligent. "I play...video games."

"Anything else?"

"Well...I go to school."

"That's not for fun."

"Not for me. But maybe for someone like you."

She shrugged. "Just because I appreciate my education doesn't mean I don't know how to have fun."

So, this is what I had gathered about Emma thus far: she was smart, she was sassy, and she thought I was a complete idiot.

I sighed irritably and stared out my window. Eight hours in the car with Emma. How could I survive *that*?

But I tried to force myself to be nice. I drew in a deep breath and smiled, facing her again. "That was clever thinking back at the diner," I said.

She looked up at me. "What are you talking about?"

"In Redding. When you spilled the coffee on Ridley."

I thought I saw the faintest trace of a smile. She immersed herself in her book once more. "I had to keep him off your trail." She paused for a moment. Then, "You know, I didn't think you saw me."

Of course I saw her. She was too pretty to miss. "Well, I did," I replied. Then, I frowned. "How did you know we would be there?"

She glanced up at Wolf in the seat in front of us, but he didn't seem to be paying us any attention.

"I live in a town just outside of Redding," she replied. "I guess you could say it was coincidence that I found you guys there."

"Coincidence?" I asked, raising an eyebrow. "That's not true. You were following us, weren't you?"

Her eyes drifted slowly, but the book didn't waver in her hand. She wasn't reading anymore. "My father told me where to find you," she said. "He left me a load of cash and an itinerary to follow before he…" She swallowed and looked down at her book. "Like I said before, he knew someone was onto him. He'd been preparing to send me away for a while. He sent me to my aunt's house, said she'd know where to take me. He left her directions to Julianna's house and told my aunt to leave me with her."

"Why would he do that?" I asked. "Why not just leave you with family?"

"Because," she said, rolling her eyes, "I would be a lot safer with the Order. If Arianne knew about me, she'd be out to get me. She couldn't leave any loose ends, could she?"

"No, she couldn't," I replied. I stared down at my hands and cleared my throat. "So, your father knew about me."

"He was very close to your father back in the day," she replied. "In fact, he helped your mother settle in after they…left each other."

What she meant by that was, "After you were born." I couldn't help feeling like everyone thought of me as some kind of unspoken tragedy. I guess this was true in a way, because as Wolf had so clearly pointed out to my mother, none of this would have happened if I hadn't been born.

She lowered the book in her lap and stared down at the floorboards. A tiny smile crept over her lips. "Growing up, he would tell me stories about the Dragonlord," she said. "He told me about Saint George and Ascalon. He practically educated me on all there was to know. He always insisted they were just fairy tales, but I hoped that somehow, they were more than that." Then, her smile faded. "I never should have made that wish. The truth turned out to be too much."

"And that's why," Wolf spoke up, craning his neck towards us, "we don't *appoint* members of the Order. Knowledge can get you killed. Especially when it doesn't belong to you in the first place."

Emma's face darkened, and her mouth tightened. I could see the rage burning behind her aqua-green eyes, the powerful urge to punch him in the face. But she simply opened her book again and continued to read.

I glared at the back of Wolf's head, wishing he would just shut up altogether. My short-lived moment with Emma—in which she had revealed something near and dear about herself—was gone in an instant.

I sighed and returned my gaze to the passing scenery outside my window.

Four long hours later, we made it to a gas station in Independence. Snow-capped mountains stretched in the distance, but before that, there was only grass and the road from which we came and would continue on.

Julianna pulled the van up to a gas pump and shifted into Park. I ripped my seatbelt off and impatiently waited to be released.

Once I was free, I stretched my limbs and yawned, thankful to be out of that cramped car. Julianna moved over to the side of the van and unscrewed the gas cap. "You have ten minutes," she called to us. "Do whatever you have to do quickly."

My stomach grumbled as the thought of gas station food sprang to mind. Sure, it was no five-star cuisine, but even a hot dog or a pre-made sandwich would suffice. I practically ran towards the mini-mart, and found Emma tagging along behind me.

A loud *ding-ding* signaled our entrance as we made our way through the front door. The mini-mart was unoccupied except for a customer in the back aisle and the middle-aged clerk, who sat on a stool with his feet crossed over each other on the counter, reading a magazine.

I made my way to the back of the store, heading for the bathroom while Emma disappeared around the aisle towards the soft drink dispenser. Four hours without a single bathroom break was a long time.

As I passed by the last aisle, I glimpsed the other customer: she was an attractive woman somewhere in her thirties—and she seemed to be up to something. She kept glancing over her shoulder, like she suspected someone was watching her. Something about her made me nervous, but I ignored it. With people chasing after us for the past few days, *everything* made me jumpy.

Locking the door behind me, I turned to face myself in the mirror. Man, did I look terrible. I wet my hands and flattened my hair, cleaning myself up as best as I could. If I was going to be traveling with Emma for the next few days, I wanted to at least *try* to look good. Fortunately for her, she didn't have to put in the effort—she would probably look good even if she rolled in the mud.

When I finished messing with my appearance, I didn't look much different. I sighed with defeat and turned towards the stall. Before I even pushed the door open, though, the screeching of a fire alarm coming from outside the bathroom startled me. I made my way out through the door to find the store filling with gray smoke.

"Emma!" I cried. "Emma, where are you?"

I waited for her response, but nothing came. I covered my nose and mouth and rushed towards the front door, passing by the store employee lying unconscious on the floor.

I came to a stop and faced him, wondering if he was dead. I made my way to his side, my heart thundering in my chest. I bent down beside him and pressed two fingers against the spot between his jaw and his throat, feeling for a pulse. It was faint, but it was there. I breathed a sigh of relief.

But where was Emma?

I rose to my feet, cupping my hands around my mouth and crying, "Emma! Where are you?" But just like before, she didn't answer. Had she left the store before I'd come out of the bathroom? Or had something worse happened to her?

I remembered the face of the suspicious woman, and my heart skipped a beat. Had *she* done this to the store employee? Had she hurt Emma, too?

The idea of it threw me into a panic. I sprinted towards the front door but found it locked. I yanked at it repeatedly, as if doing so would unlock it, but all my efforts were to no avail.

Julianna, Wolf, and David were just on the other side, only about 200 feet away. I screamed for them to come to my rescue, wishing they would glance my way, but they didn't seem to notice at all. I doubted they could even hear the fire alarm wailing from where they were. I was trapped.

I stumbled towards the phone behind the clerk's counter, but there was no dial tone. The line had been cut. Whoever this woman was, she knew what she was doing. Perhaps it had all been in the effort to abduct Emma.

I tried to keep my head level and my heart rate normal, but it was hard. The smoke had become black, making it even harder to breathe. I pressed a hand to my mouth and sank down to my knees, knowing that the smoke would rise.

There had to be another way out. I glanced up at the blurred neon "Exit" sign at the back of the store. Without thinking twice, I leapt to my feet and sprinted towards the door. A cloud of black smoke was drifting down the aisle from the women's bathroom in the back, growing thicker and thicker with each passing second. I pressed my nose and mouth into the crook of my elbow and jumped across the black cloud towards my escape route, my stomach settling with relief as I approached the door.

But when I tugged on the handles, it didn't budge. That woman must have locked it from the outside, too.

I turned around and leaned against the door as the smoke continued to grow, creating a barrier between the front and back sections of the store. Then, an orange flickering filled my vision. I finally saw the flames, rising higher and growing larger. I could feel the heat on my skin even beneath my sweater and jeans, threatening to burn and blister me in seconds. I was cornered by the fire.

I thought to sneak past the flames, but I knew if I even tried, I'd gain some terrible third-degree burns. My heart pounded in my chest as I backed towards the wall.

I thought that the sprinklers overhead would have already come on by that point, but they hadn't. And if they hadn't yet, they wouldn't. The woman must have tampered with those, too, though how she'd known we would stop at this particular gas station was beyond me.

Even with my mouth pressed into my clothes, I could still feel the smoke filling my lungs. I coughed something hideous, gagging and choking. My eyes felt like they would burst right out of my skull. I wondered where the fire extinguisher was, but I didn't doubt that she had either taken it or hidden it.

I climbed down on my knees and ducked my head as low as I could. That was when I heard a crash—*barely* heard it—in the distance, and assumed that the glass had been broken on the front door. I heard male voices shouting in panic and vaguely made out the shape of two people moving beyond the flames. Wolf came through, dragging the unconscious store clerk out the door. David craned his neck, searching me out through the flames and smoke.

I waved my arms back and forth to get his attention, but even in that small moment, the smoke managed to snake its way into my lungs. I crumbled over, gagging again.

Then, I saw a blur of black fly towards me and cover the flames. David stood on the opposite side of the flaming blockade, stamping his jacket into the wall of fire. He reached a hand forward, dragging me to my feet and across the open space. I stumbled over my feet, hacking up a lung as he steered me out of my corner.

While I had been trapped by the flames, the fire had claimed almost all of the store. I could smell donuts burning and hot dogs crisping. The flames rose threateningly on either of our sides, stretching over us like arms trying to grab us and pull us in. David covered his face and guided me towards the door as the flames continued to consume the mini-mart.

We stumbled out the door and into fresh, open air. Once we were a safe distance away, I collapsed onto my hands and knees, gagging, spitting, and choking for what must have been five full minutes. I stared down at my hands and clothes, which were blackened and grimy from the dark smoke. My chest swelled with pain, and my eyes stung. The bare skin on my face, hands, and neck cried out in agony, burning from the fire's damage.

But I couldn't relax just yet. I seized David's arm and stared up at him. "Emma," I croaked. "Where is she?"

"She's safe," David replied, helping me to my feet. "Arianne got away, but Emma is safe."

Arianne. That was the woman who worked with Cain and Ridley. How had she found us?

Knowing that Emma was safe, though, gave me leave to focus on my own pain. I continued to spit and gag until I could breathe normally once more. When I finally felt like I had rid my lungs of the smoke, I looked up and surveyed the scene. The unconscious clerk lay on the ground a safe distance away. Black clouds of smoke snaked their way out the front door, and red flames danced from within. A smoke signal rose over our heads, putting us on the map for whoever might want to find us. I knew we had to get out of there right away.

David clapped a hand on my shoulder. "Are you all right?"

"I'll be fine," I replied. "Where is Emma? And what happened?"

"This way," David said. He led me around the building to the back exit, where I would have been able to flee through if not for Arianne.

I came to a halt as we rounded the corner and sighted a half-unconscious Emma lying across Julianna's lap. "What happened?" I asked.

Emma looked more than a little groggy, kind of like a kid who has to go to school when he's really sick. Except she actually looked worse.

Wolf, who had been standing watch nearby, approached me and looked me up and down. "Are you—?"

"I'm fine," I insisted. "What happened to Emma?"

"Arianne Harper was here," Emma croaked, slowly sitting up. "*She* did this. I couldn't mistake her for anything."

"Take it easy," Wolf said. "Obviously, we know it was Arianne. That much is certain. But what was she doing here? How did she find us?"

"She must have recognized Emma," Julianna mused, rising to her feet. "Tell us exactly what happened."

"I was getting a drink," Emma replied, "and the next thing I knew, I *saw* her. She was in the store with us!"

"Where was Logan?"

"He went to the bathroom or something," Emma said. "I don't know, but he wasn't there."

"You don't think she knew who *he* was, do you?" David asked, nodding towards me.

Julianna fixed her gaze upon me, narrowing her eyes. "It's possible," she said. "Although, I'm not sure how…"

"William probably caved in and told Cain," Wolf suggested heatedly. "It wouldn't surprise me."

I glared at him. "He wouldn't. He knows what's at stake."

Wolf raised his eyebrows and grinned. "And you would know how your father would handle something like this, wouldn't you, Logan? Since you guys are so close?"

I wanted to hit him, to punch him in the stomach and knock him over, but I kept my fists clenched tightly at my sides.

"That's enough," David interrupted with a sigh. "We need to get out of here right now. We're sitting ducks here."

He turned and headed towards the van in the distance while Julianna helped Emma to her feet. Wolf glanced at me, annoyed, then followed after David.

"Let's go, you two," Julianna called, following after the others once she was certain Emma could stand on her own two feet.

I placed a hand over my chest and drew in a slow, deep breath. Emma approached my side. "Are you all right?" she asked.

I nodded. "Yeah, I think I am…" Then, I drew back with a frown. "Wait, what? I should be asking *you* if you're all right."

"I'm fine," she said. "Arianne put a wet rag over my nose. I don't know what it was soaked in, but it would have knocked me out if I hadn't put up such a fight."

"How did she get away without you?"

"Once the others noticed the fire in the store, they realized we were still in there," she explained. "Luckily, they found me before Arianne took off with me. She left me behind so she could escape."

"What did she want with you?"

"I don't know," she muttered, staring down at the ground with concern. "She must know who I am. She must've realized I'd gotten away that night."

"Well, good thing she was in a hurry," I said.

"Yeah," Emma said. "Good thing. For *her*."

Then, she turned and headed towards the van, her brief moment of compassion and transparency floating away with the wind.

The loud, annoying whir of vehicle alarms echoed in the distance, and I looked up to see two red fire trucks and two police cars speeding down the road from which we had come. By that point, the clerk had come back around, although he hadn't gotten up from where Wolf had left him. He remained seated in the middle of the parking lot, staring up at the mini-mart as it continued to burn. I felt sorry for him—he'd have quite a bit of trouble explaining to his boss what had happened.

We climbed into the van and buckled up. Julianna fled the gas station like we were criminals on the run—after all, I felt like one. Emma was a victim of an attempted kidnapping, the clerk a victim of attempted murder, and we witnesses to arson. The police would want to question us, but Julianna obviously wouldn't let that happen. We had managed to sneak off just in the nick of time.

I glanced at Emma, who was staring out the window. Her book lay on the seat between us, forgotten and discarded. "Hey," I said softly. "Are *you* all right?"

She faced me, but her eyes drifted towards the space between us. "I already told you I'm fine," she said. "Why do you ask?"

Sure, she hadn't been killed or seriously injured, but there was more to it than that. She must have felt terrible, seeing her father's murderer for the first time since his passing. And to know that Arianne had gotten away on top of it? Well, she couldn't be doing well.

"Well," I said, "because of Arianne. I mean, aren't you…?"

She stared at me, her eyes empty and emotionless, betraying the anger and hatred for Arianne buried inside of her. An ache filled my heart as she stared lifelessly at me, but more *past* me than anything.

I forced a sympathetic smile and shook my head. "Never mind. Forget I asked."

She stared at me for a long moment, then returned her attention to the world speeding by through the window, all sense of fear and terror gone as if it had never existed.

CHAPTER NINE

THE FINAL PIECE

By the time we arrived in Ontario, the sun had begun to set. Julianna pulled the van down a narrow dirt road that forked off the main road. We rumbled along, guided by a wooden fence. Eventually, trees sprang up on our side, separating us from the highway and the life that existed beyond it.

The road widened and continued deeper into the forest, underneath the protective watch of the trees rising around us. Orange sunlight streaked in through the branches, flickering and warming the interior of the van through the windshield.

Further down the road stood a brown barn, run-down and collapsing underneath the weight of abandonment. Bald patches scattered the roof, exposing the termite-infested planks of wood that held up the remaining shingles. The front door hung by a single hinge, and looked like it would fall off at any second. The place might have been nice and quaint some time before, but now it was eerie and desolate.

And as I suspected, I would have to venture inside.

Julianna pulled the van to a halt outside of the barn and we filed out, stepping into the chill of the evening air. "So," I said, "where are we exactly?"

Julianna looked towards the barn. "The location of the final trial."

"In there?" I asked, raising an eyebrow.

"What's wrong?" Emma spoke up, approaching my side with her hands shoved into her jacket and her cheeks pink. "Are you afraid it's haunted?"

Well, I was glad to see she was feeling better. "No," I snorted. "I've already almost been drowned and burned alive. What can ghosts do to me?"

She grinned at me and followed after the others. With a sigh, I tagged along. Secretly, I wished she could come along with me and watch me complete the final trial like a stud. That might shut her up.

We pushed past the rickety front door of the barn and entered into the darkness. I heard a round of clicks, and David, Julianna, and Wolf played the light of their flashlights off of the walls and the balding ceiling.

For a moment, I really did think the barn was haunted. In the center of the room, surrounded by dead grass and a stale, nauseating odor, stood a stone well. There was nothing else inside the barn, almost as if the place had been built around it.

David approached the edge of the well and shined the light down into its depths. He whistled and stepped back. "It sure is deep down there."

Julianna tucked her flashlight into her pocket and reached forward, gripping the crank over the well. A rope was coiled around the cylinder above the well's hollow, seemingly infinite in length. She tugged on the crank several times before it budged, and the tail of the rope slowly began to descend towards the well.

David pulled the rope over the edge of the well as Julianna continued to crank the lever. When she stopped, at least ten feet of rope lay in a heap on the ground aside the well. She stepped back, brushed her hands together, and faced me. "Are you ready?"

"For what?" I asked.

"You're going down there," she replied. "What else would we be doing here?"

Why did I always have to go into the darkest of places?

I sighed and approached the well, leaning over the edge and staring into darkness. "What's down there?"

"I don't know, Logan," she said. "None of us have seen the trials. We weren't the ones who hid the pieces of Ascalon. But I promise, you'll be fine. Take this."

She handed me her flashlight. I drew in a deep breath and pocketed it, forcing myself to at least appear brave.

David approached the crank and leaned against it, eyeing me expectantly. "We're ready when you are," he said.

I glanced at Emma, hoping for some words of encouragement. "Stay alive, Dragon Boy," she said.

Well, that was helpful.

I rolled my eyes and crawled over the lip of the well, dangling my legs into the hollow. The well wasn't much wider than me—I was thankful that I wasn't claustrophobic.

I drew in one last deep breath and pulled the rope over the well, wrapping my hands tightly around it. Wolf positioned himself opposite of me and gripped the tail of the rope, tying the end into a looping knot. Then, he gestured for my foot and slipped the loop over my shoe. "You're good to go," he said, patting my foot.

I nodded my thanks, too anxious to speak. Then, I scooted over the lip of the well and dangled over the darkness. David gripped the crank with both hands, his forehead wrinkled in concentration. My life rested in his hands—literally.

"Slowly now," Julianna said, and David began to turn the crank. I wrapped my hands around the splintery rope and stared up at Wolf as I descended into the well. "When you're ready to come back," he said, his voice becoming distant, "tug on the rope a couple times and we'll know to pull you up."

"Got it," I returned, although I wasn't really listening. The walls seemed to close in around me with each inch that I descended, and what little light had been above me continued to fade. My heart thundered in my chest, and my hands became sweaty and clammy.

The air grew damper and colder as I continued to descend. My mind began to race with thoughts over the possibilities of the next trial. With my luck, I'd have to wrestle a lion or fight a giant robot—at this point, anything was possible. I just hoped it would end quickly, so that we could get on with the really important stuff—like facing Cain Hunter and rescuing my father.

Finally, I found my footing beneath me. I could see the faint glow of flickering torches down the dark passage that stretched before me, and for the umpteenth time, I wondered who it was that spent his time traveling between the trials to make sure the flames remained lit for the sake of suspense. And what were the job requirements for something like that?

I yanked twice on the rope to indicate to the others that I had reached the ground, and the rope hung still. I puffed up my chest and marched bravely down the hall towards the light in the distance.

At the end of the passage, I found myself standing inside a small chamber not much bigger than my closet. The lit torches hung on both my sides, and before me was the blank canvas of a smooth, white wall. Near the bottom of the wall were two empty iron sconces. There were no doors, no windows, and no obvious ways out. I considered that maybe Julianna had been wrong about the shaft's location.

My eyes fixed upon the sconces near the bottom of the wall, and something inside my brain clicked. I shoved my hands into my pockets and searched through their depths, discovering a shiny quarter, my wallet, and a week-old receipt from a sandwich shop in Ashland. I coiled the receipt into a narrow funnel and moved towards the torches on the wall, lighting the edge of the paper just enough.

Then, I carefully moved towards the sconces near the wall, lighting each of them.

Some kind of magic triggered by the flames in the sconces caused words to appear on the wall, gold and calligraphic as if an artist himself had painted them in the chamber. I stepped back—quite pleased with myself—and observed the appearing message:

The eyes of the beasts see with light.

Well, so much for that. I considered turning around and heading back towards the well, telling the others that I couldn't figure out what to do, but then something irreversible happened.

The panel upon which I stood flipped over and dropped me into an underground room. I cried out as I went face-first into the ground.

After spitting out a mouthful of dirt, I dragged myself to my feet. The panel had dumped me into a small brick room with a sloping pathway before me. I set forward, following the dipping tunnel to the end where I found myself standing outside of a massive chamber.

The chamber closely resembled the crypt, but it lacked that particular eeriness. Two tall stone pillars stood on the east and west ends of the room, stretching nearly fifty feet high to the darkened ceiling above. At the north and south ends of the chamber, the stone heads of a pair of dragons jutted forward with their mouths open. Their bodies were woven along the walls, curving delicately towards their heads, as if they had been cemented into the wall itself.

A soft purple light emitted from the left eye of the north dragon, and from the right eye of the south dragon, forming an angled, crisscrossed path towards the ground.

The eyes of the beasts see with light. I still had no idea what it meant, other than the fact that mystical beams of light protruded from their eyes, but that didn't do much to help me.

I trudged my way into the chamber, observing the high walls and the creepy way the dragon seemed to be watching me. I stopped and faced the north dragon, standing tall and narrowing my eyes at him. "You're not so scary," I muttered. "After all, you *are* trapped inside stone."

Then, I thought, maybe Bolla was trapped in stone, too, along with all of the other great dragons.

I turned my back on the stone dragon and paced the chamber some more, searching for any kind of clue I could find. Unlike the previous two trials, the ornamental box that held the piece was nowhere around, which could only mean it was hidden.

That was when I tripped over a hole in the ground and tumbled to the floor, scraping my knee. I cursed under my breath and jerked my head towards the hole, eyeing it accusingly, as if tripping me had been its only purpose for existence.

But something struck me as odd about it. I crawled on my hands and knees towards the hole, peering down inside. It was a perfectly carved four-inch square. The faint purple light of something like an amethyst stone flickered from within. I reached inside and tried to tug it out, but it was wedged in there tightly.

I ran my fingers along its edges, trying to visualize exactly what it was. It had a flat, disk-like shape to it, and I could feel the cold edges of metal surrounding its base, like some kind of rod holding it up.

The eyes of the beasts see with light. I peered up at the dragons, searching back and forth between their eyes and the hole in the ground. Then, I stumbled to my feet.

I figured that if I could get that amethyst disk out of the ground, the beams of light from the dragons' eyes would somehow answer my questions.

I ran a hand through my hair and continued to pace through the chamber, looking all around me for more answers. Then, I noticed a set of handles at the base of the pillar on the west side of the chamber, so small that I had nearly missed them.

I jogged my way towards the pillar and examined the handles, the base of the pillar, and the crevices carved around it. I tugged on the handles and found the base of the pillar move just slightly, rotating towards the right.

"Here goes nothing," I said, and I turned the pillar further to the right. A loud, dull groan followed as stone moved against stone. Interestingly enough, the *entire* pillar didn't move—only the bottom section rotated.

Another groaning noise was followed by rumbling, and I turned my head towards the sound.

The amethyst disk emerged six inches from the ground, clasped in the claws of the golden rod. The rod had been fastened atop the familiar ornamental box that held my prize, although this one was longer and narrower. Judging by the shape of the box, the shaft was at least six feet long.

Well, if the disk was going to reach the beam of light, it would have to go a little higher. I continued to twist the pillar until it lodged into place once more after a quarter rotation. The disk rose another six inches. I twisted the pillar again, and the disk continued to rise.

As I twisted the pillar back to its original place, the disk ascended towards the light. The purple beams of light projected through the mirror and out the back.

My heart skipped a beat as I made my way towards the ornamental box, cautious about celebrating something that may or may not have been worth the trouble. I moved around to the front of the box and saw the button on the top panel. This time, the image was of a dragon's head with its mouth gaping open.

I pushed the button, and the doors opened with an almost inaudible *click*. The wooden shaft of Ascalon sat nestled inside the box.

I retrieved the piece and examined it with reverent awe. It was the last piece—the *last* piece. No more trials, no more death-traps, and no more solving riddles that were beyond my brain's ability to process. I was home-free. The final trial had been a lot less difficult than I had imagined.

Or, so I thought.

I should have remembered by that point that nothing about the trials was ever easy, even when it seemed like they were. I also should have remembered that neither of the previous two trials had allowed for easy escape, and therefore, the third trial wouldn't be any different.

The beams of light immediately extinguished, as if someone had flipped them off with a wall switch. I jerked my head all around in search of the approaching threat, gripping the shaft for my life.

I knew well enough by that point to run rather than wait for the inevitable death-trap coming for me. The problem was, I couldn't go back the way I came—my escape was sealed off by the floor through which I'd fallen.

Then, the worst thing imaginable happened (I know I've said that before, but this was *really* terrible!). The eyes of the north dragon began to glow red. A rumbling noise followed, shaking the ground upon which I stood. Moments later, hot molten lava began to spew out of the mouth of the north dragon.

That's right. Lava.

My instincts took over, and I sprinted away from the waterfall of lava coming my way. Unfortunately, I couldn't outrun it—I would have to get above it.

I made my way towards the south end of the wall, searching desperately for some kind of escape as the lava crept closer and closer. I didn't doubt that the entire chamber would flood before it ceased.

I had nowhere to go except up, and I wasn't even sure that was a viable option. However, I had no other choice—I faced the south wall, examined the notched edges of the dragon's body, and began to climb along its spine.

The horns along its body served as small anchors, helping me to get my grip and footing. The stone was slick, though, and I almost slipped and fell on several occasions. I forced myself to climb, climb, climb and not look down, gripping the shaft in my left hand so tightly that I thought I would snap it in half. One single thought kept me going: *It's the final piece.*

The lava continued to rise, chasing me higher and higher until I reached the south dragon's head. I straddled its neck and gripped its ears, peering down at the scene below me. The heat rose, and sweat dripped off my face. The entire chamber had been filled like a swimming pool—one that I would never, ever want to swim in, even on the coldest of days in Ashland.

I was out of ideas, and for a moment I considered that I had never been meant to live through the third trial. Maybe the Order had been wrong about a small detail somewhere. Maybe no one was ever supposed to retrieve Ascalon again. Maybe it had been left alone for a reason, and there was no way out of the lava chamber.

Then, it occurred to me that only one of the dragons was spewing lava.

I didn't bother testing my speculation. If it didn't work out, I would be dead anyway, and

Ascalon would be lost forever. I only had enough time to act once. Only once.

I shimmied forward on my stomach along the snout of the dragon's head, wrapping my hands around its open mouth. I crawled until I was at the very tip of its nose and leaned my head over, peering into its open mouth. Then, I tossed the shaft down into its throat. It clattered against the stone wall, but the sound faded a moment later as it disappeared down the dragon's throat.

Bingo. I inched my way as far as I could and gripped the dragon's mouth as tightly as possible. Then, I rolled over on my side until my feet dangled over the lava pool. I swung my left leg out and hooked my foot on the dragon's jaw, pulling myself inside and exhaling with relief.

I turned on my hands and knees inside the mouth of the dragon and peered down at the scene below. Across the chamber, the north dragon had finally stopped spewing lava. If I had been a second slower, I would have been at the bottom of the lava lake. I tried not to think about it and turned towards the dragon's throat.

My hand immediately slipped on the steep edge, and I tumbled forward on my stomach, screaming the whole way down the chute. Like a bad water slide, it was steep and very narrow.

A panel at the bottom opened, triggered by my weight. I slid out of the chute and was dumped through a hatch into the first chamber where the magic message had appeared.

I lay on my stomach, groaning in both pain and relief. The shaft lay at my side, the prize I had nearly lost my life to. At that point, though, it didn't matter.

We finally had all three pieces of Ascalon.

I tucked my foot into the loop of the rope and clung tightly, yanking twice to signal that I was ready. A moment later, I was lifted through the air towards the light above. I clasped the shaft in my hand and looked up, awaiting the face of my rescuer.

I hadn't expected it to be Ridley Bancroft.

He grasped the crank with some effort, smiling politely at me in that eerie way of his. My breath caught in my throat, and I almost released my grip on the rope. "Careful," he warned. "You wouldn't want to fall down."

Behind him, Julianna, Emma, and David were forced onto their knees near the entrance of the barn with their fingers laced behind their heads. Arianne paced behind them with a pistol in one hand and a knife in the other. A smug grin was spread across her face. Beside her stood Wolf, also with a gun at hand.

I was trapped. The only way out of my predicament was back down the well, but that wouldn't get me anywhere, and Ridley certainly wasn't going to allow me to go back down there.

He reached a hand towards me. "Let me help you," he said.

I stared at his hand as if it were infested with boils, diseased and disgusting. If I *had* to follow his orders, I would do it on my own terms. I swung my legs forward and notched my foot against the lip of the well, pulling myself over the edge and ignoring his offer.

I backed around the edge of the well, cocking the shaft back in my arm to use as a weapon if needed. Sure, it wouldn't do much damage, but getting hit in the face wouldn't be pleasant either.

"I wouldn't do that if I were you," Ridley warned. He reached into his jacket and removed a gun, waving it at me.

I glanced at the others, at the defeat in their eyes. Julianna fixed her deadly gaze upon Ridley, and I half-expected her to leap forward and choke him. But with Arianne standing right behind them, no one had any advantage.

I met David's eyes, searching for some answer behind them, but he lowered his gaze in shame.

At that point, I didn't dare look at Emma. No one could help me, and whatever answers they had, I wouldn't want to hear.

I knew what was going to happen, and I couldn't fight it.

Finally, I turned my attention to Wolf. "What are you doing?" I demanded.

A sly grin crossed his face. "What do you mean?"

"Why aren't you on your knees begging for mercy, too?"

Wolf stretched out his arms. "Isn't it obvious, Logan?"

My grip tightened on the shaft. It *was* obvious—that was the painful part.

"I've been the perfect distraction this entire time," he went on. "Didn't you wonder how Ridley and Arianne continued to find you?"

I glared at him. "You were feeding them information. You led them to us."

"That's exactly right."

"How?" I said in a small voice. "How could you betray us like this?" I suppose I should have asked myself another question: how had his betrayal slipped past us for so long? He must have been scheming with Cain for thirteen years, or perhaps even beyond that. How was it possible for someone to be elusive for so long?

"Don't make this personal," he said. "Cain is like a brother to me. I did what I had to do."

"For your *family*, right?" I spat, shaking my head. "You said the Order was like a family, but you weren't talking about us, were you? You were talking about Cain all along. It's always been about Cain."

"Save your ramblings for someone else," Wolf shot back. "I'm no different than you, Logan. You're doing what you have to do for your father, and I'm doing what I have to do for my friend. Don't be a hypocrite."

"But what I'm doing isn't wrong."

"Blindly following orders doesn't make you a saint," he said. "It makes you ignorant."

My stomach sank. He was right, but I couldn't admit it. "So, why didn't you just kill me when you found me? Why did you waste all this time when you could have just delivered my body to Cain?"

"We needed the pieces of Ascalon, and they could only be retrieved by the Dragonlord." He smiled sympathetically at me. "Don't feel too bad, Logan. At least in the end, you can say you were blissfully unaware of what you were doing."

I remembered that David had once told me that Wolf was good at what he did. Unfortunately, he played for the wrong team. His betrayal was a painful stab in the gut.

"Now, listen here, Logan," Ridley said, interrupting our argument. "We are going to offer you two choices, and you are going to have to pick one. I suggest you don't make things any harder on yourself than you have to. Do you understand?"

I glared at him.

"I'll take that as a 'yes'," he sighed. He began to pace the space near the well, making his way towards me. "You're coming with us, whether you like it or not. Cain expects you delivered to him alive." I shuddered at that thought—I didn't know if Cain wanting me alive was better or worse than him wanting me dead. "It's up to you whether your friends live through today or not."

"Up to me?" I scoffed. "I'm no idiot. I know you're just going to kill them anyway."

"Don't presume us to be so cold-hearted," Ridley scolded me. "Show some faith. It might shock you to hear this, but we are not bloodthirsty murderers, and neither is Cain."

"The only reason you wouldn't kill them is because Cain wants to do it himself."

After a moment, a smile settled across Ridley's lips. "How very intuitive of you. Although, if you *do* give us a hard time, Cain has granted us permission to bring the four of you back with whatever means necessary. He wants you alive—he never said you had to be in one piece."

He might not kill us, but he would certainly make sure we suffered.

"What do you want from me, then?" I demanded.

"Your cooperation," he answered. "Come along with me—*without* putting up a fight—and I'll spare your friends."

"That's a lie if I've ever heard one."

"Well, whether or not you cooperate, you're coming with us," he said. "The question is, do you want to come quietly, or be the cause of their suffering?"

I stared down at the ground, fairly certain that my heart had stopped beating. I almost wished it would, so everything would end.

I wasn't willing to put the others at risk, and after the countless attempts on our lives, I didn't doubt Ridley and Arianne would go through with exacting some kind of excruciating punishment upon them, especially since nothing stood in their way.

"Don't listen to him, Logan," Julianna spoke up. "Our lives don't matter. *Yours* does."

Arianne pressed the muzzle of the gun against the back of Julianna's head. "Shut your mouth," she warned in a chillingly polite voice, "or you'll be spitting bullets out of that pretty face."

Julianna didn't seem fazed. She locked her eyes with mine, struggling to communicate some secret message with me. I knew she was right, but I couldn't bring myself to agree with her.

I stared down at the shaft in my hands, wondering if their lives were worth it. I knew they were, but we had come so far for Ascalon. I couldn't hand it over so easily after the trouble we went through to get it…

"The Order exists to protect *you*, Logan," David added. "If *you* die, everything else doesn't matter—" Arianne cut him off, smacking him in the back of his head with her gun. He groaned and grimaced against the pain. Then, Arianne leaned in towards him and wrapped an arm around his neck, sliding the shiny, silver blade of her knife against his throat. "Not another word," she ordered.

I looked at Emma, at the tears in her eyes. At the hatred boiling behind them as she contemplated the many ways she could destroy Arianne, her father's murderer.

Then, I looked down at the shaft in my hands once more. It felt like it weighed a hundred pounds—the weight of four lives was buried within it. All I had to do to save them was hand the piece over, give in and let Cain do with me what he would…

"We don't have all day, Logan," Wolf said. "Make your decision."

I swallowed hard and took another step back. Then, I placed a hand at each end of the shaft and held it horizontally over my knee. "Let them go."

Ridley glared at me. "Just what do you think you're doing?"

"I'll break it," I warned. "I swear, I will. Without Ascalon, Cain can't resurrect the dragon."

"And without Ascalon," Ridley said, "you can't stop him even if he does. Do you really think that lance is his only means of attaining power?"

I hesitated. "You're bluffing."

He shrugged. "I guess you'll find out if you break the shaft, won't you?"

I stared down at the wooden rod in my hands, thinking of how easily I could end everything if I just snapped it in half. But was what Ridley said true? Could Cain find another way without Ascalon, and leave me up a creek without a paddle?

"Come, now, Logan," Ridley chided. "Don't be ridiculous. It's just a little stick. Your friends' lives aren't worth risking over something so trivial."

"Shut up," I muttered, my heart racing. Ridley was like a pesky gnat in my face—I couldn't think with his mouth flapping in the wind like that.

"We're wasting time," Wolf sighed. "The kid isn't going to budge. I've spent enough time with him over the past few days to realize it. He's tougher than he looks."

"That's enough from you," Ridley said. "I've got this handled."

"I don't think you do," Wolf argued.

"Shut up, Marcus," Arianna hissed. "Don't make things any more difficult."

"In case the two of you forgot," Wolf said, "*I* am the ghost in the machine. I am the only one

Cain trusted enough to stay behind and clean up the messes you left when you were excommunicated thirteen years ago. I think that gives me seniority."

While they continued to argue, I glanced at David. There was a look in his eyes, something like determination. They were distracted by their own struggles for power. That gave us an opportunity to get the upper hand.

"I'm taking over now," Wolf announced, making his way towards Emma. He yanked her to her feet, ignoring her cries and protests. Then, he wrapped an arm around her shoulders and pressed the gun into her side. "Let's get things moving a little faster," he said. "Logan, what's it going to be?"

"Wolf!" Ridley barked. "Let her go!"

I didn't think that Ridley would allow Wolf to get away with killing Emma, but that didn't make me feel any more comforted. My blood was racing so fast, I thought my heart would explode. For a moment, time seemed to stand still.

"You've got until the count of three," Wolf said. "One…"

Ridley then aimed his gun at Wolf. "Let her go, or you'll be the first one I shoot."

"Two…"

My hands shook. My heart pounded in my chest. Wolf's finger tightened on the trigger, and tears streaked down Emma's cheek.

"Three—"

"STOP!" I cried, raising my arms defensively. "Stop, right now!" The next sentence caught in my throat, resisting as I tried to force it out.

Wolf raised his eyebrows. "Yes?"

"I'll do it," I muttered through clenched teeth. "I'll go with you."

A devilish grin appeared on Wolf's face. "Wonderful," he said. "Hand over the shaft."

Ridley shot him a sidelong glare before facing me and holding out his hand. I might have protested if it weren't for Wolf, who still had the gun pressed into Emma's side. I didn't doubt he would kill her—that was just the way he worked. He didn't care what Cain would do to him so long as he was able to have his fun.

I reached a shaking hand forward and extended the shaft towards Ridley, who took it and admired it with wide, reverent eyes. "The final piece," he whispered triumphantly. "When was the last time Ascalon saw the light of day?"

"It's been 150 years," Wolf reminded him, finally releasing Emma. She took a timid step forward and glanced all around her like a scared doe in the meadow, unsure of where to go.

Once Ridley was done admiring the shaft, he redirected his attention towards Wolf, glaring hatefully at him. "Cain will be hearing about this," he said. "Your recklessness is the last thing we need right now."

Wolf flashed a smug grin. "I look forward to hearing the verdict."

With their focuses upon each other, it gave David the opportunity to attack.

In the blink of an eye, he unlaced his hands from behind his head, drew them down across his face, and seized Arianne's wrist. Then, he flipped her over the top of him, dropping her flat onto her back like the unfortunate opponent of a cage-fighting champion. The knife cluttered out of her hands and onto the ground, and David leapt to his feet.

Before anyone could fully comprehend what had just happened, David had plowed into Wolf. Wolf had raised the gun a second too late, and he and David tumbled to the ground, wrestling for power.

Arianna had quickly scurried to her feet and reclaimed her knife. Before anyone else could make a run for it, she had already drawn her pistol and pointed it at Julianna. Ridley drew a second gun from his shoulder holster and aimed one each at me and Emma. "Don't move," he ordered. "This is between the two of them. The rest of you aren't going anywhere."

I already knew that no matter what happened between David and Wolf, we had lost. David had thought he'd have the opportunity to stop Wolf—or at the very least, turn the tables and use his life as a bargaining chip—but whether either of them died, the rest of us were still captured. His struggles were in vain, just as the outcome would be.

As they continued to wrestle, David pressed a hand to Wolf's face while Wolf tried to gain proper control of the weapon in his hand. Then, David's free hand went towards the weapon. They fumbled with the gun and struggled over it until a loud *bang* went off. My heart skipped a beat and I startled.

David cried out in pain as Wolf climbed off the top of him and returned to his feet. His slicked-back hair had become messy, and dark gray tendrils hung over his forehead. His eyes raged with hatred, and he aimed the gun at David once more.

Ridley aimed his weapon at Wolf, leaving Emma out of harm's way. "Don't do it."

Wolf glared at him before taking a step back and holstering his weapon. "We've wasted enough time," he said, his chest heaving. "Let's get out of here."

"I agree," Ridley said. "Can I trust you not to shoot our hostages, Marcus? Or do I have to take both David and the girl to the van myself?"

Wolf ran a hand through his hair, flattening it and making it look neat once more. "I can handle the girl," he snapped. He marched towards Emma and yanked her by the arm, shoving her towards the exit of the barn. She glanced at me over her shoulder before leaving, just in time for me to see the genuine fear in her eyes. Then, she was gone.

"He's going to get us killed," Arianne said, dragging Julianna to her feet. "We've got to get the lance back to Cain immediately. Tomorrow is Saint George's Day, and we've already wasted enough time."

"I'll speak to Cain as soon as we get back," Ridley said.

"Please, Ridley," Arianna begged. "Marcus is right and he knows it. In Cain's eyes, he can do no wrong."

"We'll see about that," Ridley muttered, watching as Arianne guided Julianna out of the barn, her claws digging into the back of Julianna's neck.

Ridley made his way towards David and stood over him, staring down at him with an expectant gaze. "It seems to me like you're alive," he said. "Am I right?"

Slowly, David pushed himself to a sitting positing, all the while clutching at his bloodied left arm. "It's just a flesh wound," he grunted.

"Wonderful," Ridley said. "So, you can walk."

David dragged himself to his feet, ignoring the gun in Ridley's hands. He made eye contact with me, but I looked away. I didn't want to see the guilt in his eyes, and I didn't want him to see the disappointment in mine.

"Come along, Logan," Ridley said, ushering David forward. I glared hatefully at him for a long moment, hoping the rage in my eyes would convince him that by the time this was over, he and his friends would be goners.

Ridley had me march directly behind David as we made our way out the barn. He followed us at the back of the line. "Don't get any ideas about forming a mutiny up there," Ridley warned. "Cain may want you alive, but that doesn't mean I won't shoot you."

As we emerged from the barn, I saw that the van was still parked off of the road from which we arrived. Alongside it, two other vans were parked. I could see Emma's silhouette in the back of one of the vans, wrists bound and mouth gagged. Julianna was tied up in the back seat with her, although much more reserved. Her eyes, though, were empty and blank. This was probably the first time in her life that she had been overcome with defeat.

Arianne came around the side of her designated van and dragged David away from Ridley's watch, shoving him into the back of the vehicle. Then, she locked the door and climbed into the driver's seat. She nodded towards Ridley and said, "See you there."

Then, she turned over the ignition and peeled off the road. The Order disappeared from my range of vision in a matter of seconds.

Wolf had taken control of the second van, waiting nearby with the engine idling. He and Ridley made eye contact for a moment, each shooting the other a deadly glare. Then, Wolf shifted into Drive. "If I get there before you," he said, "I'll be sure to tell Cain all about what happened."

Ridley's eyes narrowed into slits. "I'm sure you will."

Wolf grinned at him, then pulled onto the road and followed after Arianne, disappearing in seconds.

Ridley threw open the side door of the other van and gestured for me to enter. "Into the back seat," he commanded.

I began to climb in, but before I entered, his hand wrapped around my neck. A wet rag was pressed over my face, covering my nose and mouth. The overpowering, nauseating odor of sour lemons met my nose, making my stomach turn. I squirmed and wrestled for my freedom. My arms flailed in an effort to strike Ridley's face or stomach, but my strength was no match for his.

My limbs began to tingle, and my energy quickly dissipated. After a few moments, my arms stopped waving, and my eyelids drooped. The world around me grew darker, and the sounds of my own grunts and struggles faded into nothing.

Then, I slumped forward and passed out.

CHAPTER TEN

FAMILY TIES

"Wake up, Logan."

I could hear a voice calling, but my head was heavy, and my neck ached like a bag of bricks had been tied around it. My arms and legs were stiff, and my fingers felt like they'd been soaking in a bucket of ice for several hours. Every inch of my body was tormented.

I felt someone lightly slapping my cheek, and I startled to full consciousness. My eyes flickered open, but the room around was nearly dark. I could see the silhouette of someone standing before me, but I couldn't make out his face yet. Narrow streaks of light from the small lamp hanging overhead did little to illuminate his features. The gentle light strained my eyes, and I squeezed them shut again.

"Stay with me, kid."

Kid? There was only one person who called me that.

He gently slapped my cheek again, and my eyes flickered open once more. My head bobbled like it was hanging on by a thread of skin and might fall off at any moment.

"Wolf?" I croaked. It had to be him, but I couldn't be sure. My brain wasn't functioning properly, and my mouth was as dry as if I'd stuffed ten cotton balls inside of it.

"It's me, kid," he returned.

"Help…me…"

I heard him shuffling in the distance, but he didn't come to my rescue—maybe he hadn't heard me. I tried to repeat my request, but I found it to be too exhausting.

"It will all be over soon," he said.

I tried to move my arms again, but they were as stiff as they had been moments ago. Something was holding me in place. My wrists felt as if they'd been rubbed raw, and my shoulders throbbed. *Focus, Logan,* I told myself, *You've got to focus.*

I drew in a slow, deep breath and forced my eyes open. I focused my gaze on Wolf's face before me and clenched my fists so tightly that my fingernails cut into my palms. But no matter how I struggled, no matter how I fought, my vision remained clouded, and my limbs felt like jelly.

A door opened and closed repeatedly, and someone moved in and out of the room. I must have dozed off again, because my body felt stronger when I awakened. How long had I been out?

Thankfully, my mind was more alert when I awakened, but I was aware of every inch of pain that my body had endured for…well, who knew how long?

My arms were tied behind my back with splintery rope to the rungs of a metal chair, and my ankles were tied to the legs of the chair. My wrists were caked with dried blood—I must have been fighting against my restraints in my sleep. My neck ached, probably from having slept hunched over all night. My eyes swelled like bursting water balloons.

I remembered speaking to Wolf a few minutes ago—or had it been hours ago?—but he was nowhere in sight anymore.

And then, an itching arose in my brain: Wolf wasn't my friend. He was a traitor. With my own two eyes, I had watched him threaten Emma. I had listened to him proudly confess his betrayal.

And where were the others? Where were Julianna, David, and Emma? I remembered that they had been captured and taken away by Arianne and Ridley—or had that been another one of my strange dreams? I couldn't remember anything to save my life. The last image that popped into my mind was of the barn and the well where the final trial had been located, where I had found the final piece of Ascalon. Beyond that, though, everything was a blur.

"He-Help!" I shouted. My throat was raw, like I'd been screaming at the top of my lungs for hours on end. "Help me!"

I knew I was at Cain's mercy—he had finally found us and imprisoned us. But why was I still alive? And why couldn't I remember facing him?

"HELP ME!"

I shook the chair, throwing my weight back and forth. The metal legs banged noisily against the cement floor, bouncing sharp echoes off the walls. The movements dug the ropes into my wrists even further, but I ignored the pain.

I continued to shout and shake the chair until I finally heard hasty footsteps coming towards the door to my cell. A clanking noise and a screech followed, and the heavy metal door opened.

Standing in the light was Wolf, the person I hated the most at that moment. I glared at him with as much as hate as I could muster. "You," I breathed.

I saw something on his face that I hadn't expected to see: guilt.

"What are you doing here?" I demanded. "I thought you would have killed me by now."

"Cain wanted you alive," he said. "And it's about time the two of you talked." He marched towards me and began to untie my ankles.

"Where are the others?" I asked.

He didn't answer, but the loosening of the ropes around my wrists was a good enough response, anyway. The muscles in my shoulders tightened and ached as I cradled them into my stomach. I avoided looking at my wrists for fear of becoming sick. The sight of blood or severe wounds always made my stomach turn.

I drew in a determined deep breath and rose to my feet with my fist cocked back, prepared to strike Wolf in the face, but my legs immediately gave out. Wolf stepped to the side as I tumbled to the floor. "Don't bother, Logan," he said. "It won't get you anywhere."

My arms and legs shook as I tried to push myself to my feet again. Not wanting to waste time, Wolf yanked me to my feet and grabbed me by the back of the neck, shoving me towards the door. He pushed open the heavy metal door and led me down the narrow path.

By the looks of the place, we were underground. The hallway beyond my cellar was a low cement tunnel that looked like it had once been part of a sewer line. We followed the tunnel to the end and turned to the right, making our way down another path that led towards a door at the end. Wolf pushed it open to reveal a room as big as the foyer of Julianna's home in Tahoe. But, to my dismay and horror, it looked nothing like Julianna's home.

I wasn't sure if it had once been a cave or a tomb, but either way, it was as engrossing as it was terrifying. The perimeter of the room was a perfect circle, with dark hallways leading off from every direction. The dome-shaped ceiling stretched so high that the darkness above enshrouded its infinite depths.

"Where are we?" I asked.

"Bolla's tomb," Wolf replied. "What a wonder it will be when we, of all people, are the first to witness her resurrection." He yanked on the back of my neck, pulling me to a halt. "And it's all thanks to you, kid," he said with a devilish grin.

The center of the floor was consumed by a pitch black void. It looked like it had once been a deep, unending pit, but it had been covered by a thin, fragile glass for protection. I was sure that it could easily be shattered if someone walked over it.

I had seen the place before in my dreams, and it was no less terrifying in reality. There was something about the deep pit, though, that really made my insides stir. Everything around me suddenly felt as if it had been frozen in place, and my ears began to ring. A strange, intense power began coursing through my body, ridding me of the pain and fatigue.

I felt powerful. I felt strong. I felt dangerous.

It was a sensation that was both overwhelming and treacherous. I *liked* feeling so powerful that no force of the universe could stop me. But on the other hand, it was dark, like something that could corrupt me in the blink of an eye.

Come...

A dark voice echoed in my head. It was chilling down to the bone, cold and evil.

Come this way, Dragonlord...free me...

I shook my head, trying to clear my mania. I was probably just tired and still rather delirious.

Release me...let me serve you...

I stared down at the pit, almost certain that it was coming from within.

"You hear something, don't you?"

I looked up and saw a tall, younger man—possibly in his late twenties—standing at the mouth of one of the adjacent hallways. He had dark brown hair that hung in tendrils around his forehead and around his neck, like he had begun to grow it out, but had not made much progress yet. His icy blue eyes were not cool or calming like my mother's, or even fierce and strong like Julianna's—they were cold and chilling, dark and calculating. Swirls of gray passed behind them, a terrible storm on the brink of eruption.

He was, as a lot of women might think, handsome, but the eeriness of his dark stare made even Wolf seem like a saint. He watched me with eyes that could see right through me or burn me alive. I shuddered, and found the sudden surge of strength that I'd experienced begin to flounder, as if it was warring for both of us.

Passing by him on the street, he might have been just another person. He was casually dressed, in dark jeans and a blazer. His hands were tucked into his pockets, like he was strolling through the park. But there was a cold, fearful assurance in me that told me he was Cain Hunter.

By the way everyone spoke of him, I had always imagined that Cain was a big, buff wrestler, or that he had three heads and talons instead of fingers. I hadn't expected he would look like any other regular guy.

Part of me wanted to laugh that he looked so harmless—the other part of me remembered there was a reason he'd been cast out from the Order, and that he'd kidnapped my father and wanted me dead.

He paced around the perimeter of the enclosed pit, staring down at it with a subtle, entranced smile. *You hear something, don't you?* How could he possibly have known that? Unless everyone else could hear the voices, too…

"You're Cain Hunter," I declared. "You're the one who kidnapped the Dragonlord. You're the one who wants him dead."

He stopped pacing and looked up at me. His smile widened. "You're right about the first two parts."

I raised my eyebrows. "And the last part?"

"Well," he said, "we'll see how things go after today."

"Do you need anything else from me?" Wolf asked behind me.

Cain waved a hand. "No. Thank you, Marcus. You may go."

Then, Wolf turned away, exiting through the door we had come through.

I was alone with Cain Hunter, my enemy. The man who had kidnapped my father and had threatened the lives of my friends. The man who had been pursuing me since my birth. I was alone with him, and as far as I knew, he was unarmed.

Unfortunately, so was I. I could strangle him, or I could try to beat him up. But he was a full foot taller than me, and I was almost sure that Wolf was waiting just outside the door to come back in and put me to sleep if necessary. I didn't stand much of a chance.

Cain paced the room again until he stood opposite from me on the other side of the pit. "Do you know what tomorrow is, Logan?"

"No," I replied sharply. "I don't. I've been locked in a cell for who-knows-how-long."

Cain chuckled at this statement, as if I had been trying to be funny. "Well, I'll tell you what tomorrow is," he said. "Tomorrow is April 23rd. Saint George's Day."

The day when the Dragonlord is most needed, as Wolf had once told me. The day when the powers of the great dragons stir. The day when the Dragonlord is invincible.

The next day would either be the day of my reckoning or of my downfall.

I shrugged, trying to play off my knowledge. "What about it?"

"Come now, Logan," he scolded me. "Certainly our friends in the Order have told you all about it. You know what significance this day carries."

"It's the Dragonlord's busiest day of the year."

"It's also the day of Bolla's rebirth," he added, gesturing towards the pit. "She lays in wait for her lord to come and free her."

I scoffed. "Don't tell me you think the Dragonlord will help you resurrect her."

"I don't expect that at all," he replied. "It's merely a speculation."

I drew in a deep breath. "Where is William Lockwood?" That was what I was really interested in, not Cain's obsession with dragons.

He stared thoughtfully up at the ceiling, as if trying to remember where he'd put his car keys. "He is safe," he answered. "*Alive*, and safe."

"How do I know you're telling the truth?"

He spread his arms into a shrug, smiling faintly. "Well, how else would I have set the true Dragonlord on his path towards me?"

My mouth dropped open, and I felt like I'd been punched in the face.

Cain hadn't kidnapped my father because he thought he was the Dragonlord—he'd been luring me out to come after my father so that he could kill *me*!

I should have known. I should have seen it coming, but I had thought playing off my identity would help me. Unfortunately, he had already known the truth. All of the Order's efforts to protect me had been in vain. If the others were even alive, I wouldn't survive to tell them this.

"How did you know?" I asked.

"How did I know you are the Dragonlord?" he said. "Wolf discovered the truth several months ago. He's been working with me since I was excommunicated from the Order at the age of sixteen. I'll admit it took quite a bit of research and digging to discover your father's little secret."

"Meaning me," I said.

"That's right. But besides all that, William Lockwood has caused me enough trouble over the years. I wanted to have my fun with him while I waited for you to show up. Thankfully, you made it in time."

"So, my father could be dead."

"I promise you: he isn't," Cain insisted. "I know the Order has told you all about what an evil person I am, but I *can* be a nice guy. And since William went through such trouble to protect you and keep you alive, I suppose there's no harm in allowing you some father-son time."

"How generous of you. But I'm already here, standing before you." I outstretched my arms, surrendering. "Why not just kill me now?"

He stared at me, waiting for me to figure out something that was right before my face. "Because there may not be any sense in killing you. Not yet, anyway."

"And why is that?"

He began to pace around the pit once more, staring into it as if he could see Bolla within its depths. "I'm surprised you haven't asked me why I decided to wait out these past several months when I so easily could have killed you and been done with it."

"I know why you haven't," I said. "Because the pieces can only be retrieved by the Dragonlord. If you'd killed me, Ascalon would be lost."

"That's only half-true," he said. "You were never my only means of retrieving Ascalon."

I blinked. "What do you mean?"

A small grin crossed his lips. "You know, Logan, I was thirteen years old, too, when I found out. I understand what you're going through."

"Found out?"

He stared at me through those cold, blue eyes for a long moment. "When I found out that I was a Dragonlord, as well."

I laughed. "That's impossible. My parents only had one child: *me*. And you're way too old to be my brother."

"Don't be so narrow-minded," he scolded. "Do you really believe that there can only be one Dragonlord?"

My stomach turned. Certainly, he couldn't be telling the truth. There was no way the Order could have missed such an important detail. There was no way they could have forgotten that another Dragonlord had been born. Such a careless mistake could cost everyone's lives. There was no way…

"That's what I've been told," I answered.

"Then, consider me the forgotten one," he said. "My grandfather, Silas, disowned my father when he was a child. He was afraid of my father, afraid of the darkness in his heart." He scoffed. "Wretched old man. I hope he died a painful death."

My heart skipped a beat. "S-Silas?"

Cain grinned. "Does that name ring a bell?"

It certainly did. *My* grandfather's name was Silas. Silas Lockwood.

"That…That doesn't make sense," I stammered, my mouth suddenly dry.

"It makes perfect sense, Logan. My father, Ethan, had a brother, only a year or two younger than him. But Silas disowned my father when he was about eighteen years old. Ethan went mad with his desire for power. He knew what he was capable of, what he was destined to be."

He glared down into the pit, imagining the face of his grandfather. "And Silas never spoke of him again, like he was some kind of forgotten epidemic that could never be resurrected."

"No." I shook my head. "No, that's impossible. The Order would have known if there had been two Dragonlords…"

"The Order made a foolish mistake," Cain snapped. "They erased my father's name, his memory, from history, as if he had never existed. As if William had been Silas Lockwood's only son. They assumed that if Ethan was taken away from the source of his power, he would lose sight of it, and condition himself into normalcy." He shook his head, and a dark grin spread across his face. "Well, do you think someone can ever really forget who he truly is?"

"Ethan…" I repeated. "Ethan Lockwood."

"Ethan *Hunter*," Cain corrected. "He eventually changed his name so the Order could not track him down. They'd kept a watchful eye on him over the years, but my father knew what he was, and he wouldn't let the Order of Ascalon keep him away from it. He disappeared overnight, right off the map. And the Order was left chasing its tail."

So, here was the bitter truth: Cain Hunter was my cousin. My father had had a brother once, an uncle of mine that was hungry for power. And my grandfather, Silas—who I had always imagined to be a cute old man with stories of the wars and tales of the first baseball team he played for—had given up his son on a whim.

If there was ever a time to be ashamed of my family, it was at that moment. So many secrets, and they were being revealed to me by the same person who wanted me dead. By my cousin.

My cousin.

I shook my head as tears formed in my eyes. "No, the Order wouldn't do that. They would try to help him."

"Do you really think the Order is full of saintly people, Logan?" Cain asked. "After all, *you* didn't know who you were until a few days ago."

"That wasn't the Order's fault," I argued. "It was…well, my mother and father were trying to protect me…"

"I know Julianna Thorne puts on a wonderful face for *you*," he said, "but beneath that pretty smile, she'd push you off a cliff just as soon as she would push me."

"You brought this on yourself," I said. "You're the one who tried to kill my father, and that's why the Order kicked you out. *Not* because you're the son of Ethan Hunter."

His face suddenly flushed, beet red with anger. "Do you think if they'd known who my father was, they would have welcomed me into the Order with open arms?" he shouted. "They were on a witch hunt, and *I* was the target! They'd been looking for Ethan Lockwood for years, but they'd never found him, so they settled for *me*. My issues with your father gave them a reason to blame me. I *hated* that man, and I still do."

His rising voice and glaring anger startled me, and I glimpsed the reason why the Order feared him. He was controlled by his desire for revenge, his desire for power.

"So, how did the Order find out that you're a Dragonlord?" I asked calmly, trying to keep him from losing it again. It must have worked—the storm clouds behind his eyes settled and he resumed his composed demeanor.

The grin that spread across his face, however, might have been worse than his raging temper. "They haven't," he declared proudly. "Both of my parents died shortly after I was born, and I was raised by my godparents until I was sixteen, when I joined the Order.

"On my thirteenth birthday, my godfather gave me the journals and letters that Ethan had left behind. His letters urged me to seek out the Order and join them, and not to take 'no' for an answer. After a bit of difficulty, I managed to make my way into their silly little club. I stuck around long enough to get my bearings, and when the time was right, I finally set his plan in motion."

"The Dragonlord is supposed to keep the great dragons entombed," I argued, "not steal their powers for himself. What good will that get you?"

He drew back in shock, as if I should have already known the answer. "Well, what fun is there in being a tomb keeper?"

"And what honor is there in destroying peace?"

He narrowed his eyes at me. "Honor? You serve the Order in the name of honor even after what you've learned about my father? Even though, at the back of your mind, you know you're just being used as a pawn in their game against me?"

My stomach sank in the same way it did when I failed a test. It was a disappointment in the truth more than in myself, because even though I was responsible for my own actions and the outcome of my trials, the outcome itself was absolute.

And the absolution in Cain's argument was too strong to argue against.

Somewhere along the way, I had already thought about these things. I had already considered that the Order would toss me aside once everything was over—if I survived.

And for that matter, did they even care if I survived? Or did they only care if I stopped Cain?

And if they discovered that Cain and I were related, would they toss me aside like they had done to his father? Was it possible that somewhere in the midst of Cain's insanity, he was right?

No. I couldn't think like that. Even if the Order was using me, it didn't justify Cain's terrible actions. Even if I was just a tool, I was still doing the right thing.

At least, I hoped it was the right thing. The truth about Cain's father made me sick. How could I trust people who had been so cold?

I shook my head clear of the conflicting thoughts. "It doesn't matter if they're using me," I declared. "It doesn't excuse what you're doing."

"I'm just doing what I'm supposed to do, Logan," he said. "There's a reason why we can feel the great dragon's power, why it fulfills us and completes us. There's a reason why we can hear it calling to us. We weren't meant to defy the nature of who we are. We are Dragonlords, and with our power and the power of the dragon under our command, we can rebirth a species that has long since been extinct." His eyes lit with passion, and an entranced smile spread across his face. "I want nothing more than to carry on my father's legacy."

I stared thoughtfully at him. "You pitched this idea to my father, didn't you? Thirteen years ago?" His smile slowly faded, and he narrowed his eyes at me. "He wouldn't go along with this crazy plan either, so you decided to kill him. And now, you're pitching it to me, hoping I'll jump on board. Aren't you?"

He shrugged pleadingly. "Why deny yourself, Logan? This is who you are. This is where you belong."

I hesitated, lowering my gaze towards the pit before me. I could feel Bolla's power as I stared into the pitch black void, could feel my fingertips tingling and my heart pounding in my chest. The power was overwhelming, and I knew that it could easily fold in on itself and darken my heart. I would become just like Cain: alone and consumed by vengeance.

I didn't want that. Unlike Cain, I had others who I couldn't risk everything on. My mother, my father, even the Order—they were enough to keep me focused. The power of the dragon wasn't enough for me to turn on them.

I looked up at Cain, hoping I could somehow get through to his black heart. "Don't you want to prove that you're not like your father?" I asked. "Don't you want to show them who you really are?"

He glared and pointed a threatening finger at me. "My father was a brilliant man," he argued in a low, heated voice. "He knew who he was, and so do I. Don't try to dissuade me from doing this. You won't take this away from me, Logan."

"You don't know what you're doing, Cain!" I protested. "You don't know that you can control the dragon. This entire plan of yours could collapse in a second!"

He scoffed. "You have such little faith. Do you really think that after thirteen years, I'd risk such a foolish mistake? This is all I have left for myself, and I'm going to make it happen. And not even *you* will stand in my way."

I shook my head. "I won't let you do this."

He grinned and began to pace towards me. I wanted to back away, to run down one of the halls in the distance behind him, but I stood my ground. I couldn't show him I was afraid.

He stopped walking and stood before me. I could feel his warm breath on my face, and a chill ran down my spine. I held his cold gaze, willing myself not to break eye contact.

His mouth twitched as he contemplated the many different words he could say. I expected him to threaten me with death or scream in my face, but his final verdict was simple and calm:

"And you're going to stop me?"

Then, he socked me in my stomach.

For looking so harmless, he certainly packed a punch. I sank to my knees, clutching my stomach and drooling out of the corner of my mouth. My vision blackened, and I lay crumpled on the floor in agony.

Now, let me clarify something: I had only been in a few fights before, but I usually held my own. In my defense, though, I was still a little drugged from whatever Wolf had given me, and Cain was about ten times stronger than any school bullies. Plus, I wasn't expecting him to hit me—he played the cool-and-collected role so well, I hadn't seen it coming.

I felt pathetic, lying on the floor in pain before my enemy, but I wasn't going to fight him. He would have knocked me out with one more hit.

So, I remained on the ground, hoping he would just send me back to my cell.

Either that, or just kill me and end the pain immediately.

"Marcus!" he called. The door opened and Wolf entered, making his way towards me. He bent down near me and pinned my arms down by my sides. I writhed against his restraints, but he was too strong. I was completely vulnerable and powerless.

Cain walked towards me and bent down beside me on one knee. He rustled through the pockets of his blazer until he removed a syringe and a small vial of clear liquid. He inserted the syringe into the vial, returned the vial to his pocket, and flicked the needle twice. Then, he turned my head over, exposing my neck.

I wriggled and thrashed my head this way and that, but Cain seized my chin and stilled me. I had never felt so weak and powerless in my whole life.

I was terrified. Unashamed, and completely terrified.

"I'm sorry about this, little cousin," Cain said. "But you had your chance. You did this to yourself."

I felt the cold pinch of the needle entering my neck. My heart skipped a beat, my stomach flipped, and I screamed. It was the only thing I could do, the only way I could free myself from the torment. It was the only thing that Cain couldn't take away from me.

A moment later, he removed the needle and drew back. Wolf released me, and I rolled over on my hands and knees, rising to my feet. I charged towards Wolf first, because I hated him the most. But as soon as I took two steps in his direction, I tumbled forward.

I fell face-first onto the ground, my vision wavering so intensely that the fall felt longer than it actually was. My limbs went numb again, and everything around me became foggy.

Oh, no. Not again.

I hated having no control over my own thoughts and body. I hated being unable to defend myself. I wished Cain had killed me and gotten it over with. Whatever he planned to do with me was worse than immediate death.

My mind commanded my body to rise and fight, but lying flat on my stomach, I could see that my limbs wouldn't move. I was paralyzed.

"That should last for a few hours," Cain's distant voice said. "Put him in the cell with William, and then…"

I never heard the rest of the sentence. I passed out a second later.

CHAPTER ELEVEN

REUNION

I was really getting tired of awakening in terrible pain in cold, dark cellars.

Thankfully, the effects of the sedative that Cain had given me didn't last as long as whatever I had been given the night before, although I still felt pretty dizzy and weak. I awakened on a cold cement floor, spread across a mess of itchy blankets. A lamp overhead illuminated my cell, revealing just how small it was.

I sat up, but found my head spinning. As I wavered, a pair of strong hands clasped my shoulders to steady me.

"Careful," a deep voice gently commanded.

I startled, nearly jumping out of my skin. I whipped around, springing to my feet and backing towards the wall of my cell.

The man rose to his feet, staring at me with a gentle smile. He looked like he was in his late forties, with dark brown hair and soft blue eyes. His clothes were dirty and worn, dark circles had formed under his eyes, and his face was covered in stubble. But beneath his disheveled appearance, I could tell that he was strikingly attractive.

Then, it hit me. He was the man in the picture with my mother.

"You're my father," I blurted out. "You're William Lockwood."

He picked at his fingernails, staring down at them as if I had not spoken. Then, he said, "Sometimes I wonder if it was the only option."

"If you had left me with the Order, Cain would have killed me anyway."

"The Order would have protected you, and I would have, too." He looked up at me with solemn eyes. "And because of my poor choices, I won't get back the last thirteen years with you."

A lump formed in my throat, and I had to swallow it to keep from saying, "And neither will I." He was determined to blame himself, although I didn't blame him at all. I had spent my entire life wondering why he and my mother had left each other, but he had been gone for our safety. Certainly, that didn't deserve conviction.

I didn't know how to tell him this, though. He was my father, but I didn't know him.

So, I changed the subject. "Cain Hunter is your nephew."

He lowered his gaze in shame, as if he could have somehow prevented this truth and had done nothing to stop it. "He told you."

"Did you know all along?"

He shook his head. "Don't you think if I had, I would have told the Order? I never knew what became of my brother after he was…sent away. And any family beyond him was lost, as well. Cain revealed the truth to me upon my capture."

I nodded, realizing that he was unfortunately right. "He told me everything," I continued. "About Silas Lockwood, and about the Order's influence on his decision to disown his son." I stared down at the cement, wishing it had the answers I sought. "I don't understand. The Order is supposed to protect the Dragonlord. But they cast him out without second thought. They could have given him a chance before sending him away."

My father smiled. "I'm proud that you are thinking so mercifully," he said, "but Ethan Lockwood—Ethan *Hunter*—was not a man who could be reasoned with."

"He was only eighteen," I said. "He was still just a kid."

"That's true," he agreed, "but the man he became was nothing but a dark shadow. And his son has followed in his footsteps since his birth. Ethan and Cain are one and the same, and neither can be persuaded. They are set in their reasoning." He sighed. "And as with his father, it will be the death of Cain."

Cain hadn't told me how his father had died, and the missing truth brought forth a nagging itch in my brain. "What happened to Ethan?"

My father looked up at me. "Shortly after Cain was born, he returned to destroy the Order and kill me, but we managed to get the upper hand. He came back on Saint George's Day with the intent to resurrect Bolla, after having been missing for two years."

"Missing?" I asked irritably.

My father shuffled his hands. "After having been *gone* for two years." He hesitated, twisting his hands in his lap. "I stopped him."

A chill ran up my spine. "You killed him, didn't you?"

He remained silent for almost an entire minute before responding. "I knew the day would come when it had to happen," he said, in a voice so low that I had to strain my hearing to understand him. "But after he disappeared, I didn't know when. Every day, I waited for him. Every day, for two years."

He drew in a quiet breath. "I was eighteen years old, and I killed my own brother. And the worst part is, I don't think Cain knows it. He never knew what became of his father."

It had to happen, he said. And I suppose it did. Who else could have stopped the Dragonlord, but another Dragonlord?

Was this a foreshadow of my and Cain's intertwined destinies? Would I have to kill him for the world to live in peace, if he didn't kill me first? Would I have to live with the stain of his blood on my hands?

I looked at my father, at the weight behind his eyes. He'd killed his own brother. He'd given up his peace of mind for the world's safety. He'd given up his only son so that I could live away from harm. He had sacrificed so much of himself for everyone else, had ridden pieces of himself that he could never get back.

It was in that moment, looking at the scars behind my father's eyes, that I knew my life would be anything but easy. Cain and I were both Dragonlords, at war with each other for two different things: one for power and revenge, and one for honor and peace.

I could be him. I could be Cain Hunter, if I only gave in to the power of the great dragon. It would not be so difficult. In fact, it might make things easier. But was the right thing supposed to be an easy feat to come by?

"How did it happen this way?" I asked. "How did you and I end up on this side of the fence, and Ethan and Cain end up on the other?"

My father stared thoughtfully down at his hands. "There is good and bad inside of all of us," he said, "but not everyone chooses to fight for what is right."

I thought about the surge of power I'd experienced near Bolla's pit. "Were you tempted by her?"

My father met my gaze. "Yes, as all Dragonlords are. But we cannot give in to their treacherous power. They do not mean well, no matter how comforted they make us feel."

I picked at the edge of my blanket. "I liked how it felt. Her power was…captivating."

He set his mouth in a straight line and locked eyes with me. "You must be careful, Logan. The great dragons will call to you at all times, but especially now—so close to Saint George's Day—you will feel their power even more. Don't let it consume you."

I nodded. "You don't have to worry. I won't push my luck."

"Even so," he said, "do not tempt fate. I don't believe you would ever choose to follow in Cain's footsteps and pursue the power of the great dragons, but sometimes, you will want to give in regardless. It is part of who you are and it always will be, so long as you are a Dragonlord."

I didn't like the way that sounded, like I couldn't control myself even if I wanted to. But I pushed it to the back of my mind.

I sighed and straightened up. I looked around the edges of our cell, at the metal door, and at the ceiling. "How are we going to get out of here?"

My father searched the room, too. "I don't know," he sighed. "I've been in here for the past four days. The cell is locked from the inside out."

I carefully rose to my feet. My father watched me, prepared to leap to my rescue if I needed it. My legs were still weak and shaky, but sitting on the ground wasn't making me feel any better. I needed to get up and move.

I paced the wall of our cell, using a hand to guide and steady me. There had to be a way out—there always was.

I examined the hinges and the handle of the door, but nothing seemed to stick out. I looked up at the ceiling, which rose several feet above us, and down at the ground. Still, nothing.

I sighed and leaned against the door, folding my arms over my chest. "We're trapped," I muttered.

Which meant only one thing: we would both die in a matter of hours. As soon as the sun rose on Saint George's Day, Cain would execute us, and Bolla would rebirth. The game was set—we only had to wait.

"After getting this far," I said, "we end up stuck in a jail cell, awaiting our executions."

My father didn't say anything. He probably felt it, too.

I prayed that somehow, the Order had survived and was on their way to find us. Unfortunately, though, even I had no idea where we were. I didn't even know if they were still alive. Heck, we could be in another country, and the Order could be thousands of miles away.

There was no way we would survive. Death breathed down our necks, waiting for dawn's early rays to give it permission.

I groaned. "So, this is it, then? We're just gonna wait for Cain to come for us?"

My father shrugged helplessly. "What do you suggest we do, son?"

My heart skipped a beat. *Son.* I tried to push it to the back of my mind. "I don't know, but we have to *try* to get out of here. There *has* to be a way out!"

He sighed and rose to his feet. Looking up, he searched the perimeter of the cell once more, hoping he'd missed something that he hadn't seen before. Then, he pointed to the ceiling. "It looks like there is some kind of a ventilation shaft up there," he said. "I noticed it the other day, but it's too high to reach on my own." He looked at me, narrowing his eyes in deep thought. "Unless I can lift you up there…"

I shook my head. "No way. You wouldn't be able to get out if we did that."

He sighed and approached me, forcing a smile and placing a hand on my shoulder. "Logan, *you* are the one who Cain wants. *You* are the Dragonlord. *Your* survival is imperative. I've already served my time as the Dragonlord, and now, all I care about is getting you out of here. *Alive*."

I stepped back, and his hand fell off my shoulder. "Are you crazy? After thirteen years, I've *finally* found you, and you want me to run scared and leave you to die?" I shook my head. "No. Either we both go, or neither of us goes."

"Only you can stop him," my father insisted. "If you are dead, then what hope can the world have?"

"The world can find a new hope," I argued. "I'm not giving you up for them."

He sighed and stepped back, closing his eyes. Had he honestly expected me to go along with something so absurd?

"I've spent the past thirteen years of my life doing what I had to do to keep you alive," he said. "Now, when the time is most important, you think it best to argue against me."

"Well, it's the first time in my life I've been able to argue with my father," I shot back. "And I hate to burst your bubble, but the past thirteen years without you wasn't *my* choice. *This* is, and I'm not going to do it. If Cain wants to come for us, then let him try."

He didn't say anything. He only stared down at the ground, either ignoring me or processing my words.

Then, he turned and faced me. His eyes were lit with passion and determination. *This* was my father, not the man sitting in the corner awaiting death's approach.

"The sun will rise in only a few hours," he said, "and Cain won't come until then. If you get out of here, you will have time to find a way to get me out."

I narrowed my eyes at him. "That's a pretty big gamble."

"It's the only compromise I will make on this, Logan," he said. "Accept it, or I will toss you up into the ventilation shaft myself."

I folded my arms over my chest, glaring at him, but his convicting stare did not waver. I might have been looking at my own reflection, only thirty years into the future.

He wouldn't budge, I could already tell. I hadn't gotten my stubbornness from my mother alone, that was certain. So, I folded. "Fine," I muttered.

He grinned. "Good." Then, he moved towards one of the walls and looked up at the ceiling. "Now, we'll have to—"

"Wait."

He looked at me, watching as I shuffled my hands together. Then, I drew in a deep breath and dived into him, wrapping my arms tightly around him.

He hesitated for a moment, then put his arms around me. It was a strange and foreign feeling, but if things should go wrong, it would be the only experience with him that I'd ever remember.

"I'm sorry this took so long," he said quietly.

I didn't respond. He would never stop blaming himself.

I pulled out of the embrace and stood tall, drawing in another deep breath. His previously firm, determined expression had faded, replaced with solemn, shadowed eyes. I tried not to look at them.

I marched around him and moved towards the wall. Then, I turned to him. "Ready?"

He stared at me for a moment, possibly rethinking his idea. Then, he nodded and moved towards me.

I lifted a foot as he bent down with open hands. I stepped into his grasp, and a second later, I shot up towards the ceiling. Either he was incredibly strong, or I was puny and lanky. Maybe both were true.

He cradled my feet near his chest and watched as I patted the ceiling. My fingers grasped the grate over my head, and I shoved as hard as I could. The grate dislodged with a screech, and I pushed it aside into the vent. Then, I pulled myself inside and crawled into the narrow tunnel.

I turned on my knees and stared down through the opening. My father peered up at me from below. "Are you sure you'll be all right?" he asked.

"I'll be fine," I promised. "Hold on for a little while. I'm going to get you out of here."

"Logan, wait," he called as I turned away. I gazed down at him once more. "Be careful," he warned. "And if things get too risky, get yourself out immediately."

I shook my head. "I'm not going to leave you. We go together."

He stared at me with heavy eyes, as if he still expected me to give in without a fuss. That would never happen. After all, if I couldn't live my life with him, then why would I want to live it without him?

I forced myself to turn away from him and began to crawl down the narrow shaft. I tried to be quiet, but it felt like the vent would snap in half under my weight.

It barely occurred to me that I had no idea where I was going. I had seen in movies where the heroes escaped through the vents and ambushed their enemies from above, but those guys were usually special agents or spies, and they knew what they were doing. I didn't.

So, my best chance rested with continuing forward until I fell through the vent, or until I found an opening to escape through. I preferred the second option.

I passed over several grated openings like the one I had crawled through, but every room beneath was just as dark as the next. I didn't want to end up stuck in another empty cell.

After crawling for another ten minutes, I glimpsed a dull light coming through one of grates. I stopped above it and peered into what looked like a long, empty hallway. I figured it was my best bet—I just hoped that no one was nearby.

I grasped the grate and yanked on it until it came free, shoving it aside. After taking a quick peek into the hall below me, I dropped myself down below and hugged the wall. I searched in both directions for anyone who might be approaching, but luckily, the coast was clear.

At least, I had thought so.

A hand clamped over my mouth and dragged me into the shadows. I tried to scream, but I couldn't find my breath.

I was going to die.

CHAPTER TWELVE

THE AWAKENING

I thought my heart would pound its way right out of my chest, but my attacker immediately released me and stepped back.

I wheeled on my feet with my fists raised to strike, but found myself coming face-to-face with David, who had a gun in his hands. "David!" I cried. "You're alive!"

He peered past me down the hallway, as if he thought someone was waiting in the shadows. Then, he returned his attention to me. "Are you all right?" he asked, looking me over with concerned eyes. "You aren't hurt at all, are you?"

I shook my head. "No, I'm just fine."

"Good," he said. "Then, let's get out of here."

He placed a firm hand on my shoulder and steered me down the opposite hallway, away from where I'd come.

"How did you get here?" I asked as he guided me forward.

"I'll explain that on the way out," he replied. "Right now, I need to get you out of here."

"Do you know where you're going?"

"Back the way I came."

Then, I halted, crying out, "Wait!" I turned towards David as he came to a stop. "I'm not leaving without my father."

He blinked. "You found him?"

"He's…somewhere." I looked up at the ceiling where I had fallen through and tried to mentally retrace my steps to his cell. "I had to escape through the air ducts and leave him behind. I'm not exactly sure which way I came from, but I suppose I came from that way." I pointed down the hallway.

"*I* will find your father," David said, "after I make sure you are safely away from here."

"We don't have time for that, David," I insisted. "Besides, it will take you twice as long to find him without my help."

He narrowed his eyes at me, giving me one of those intimidating parental looks that I'd received too often from my mother. He was trying to make me back down, but I wouldn't. I knew I was right.

Finally, he sighed. "Very well. You can lead the way."

I turned and headed down the hallway, trying to make my footsteps as quiet as possible. "Where are the others?" I asked, almost afraid of what the response would be.

"Securing our escape," David replied.

"So, Julianna sent you to find me in her place?" I asked, rather annoyed.

"Someone needed to stay behind to make sure we had a way out, and we weren't about to drag Emma through these halls."

My heart skipped a beat. "Emma? Is she okay?"

"She's just fine," he replied, "as are we all."

My heart fluttered at the thought of Emma and her long blonde hair. Her blue eyes, her high cheek bones, her plump lips…

"Are we still going the right way?" David asked, interrupting my daydreaming.

I snapped out of my love-induced trance and shook my head, looking up at the path before us. "Yeah," I said. "We'll make a left here."

We turned and wound our way through the maze of hallways. I hoped I was going the right way—if I wasn't, I would have wasted a great deal of time, *and* led David to believe I was totally incompetent.

"How long have you been here?" I asked.

"You don't remember?" David replied. "Arianne and Ridley ambushed us in Ontario. They took us along for the ride and locked us up in this place. Fortunately, we escaped our cells a couple hours ago and found a way out of here. Our escape is in the basement of a rundown hotel built aboveground. Julianna and Emma are waiting for us there."

I felt a little angry hearing this. "Julianna should have come looking for me herself. She is the leader of the Order, after all."

David didn't seem to think of it that way. In fact, he seemed rather angry about my accusation. "I'd watch my words if I were you," he warned. "You may be the Dragonlord, but it's not your place to pass judgment on Julianna and her decisions."

It took all my remaining strength not to roll my eyes and fire back a retort. Maybe David thought Julianna was Queen of Everything, but I certainly didn't. She shouldn't have risked David's life on me—as our leader, she should have put herself first.

That was how I saw it, anyway.

The thought of Ethan Hunter returned to my mind, and I had to force it away to keep myself from becoming angrier. Was the Order really so concerned with self-preservation that its own leader would throw anyone into the heat of battle?

"Does this look familiar?" David asked, interrupting my thoughts.

We stopped outside of a tall metal door. The hallway continued on into the darkness beyond. I imagined that it was lined with several cells identical to the one I had been imprisoned in, although I assumed they were empty. My father and I were Cain's primary targets.

I shrugged. "I was on the other side of the door. Although, I guess it does seem a little familiar…"

Before I'd even finished my sentence, David had removed a small, brass paper clip from his pocket and straightened it out. Then, he bent down near the lock, placing his ear against the door and listening carefully as he picked the lock. After a few tedious moments, we heard an almost inaudible *click*, and David rose to his feet.

He pocketed the paper clip and slid his fingers in between the door and the wall, prying until the heavy door creaked open. My father appeared from the shadows within his cell. "You did it," he breathed, his eyes wide and his mouth hanging open.

I raised my eyebrows. "Did you think I couldn't?"

He closed his mouth and shook his head. "I guess I just didn't expect you to come so soon." Then, he turned his gaze towards David, and a smile crossed his lips. "Hey there, stranger."

David stepped forward, allowing a tiny grin to appear on his face in the midst of our troubles. They clapped each other by the forearms and shook hands. "William," David said. "You look awful."

My father grinned. "You look quite terrible yourself."

David chuckled. "It's good to see you alive, friend. Now, let's get ourselves out of here."

He stepped out of the cell and made his way down the hallway with my father and me following along. We headed down the hall, returning to the place where David and I had reunited. My father and I followed quietly after him, our gazes darting this way and that in fear of being caught.

Then, I stopped. "What good is getting out of here if Cain has Ascalon?"

My father and David faced me. "You're worried about this now?" David said. "Logan, getting you out of here alive is hard enough. We don't have time to worry about Ascalon."

"If we're not worried about Ascalon, then what *are* we worried about?"

"Ascalon will have to wait. Even if Cain resurrects the great dragon, we still have a chance to stop him, but *only* if you're alive. Let's take this one step at a time."

I looked to my father for help, but he only sighed. "David is right. We need to ensure your safety first."

I couldn't believe what I was hearing. Couldn't we escape and liberate Ascalon at the same time? If we tried to come back for the lance, surely Cain would have already resurrected Bolla, and all our efforts would have been in vain.

"We don't have time to discuss this right now," David said, turning on his heel and continuing forward. "We need to get you out of here."

My father turned and followed after him into the dark hall. I continued along behind them, but my mind didn't settle. I wasn't about to trek through those dark halls again and risk everyone's safety for the second time.

We moved down the hallway until we met a dead end. David stretched as tall as he could and tapped on the ceiling panel above him. We waited for a moment, then a panel above our heads slid open. Julianna and Emma peered down at us. Relief flooded their expressions. "You made it," Julianna said with a tired smile.

I certainly wasn't happy to see her. Not after everything I'd learned about Cain and his father, and not after her sending David in alone to find me.

Emma lowered a rope from above, noosed at the end with a small loop. I placed my foot into the loop and grabbed the rope, and together Julianna and Emma pulled me up through the ceiling. My father followed next, and David followed after him.

"My God," Julianna breathed. "William. You're alive." I straightened myself up and moved into the light where I could see everything around me, including the small assortment of weapons that they had collected in my absence. An array of guns and Emma's bow and arrows had been neatly laid in one corner of the basement. But something else caught my attention—something disgusting and appalling.

Julianna hugged my father deeply, squeezing him and whispering prayers of thanks for his safety. My face flushed with jealousy.

The woman had, in a matter of hours, lost almost all of my respect. Maybe she hadn't been responsible for Ethan's excommunication—she had probably only been a teenager at the time—but she had carelessly sent David into the sanctuary to find me, as if he were an insignificant pawn worth sacrificing on a whim.

And there she stood, hugging my father as if he were her long-lost husband, as if *they* had been together once, like my mother and my father had been.

Wait a minute—had they?

The thought had never crossed my mind until that moment. Julianna *was* strikingly beautiful, and she was the kind of woman who could get what she wanted. And my father and mother hadn't seen each other since before my birth, thirteen years ago. Thirteen years was a long time, perhaps long enough for my father to fall in love again.

Throughout my entire life, I had never considered that either of my parents could ever love anyone but each other, especially since my mother had never really been with any other men. I had seen her go on dates before, but they never really meant anything, and she always returned with the same reaction: a bored shrug, and, "He was nice, but he wasn't right for me."

In my mind, the only person right for my mother was my father, and she for him. But did they feel that way?

Perhaps I was overreacting. But I couldn't deny that seeing Julianna hug my father so affectionately—and seeing him accept it without hesitation, as if it was a familiar and common embrace—made me hate her even more.

I tried to ignore the image of them together, wrapped in each other's arms before me. I cleared my throat—perhaps too loudly and dramatically—to interrupt the disgusting, tender moment between my father and Julianna. They pulled apart from each other and faced me. "I'm so glad you're okay, Logan," Julianna said with a smile.

It was about time she noticed me.

"You," my father said, peering at Emma. She stepped forward and drew in a deep breath, standing tall. "My name is Emma Kingsley, sir."

"I know who you are," he said with a reassuring smile. "You're Edward's daughter. What on earth are you doing here?"

She swallowed, and darted her eyes away. "My father…he was killed four days ago." A silent moment passed as she collected herself. "He sent me to find you so you could help me. And, well…here you are."

He smiled sympathetically. "Here I am. I'm sorry I was too late."

She drew in a deep breath and shook her head. "It doesn't matter. What matters is that you and Logan are both alive."

"It *does* matter," my father insisted, placing a hand on her shoulder. "This won't go unpunished. Edward was—and still is—a good man."

She looked down at her feet.

To save her from the saddening thoughts of her father, I redirected everyone's attention to me. "So, what now?" I asked. "Now that I'm safe and everything, shouldn't we be trying to stop Cain?"

"Obviously, that's among our top priorities," Julianna replied. "Did he have Ascalon?"

"What do you think?" I snapped. "Ridley and Arianne took the pieces from us. Of course Cain has Ascalon."

"Logan…?" my father said. I glanced at him, at his furrowed eyebrows and confused expression.

Julianna narrowed her eyes at me, trying to remain sympathetic to the fact that I'd just been in captivity for the past two days, in spite of my attitude. "I see," she said. "Do you happen to know where he's keeping it?"

"I didn't actually *see* it," I muttered. "But he obviously has it. We'll just have to find it."

Julianna looked annoyed, but for once, she didn't intimidate me, and I didn't care. By that point, I was ready to do things on my own and be done with it. I wanted to go home, to be with my mother and have a normal life again. I wanted my ridiculous quest to end.

So, why couldn't I do it on my own? Obviously, Julianna wasn't entirely competent. Heck, *I* could probably lead the Order better than her!

Julianna sighed. "Fine," she said, facing the others. "We'll have to get back inside and find Ascalon. I'm sure Cain has it on him—he wouldn't risk leaving it lying around, even if he thinks we're still imprisoned."

I pretended to listen, but only for a moment. Thankfully, everyone's attention was focused upon Julianna and her captivating words. I backed away towards the ceiling panel and slid it open with my foot. I glanced up at the others once more, then I crouched down and dropped myself through the ceiling.

My father called my name, yelling for me to come back, but I ignored him. I sprinted down the dark hallway and away from the others.

I was going to finish things on my own.

I knew they would come after me within seconds, but by the time they got to the floor, I would be too far away to find.

I was running so fast that I thought I would surely get caught by Wolf or someone else wandering around, but the halls were deserted. I turned down every twisting hallway that I met simply to spite the others, so that if they came looking for me, they wouldn't find me.

I couldn't get any more lost that I had started out as, so the fact that I had no idea where I was going made no difference to me. I assumed that the entire place was centered around the sanctuary of the great dragon's tomb, and that the rest was just a maze of hallways, empty rooms, and cells.

Finally, I stopped running and leaned against the wall, panting for oxygen. I strained my ears to hear if anyone was coming, but the halls remained silent. I was alone, and that was how I wanted it to be. I set forward down the hall, following the dim light at the end.

The hallways continued to twist into a complicated mess. I passed several metal doors and assumed that only prison cells lay beyond them. I seized every opportunity to turn down any hall that appeared, hoping that I would find something of importance. Maybe Ascalon would be lying on the ground, gleaming beneath the light and awaiting my rescue. Hopefully, it would be that simple and convenient, but I doubted it. Nothing was *ever* that easy.

The light at the end of the hall slowly began to grow brighter, until I was certain that I was returning to the sanctuary. If Cain was anyplace, he would be there. At least, I hoped so—the sooner I found him, the sooner I could find Ascalon.

But when I reached the end of the hall, I found myself in a different place altogether. The room wasn't much bigger than a walk-in closet, and was empty save for a large stone dais positioned in the center.

Wedged into a fracture in the top of the stone was my prize, Ascalon.

The lance hummed with living energy, and was illuminated in a bright gold hue, like King Midas himself had used it in battle. Every doubt I'd ever had about the weapon's true existence was annihilated upon seeing it.

Ascalon was no myth, and dragons were as real as anything else. It just took me seeing the magnificent weapon reassembled to believe it entirely.

I reached a hand forward and wrapped my fingers around the shaft of the lance. As soon as I touched it, a powerful current surged through me. It was a different kind of power than that of the great dragon—I didn't feel tempted or coerced. Instead, I felt strong. Nothing could defy me with Ascalon in my hands.

I was so entranced by the lance that I didn't hear the footsteps approaching behind me. I turned on my heel and pointed the lance at Wolf, who stopped and stared down at the spearhead with a smirk, although he did take a step back. I guess seeing a mythical weapon at the ready could make even someone like Wolf afraid. "So you've found Ascalon," he said.

I swallowed the lump in my throat. "Y-Yeah. And I'm taking it with me."

He gave me a pleading look. "Did you really think that it wouldn't be guarded?"

My face flushed with embarrassment. "Well…I thought I'd try my luck. And I found it, didn't I? Now I'm going to take it, and you can't stop me!"

He chuckled. "I don't think that's going to happen, kid." He reached into his jacket and removed a shiny, silver pistol, pointing it straight at me. "Here's the thing: you can't die today, but it definitely won't feel any less painful having a bullet stuck in your gut. So, you can make this easy, or you can make it difficult. What's it going to be?"

I stared at the lance in my hands, then at the pistol in his. Even if I fought him, he would probably unload the clip on me, which still wouldn't get me anywhere. I should have planned things out better. I was a master at not thinking things through.

With a defeated sigh, I lowered the weapon. "Put it back where you found it," Wolf said, nodding towards the stone.

I glared at him before complying. He kept the gun level and grinned at me, gesturing with his free hand for me to step forward. "Now, let's go."

I stared at the gun. "Where are we going?"

His grin widened. Instead of answering, he stepped forward and took me by the arm, pressing the gun into my side. "You'll see in just a few minutes, kid."

There I was again, at Cain's mercy, with Wolf holding me back. The only difference was that Arianne and Ridley were present for the show. They beamed proudly and looked upon me with dark, wicked eyes. I was a meal ready to be served to their god, and nothing made them happier.

Wolf forced me to my knees and held a gun to the back of my head. I didn't think it would do him any good with the way I was feeling—kneeling before Bolla's tomb, her power coursed through my body, like a wave of great energy that could save me even from death.

Fear not, Dragonlord, she called. *He can do you no harm, if you only summon me…*

I squeezed my eyes shut, trying to force her voice out of my head. I tried to focus on something, anything, to keep me from giving in to her call, but it was too powerful. The skylight in the dome at the top of the ceiling gave way to dawn's early rays, lighting the sanctuary with a soft blue tinge.

It was Saint George's Day, and I could feel the power of the great dragon more than ever. It was intoxicating, so captivating that I felt drunk with the power that began to fill me. It was more tempting and seductive than the power I had felt while holding Ascalon, more captivating and harder to resist.

"Today is the day!" Cain shouted happily, entering through a dark hallway opposite Bolla's tomb. "And what a glorious day it is!"

A wild smile was plastered across his face. He appeared extremely alert, as if he had had the best night's sleep in ages. I knew he could feel Bolla's power, too—he was just better at controlling it and filtering it than I was.

In his left hand was Ascalon, illuminated from the shaft to the tip of the spearhead. It was fully charged, prepared to strike the great dragon down, or to release her from her tomb. If I had only been five seconds quicker, it would have been in my hands, and the spearhead would have been pointed directly between Cain's eyes.

Unfortunately, I had been five seconds too slow. I had to get my hands on that weapon if I had any chance of survival, and if I had any chance of defeating Bolla.

"William and the rest of the Order have escaped," Ridley declared, watching for Cain's reaction. He probably expected Cain to snap and stab him in the gut with Ascalon, but Cain only smiled at him. "It doesn't matter," he said. "Let him go. Let the entire Order go. You can even let Logan go!" He turned to Wolf and gestured at him. "Go ahead, Marcus. Let him go."

Wolf blinked several times, unsure if Cain was being serious or if he had lost his mind. "If we let him go, he will—"

Cain waved a hand at him. "Let him go."

Wolf hesitated before drawing back and holstering his weapon. Cain fixed his gaze upon me and grinned maniacally. "Once I awaken Bolla, he can't stop me."

I staggered to my feet. The great dragon's power coursed through my veins like lead. "Then what was the point of keeping me locked up for the past two days?" I demanded.

He grinned and gestured at Bolla's tomb. "So you could stick around for the main event!"

We heard footsteps approaching from the adjacent halls. Through three separate doorways entered David, Julianna, Emma, and my father. Each had a weapon at hand, ready to strike Cain down in a second. I hadn't wanted them to find me before, but at that moment, I was thankful they were present—even Julianna.

But Cain didn't seem concerned at all. In fact, his smile widened. He faced them and backed away towards Bolla's tomb, until he stood directly in the center of the glass covering. He settled Ascalon over his shoulder. "I'm glad you could make it," he said. "You're just in time!"

Julianna fixed her glare upon him and tightened her fingers around the grip of her pistol. "Step away from the tomb, Cain."

He laughed, unfazed. "Or what? Are you going to shoot me?"

"That's the idea."

He outstretched his arms. "Well, go ahead!"

"Let Logan go, Cain," my father warned, his position as firm as Julianna's.

Cain glanced back at me, shrugging. "He's free to do as he chooses. He's not a prisoner anymore. If you want to go, Logan, feel free to go."

I shook my head. "I'm not going anywhere without Ascalon."

He smiled painfully at me. "Well, that's the one thing I can't allow you to do, my friend. I've worked too hard to get my hands on it, and you won't stand in my way."

He turned Ascalon over and gripped the shaft with both hands, pointing the tip of the spearhead towards the glass dome.

"Do it, and it's the last move you'll make!" Julianna screamed.

Cain only grinned at her. He raised the lance over his head, prepared to drive it down towards the glass dome.

Then, I heard a gunshot. Cain staggered backwards and reached a shaking hand towards his chest, pulling down the neckline of his shirt. A dark red patch of blood had spread across his chest. His eyes widened, and he fell to his hands and knees, groaning in pain. Julianna looked on with firm eyes, but her hands were shaking.

That was it. One bullet, and the craziest guy the world had never met was done with.

Everyone immediately assumed their positions. Wolf raised the gun to my head. Arianne and Ridley turned on their heels and yanked out their own weapons, taking aim at the members of the Order.

Cain groaned again, a deep, dark growl in the pit of his throat. He reached forward and took hold of Ascalon. Staggering to his feet, he gripped the lance once more.

"Bolla…" he grunted. "Help…me…" He raised the lance over his head. Then, he drove the spear through the glass dome.

A spray of air hissed through the crack he had made with the lance. He removed Ascalon from the glass dome and stepped forward into the mist, closing his eyes and exhaling. A pleased smile spread across his face.

Even ten feet away, I could feel that the mist was anything but ordinary. My hands shook and my vision wavered. My body was overwhelmed by the excessive healing powers produced by the mist. It was only a small fraction of what was to come.

Cain opened his eyes and stepped back. He pulled down the neckline of his shirt, and the bullet wound was gone. Grinning, he stepped away from the glass dome and glanced over at me. "How are you doing over there, Logan?" he called. "Still alive?"

My chest was heavy, like something was growing inside of me and clawing its way out. The weight of Bolla's power was so strong, I thought it would crush me.

The Order stared on in complete shock. If a bullet couldn't harm the guy, then what could?

Cain outstretched Ascalon towards the pit. Then, in a dark, booming voice, he cried, "O, GREAT DRAGON: AWAKEN!"

A terrible quaking followed, so strong that even Cain had trouble remaining on his feet. Then, the glass dome shattered, and a huge black figure shot out of the pit.

The dragon swooped in circles, roaring so loudly that the others had to cover their ears. I, however, had a bigger problem to worry about.

As soon as Bolla emerged from her tomb, my limbs went weak, and I could not stand on my own two feet anymore. I crumpled to the ground, overwhelmed by the power of the great dragon.

Every fiber of my being cried out in torment. How Cain could withstand her power was beyond me. All I wanted was for the pain to stop—I could hardly focus on what was going on around me.

The dragon swooped over our heads and landed on a stone perch near the ceiling. She roared again, and her round red eyes focused upon the scene below. She stretched her wings and flicked her tail, which hammered against the wall behind her and caused several large bricks to crumble to the ground below. Her talons dug into the stone perch, and a high-pitched screech echoed across the sanctuary like nails on a chalkboard.

She really would have been a magnificent sight—that is, if I didn't have to kill her, and if she wasn't set on killing me and the rest of the Order.

Her body was armored with large black scales, each the size of my hand. Her ivory fangs bared in warning every time she snarled and growled, and her overall wingspan stretched for a length of at least fifty feet. Her eyes were the crimson color of blood, glowing with anger and rage that I didn't want to face.

Unfortunately, I would have to. I was the only one who could.

Cain seemed to be the only one in awe of the great dragon. Even Arianne and Ridley were terrified, and looked to be on the brink of fleeing. Cain stared up at the great dragon, his mouth hanging open in wonder and his eyes as wide as half-dollars. He took cautious steps forward, keeping his gaze trained upon the mighty beast above him.

He lifted Ascalon above his head, and Bolla growled low in her throat. Clearly, she wasn't happy to see the only weapon that could destroy her waved beneath her nose in warning. But Cain dropped the lance before him and lifted his hands, surrendering. "I mean you no harm, Great One," he called to her. "I have released you from your prison."

She growled approvingly, narrowing her eyes at him. She stretched her long neck forward, hanging on to every word Cain spoke.

"Will you serve me, Great One?"

She continued to growl, drawing back her long, snake-like neck. I hoped that she wouldn't go along with his plan and would bite his head off instead, but I could feel her power growing stronger in me—and that couldn't mean anything good.

She leapt from the stone perch to the ground below, shaking the earth so hard that chunks of the ceiling fell around us once more. I might have been scared if I wasn't lying limp on the floor, drunk with overwhelming power.

She marched her tree trunk legs forward, standing over Cain. He kept his gaze locked upon her and remained still.

Bolla lowered her head and studied him. Then, she puffed a cloud of smoke from her nostrils. She lifted her head high and roared.

A wide smile stretched across Cain's face, and he began to laugh with sheer delight. "Magnificent!" he exclaimed, clapping his hands. Bolla stepped back, fixing her gaze upon him and awaiting his order.

If Cain had been crazy before, he was ten times crazier with the power of the great dragon under his control. He stepped forward and retrieved the lance, facing the members of the Order. Since Bolla's rebirth, they had remained as still as statues, petrified in awe.

Cain smiled wickedly at Julianna. "Isn't she beautiful, Julianna? And to think you've spent your entire life suppressing such wonder! It's a shame, isn't it?"

The dragon directed her attention towards Julianna and snarled. Julianna kept her gaze fixed upon the beast, her mouth hanging open and her eyes wide with terror. "What have you done, Cain?" she whispered. "You've sent the world to its doom by unleashing her!"

Bolla growled again, and Cain shrugged. "The world has no idea what a gift I've given it. With the power of the great dragon at hand, imagine what can be done. Imagine nations warring for a weapon like this, fearing it when it strikes out against them. Imagine a world where humanity doesn't rule. Imagine what we can create..." His gaze drifted towards the distance, and his features shifted until his toothy grin was as dangerous as Bolla's. "Or imagine what we can destroy."

There was a look in Julianna's eyes that I had only seen once before: defeat. If Julianna's fearlessness had been conquered, then what chance did the Order have?

"So," she said, drawing back in surrender, "you're the Dragonlord's heir, too."

He bowed theatrically. "The only child of Ethan Hunter. Or as you might remember him, Ethan Lockwood." He turned his gaze towards my father and glared. "Isn't that right, Uncle? You remember him, don't you?"

My father remained expressionless, but I could see the clouds warring behind his eyes. He had said that Cain never learned of his father's true fate, but revealing it would be like unleashing a tiger from its cage. The truth about Ethan Hunter would have to die with him to protect the world from Cain's rage.

"I am the rightful descendant of Saint George," Cain continued, returning his attention to Julianna. "I am the rightful descendant of the great Dragonlords. While you've spent the past hundreds of years keeping the great beast at bay, you've only been stifling the world's growth. And here I am, to make things right."

He faced Bolla and outstretched his arms. "The Order has wasted so many years fearing this power when it should have seized it! All along, you trembled in terror over what would happen if she should be freed, and look what has come of it! The great beast serves at my command!" He laughed, thoroughly pleased with himself.

"You can't trust her, Cain," Julianna warned. "There's a reason we've spent the past several hundred years subduing the great dragons."

Bolla roared, startling Julianna. Cain shook his head in warning at her. "I don't think she likes you talking about her relatives that way."

Julianna must have realized there was no way to get through to him, so she shifted her focus from Cain to Ascalon. He glanced down at it and held it up for her to see. "You want this, don't you?" Cain smiled and tucked the spear behind his back. "That's not going to happen, Julianna."

He turned on her and marched towards Bolla. She lowered herself to the ground, and Cain climbed aboard her back. It was as if she could sense his thoughts before he voiced them, as if she had known he would want to take flight. Cain had forged a bond with the mighty beast, and she was entirely at his command.

"This reunion has been a pleasure," Cain called from high atop the great dragon's back, "but it's time we get going. Bolla has a grand entrance to make in the city. I guarantee that by the end of the day, the entire world will believe in the legend of the dragon once again!"

Bolla crouched down and sprang into the air, hovering over the ground. Her flapping wings sent powerful currents of wind against the opposite walls, vibrating the tall columns that upheld the stone perches near the ceiling.

Arianne stepped forward, waving her arms desperately. "Cain!" she cried.

"Take care of them!" he shouted back to her. "And leave the Dragonlord for me!"

Then, Bolla surged towards the ceiling, breathing a fiery funnel towards the top of the dome. Chunks of the ceiling began to collapse around her, dropping to the ground below where the rest of us were left behind. Bolla pulled her wings into her body and bulleted out through the hole in the ceiling, disappearing altogether.

Nobody moved. Not even Ridley or Arianne. Apparently, no one had recovered yet from the sight of the dragon. I didn't blame them.

But while they stood on their own two legs, healthy as could be, I lay on the ground in terrible agony. The dragon had fled, but I could still feel her strength crushing me. I feared that if I didn't get away from her tomb quickly enough, I wouldn't live much longer.

I lifted a shaking hand towards the members of the Order, who felt so far away that I doubted they could even see me. "Father..." I croaked.

Fortunately, I managed to catch Emma's attention. She gasped and came running towards me, but Ridley and Arianne were quicker. They lifted their weapons and took aim at Julianna and Emma, finally recovered from the preceding events. My father and David mirrored their actions, standing firm and ready to pull the trigger at any second.

"Don't move," Ridley warned. He gestured at Emma. "Step back. Don't go near him."

Emma stopped, but she targeted Ridley with her trademark death glare. "Don't you get it? If we don't get him out of here, he's going to die!"

"That's a chance we're willing to risk. Now, *step away.*"

"I don't think Cain would be too pleased with that," she countered. "He did say he wanted him *alive.*"

"Unfortunate fatalities occur every day," he said. "He could be just another number."

Thank you, Emma, for defending me, but harsh words wouldn't save my life, and every second wasted was a second closer to my death.

Ridley kept the pistol trained on Emma and made his way towards me. Neither his weapon nor his stone-cold gaze wavered. "We'll be taking Logan with us," he said, "and the rest of you will be dead within the minute." He glanced over at Arianne and nodded towards Julianna. "Take care of her first."

Emma seized the brief moment of his diverted attention. She whipped out her bow and an arrow from her quiver so quickly that I didn't remember seeing it. I thought she would shoot the arrow straight between Ridley's eyes, but instead, she lifted the bow at a forty-five degree angle and fired towards the ceiling.

Ridley lifted his gun to shoot her but was distracted by the rumbling that followed. He stumbled over his feet and fell to the ground as the stone perch that Emma had struck with her arrow began to dislodge. Fortunately, Bolla had already loosened the stones with her weight, and Emma's arrow had been just enough to collapse it.

"You stupid girl!" Ridley cried.

Emma readied another arrow in record time and aimed it straight at Ridley's chest. "Get away from him!" she ordered.

He glared at her, rising to his feet. Then, he lifted his weapon. She loosed the arrow, and it pierced his left shoulder.

Ridley screamed and stumbled backwards, dropping his gun and clutching his arm. The spearhead jutted out two inches from the back of his shoulder, fastened into his limb. Simply *looking* at the wound made my stomach turn, but Emma was nowhere near as unsettled. She readied another arrow for precaution and aimed it at him again, struggling to keep her footing as the stone perch and the ceiling continued to collapse.

"Ridley!" Arianne screeched from across the room. Thick ceiling chunks rained down around her, and she stumbled to and fro. "We have to get out of here!"

Ridley was in so much pain, I doubted that he even heard her. He tried to rise to his feet and run, but the quaking of the ground beneath him knocked him down once more. So, he settled for half-walking, half-crawling.

Although terrified of being crushed to death, Arianne took what potshots she could. She fired blindly at my father, Julianna, and David. They ducked when they could, but they were having just as much difficulty staying on their feet as Arianne was.

She unloaded the magazine until empty clicking was all that she received. Then, she tossed the gun aside and sprinted towards one of the dark hallways, disappearing. Ridley barely managed to crawl his way after her as a massive ceiling chunk crumbled to the ground and blocked the entrance to the hall.

I would have been relieved with them gone—well, about as relieved as I could be on the verge of death with the ceiling collapsing all around me—but one thought echoed in the back of my mind: where was Wolf?

The last I remembered of him, he was standing behind me with a gun to the back of my head, after Julianna had shot Cain. Then, he was gone. Had he fled already like the coward he was? Or was he waiting in the shadows to attack us and kill us all, like the wolf he had named himself after?

I didn't have time to ponder it. Emma rushed towards me and bent down, pulling one of my arms around her neck. She grunted underneath my weight as she pulled me to my feet. I had to admit, I was quite impressed with her strength. Sure, I wasn't the size of an elephant, but I was a full-grown boy. I couldn't have been easy to carry.

I tried to walk with her, but I only ended up slowing her down, and the shaking of the ground didn't do anything to help us. We crumbled to the floor together just as Julianna, David, and my father arrived at our sides. Julianna grabbed Emma by the hand and directed her towards one of the unblocked hallways.

My father hoisted me into his arms in one fell swoop, and he trudged after Julianna with David tagging along behind.

I saw the dark outline of the mouth of the hallway, and then everything went black.

Let me serve you, Dragonlord...

CHAPTER THIRTEEN

THE WOLF MAKES A DEAL

Once again, I found myself awakening in an unfamiliar place. Thankfully, though, I wasn't in a prison cell.

I lay on a cot with a thin blanket draped over me. The room—which wasn't much bigger than a bathroom—was nearly dark, save for the gentle streaks of sunrise cascading in through a window over my head. The walls were grayish-blue, but beneath the peeling paint were dark yellow stains. At the foot of my bed sat my father, half-asleep and slumped over in a rickety wooden chair.

Had everything that happened been nothing but a bad dream? Had I really seen a dragon? Certainly, if the world was at stake, my father wouldn't be sleeping. He would be out trying to stop the beast, and trying to find Cain Hunter…

I sat up in bed, feeling much more rested than I last remembered feeling. My father either heard me, or was tuned into my movements via some strange father-son connection. He awakened, as alert as if he had never been asleep. "You're awake," he said.

"What happened?" I asked.

He wrinkled his eyebrows. "You don't remember?"

I shook my head. "The dragon—she didn't

really come back, did she?"

My father nodded. "Yes, Logan. Cain has released Bolla from her tomb."

My heart sank. So, it hadn't been a dream. It had really happened. Cain was out there somewhere, risking the world's safety with his pet dragon.

I was so overwhelmed with the mere thought of it that all I could do was sigh. "Great," I muttered. "I hoped I had just imagined it."

My father stared at me through narrowed eyes, as if he hadn't heard me and was too busy processing whatever was going on in his mind. "You left," he said.

I mentally retraced my steps, trying to remember what he was referring to. The ceiling had collapsed…Cain had freed the dragon…I had been aimlessly running through the halls…

Oh, yeah. I definitely remembered. I had left without anyone's permission to go find Ascalon. I couldn't blame my father for being upset.

I sighed again. "Yeah, I guess I did—"

"Without permission."

I shrugged. "I wasn't going to risk anyone else's safety."

"Instead, you risked yours?" he asked angrily. "Logan, the Order exists to protect the Dragonlord. We know what we've gotten ourselves into by swearing ourselves to you. Do you think we didn't expect that there might be a few casualties along the way?"

"Well, do you expect me to be okay with that?" I fired back.

He sighed and pinched the bridge of his nose. "You don't get it, do you?" he muttered. He looked at me again and leaned forward, clasping his hands together. "*Your life* is the only one that matters. If you die, then Cain cannot be stopped, and he and Bolla will destroy everything in their path. For the past hundred years, we've moved right along every Saint George's Day without trouble, without a single black mark on the record. Now after all this time, the great dragon has risen again."

I glared at him. "So, this is my fault, then?"

"Well, it certainly never happened before you came around," he snapped. Then, he sighed and closed his eyes, ashamed. "That's not what I meant…"

"Well, maybe if my father had been around to teach me all of this stupid stuff," I shot back, "then this never would have happened."

I threw the blanket aside and marched clumsily towards the door, still somewhat weakened by Bolla's power. My father rose and blocked my escape. "Logan, wait."

If he was anyone but my father, I would have shoved him aside and thrown the door open. But he *was* my father, and he was a full foot taller than me—I had no room to challenge him. So, I backed down, staring down at the floor to avoid making eye contact.

He drew in a deep breath. "I'm sorry. I truly didn't mean it."

"It doesn't matter," I muttered. "You're right."

"I'm not. Cain has been working at this for

thirteen years. He would have figured it out at some point."

He was trying to make me feel better, but it didn't help. The fact remained that I hadn't stopped Cain, that I had walked straight into his trap and had practically handed Ascalon to him.

"We don't know what to do now," he continued, "and you are the Order's only hope. If something happens to you, then Cain wins."

What a pity, I wanted to say. After everything, I almost didn't care. The only thing my father seemed concerned about was the Order. He didn't seem concerned about me—his own son—at all.

I tried to force myself to be respectful—boy, was it hard—so I could get out of the tiny room and away from him. "I'm sorry," I murmured. "I won't do it again." But I wasn't so sure that the promise was, in fact, a promise. Knowing me, I would probably turn around and do it once more if I had to.

He placed a hand on my shoulder. "I've spent the past thirteen years without you. I don't want to lose you now."

I looked up at him and managed a tiny smile. He had gotten to me with his fatherly charm. I couldn't stay mad forever.

He returned the smile and squeezed my shoulder. Then, he straightened up. "How do you feel?"

"Just fine," I replied. "But I don't understand what happened."

"The great dragon's power is too strong for

you. You're lucky it didn't kill you."

"How could Cain stand it?"

"He has had more experience with it," my father said. "And unlike you, he craves it. He uses it to fulfill him. It's easier to give in to such a tempting power than to resist it." He raised his eyebrows and studied me. "Isn't it?"

My eyes shifted, and I suddenly felt guilty, although I didn't know why. "I suppose so."

His gaze lingered over me for a moment, as if he was trying to communicate telepathically with me. Why was he giving me that convicting look? I never should have told him that Bolla's power made me feel good—since then, he'd been acting like he needed to keep an eye on me.

Finally, he looked away and turned towards the door. "Let's go. We need to speak with the others about what we're going to do next."

There was still one thing that bothered me as it returned to my mind, something that I had to bring up before it ate me alive. "You and Julianna!" I blurted out.

My father rested his hand on the doorknob and faced me, confused.

"Uh…I mean…" I closed my eyes and drew in a deep breath. "What…What was that all about earlier?"

He stared at me, so lost that I wondered if I'd dreamed it. "What are you talking about, Logan?"

"You and *her*. Was there…*is* there something going on between you two?"

He exhaled, seemingly relieved. "Oh, *that*,"

he said with a slight chuckle.

"Well?"

He gazed past me, as if he didn't know the answer himself. "At one point, there could have been."

Could have been?

"But something has always held me back."

My heart skipped a beat. "What is it?"

He fixed his sad eyes upon me, as if every terrible memory he'd ever suppressed had suddenly flooded over him. "Your mother."

Score!

I knew I should have been a little more sympathetic—it was obvious that my father was bothered by some tormenting memory that had reawakened in his mind—but I couldn't deny that I was happy. My plan to reunite my parents was slowly coming together with Julianna out of the picture.

I knew I should have been concerned with more important things—you know, like stopping Cain and Bolla from destroying the world—but my father's revelation gave me newfound energy.

I nodded, trying to play off my genuine delight. "I'm sorry," I lied. "But…is that a bad thing?"

His eyes drifted towards the floor. "I don't know, Logan. Thirteen years is a long time."

"It's not like she remarried and had five kids," I pointed out. "Couldn't you just—?"

He shook his head. "You wouldn't understand, son. Let's leave it at that."

My heart sank, but I nodded in spite of

myself. He would come around—at least, I hoped he would.

He drew in a deep breath and forced a smile. "Now, let's go downstairs."

We had taken refuge in the abandoned hotel above Bolla's underground sanctuary. By abandoned, I mean rundown and unfit for living. The three-story building felt like it had been smashed by the hand of a giant, so that it was now compacted into a two-story building. We had to sidestep massive holes in every direction to avoid falling into a dark, dangerous pit of sharpened planks and rusty nails. Some of the windows were boarded up, but light managed to peek in through the uncovered panels, revealing a yellowish, misty fog hanging in the air.

I had only been unconscious for about an hour or two, but I feared what terrors Cain had wreaked across the city in that short time. As we climbed the creaking, unstable wooden stairs to the second floor, anxiety crept over me. Whatever mess Cain had caused and planned to cause, I was responsible for cleaning it up, and I alone. The Order would only go far enough to protect me—the rest was my job.

Heavy footsteps approached us as we drew nearer to the landing, and David met us at the top of the stairs with a pleased grin on his face. "We've caught ourselves a wolf," he said. I hesitated in mid-step.

Wolf. They'd caught Wolf.

But the wolf was impossible to catch. How had they managed to do that?

My father darted up the remaining steps in his path and disappeared around the corner, and David waited for me to follow.

As soon as I reached the landing, I saw him. Wolf was tied to a chair with his hands restrained behind his back. The Order stood in a half-circle around him, and he was at their mercy. I should have felt safer knowing that, but something didn't feel right.

I remembered wondering where he'd fled to when the sanctuary had begun to collapse—certainly, he would have had time to escape. So, how had we managed to catch him?

Wolf fixed his eyes upon me, and a chill ran up my spine. Sensing my apprehension, he offered a chilling grin to intimidate me even more. I glanced away.

I tried to feel more at ease despite my fears. Julianna knew what she was doing. She had to know something was up.

"Good to see you, Logan," Wolf said.

My father stood protectively before me, blocking me from his view. He glared at Wolf, a look so cold that it would have made me back down. Wolf, though, was a lot more resilient. His disturbing smile widened.

Julianna paced the floor before him, deep in thought with her arms folded over her chest. "I just don't understand, Marcus," she said. "All this time, you've been working for Cain. How did you manage to elude us for so long?"

Wolf looked up at her and grinned. "You're not too difficult to slip past, Julianna."

She narrowed her eyes. "Thirteen years is a long time."

He shrugged. "Maybe you're slipping. Maybe you're not as good as you used to be. Either that, or *I'm* just good at what I do."

"Well, isn't that the truth?" she muttered. "How did you end up separated from Ridley and Arianne?"

"I fled the sanctuary before it came down."

"And you stuck around to wait for us?"

"I did, actually," he replied. "I have a message to deliver for Cain."

"A message," she repeated. "One he couldn't have delivered himself?"

"He figured it would settle better if I did it myself, since the rest of you aren't too fond of him."

"So, he left you behind," she said, pronouncing each word slowly for full effect.

Wolf didn't seem bothered. He shrugged again. "I'll leave when I want to leave. Despite what you think, these binds"—he shook his bound hands behind his back—"aren't going to do much to keep me here."

Julianna smirked at him. "Just like a wolf. So elusive."

He smiled back at her.

"All right, then," she said. "Give us the message, and we'll reconsider leaving you here to rot."

He shook his head. "Sorry, Julianna. It's for

Logan's ears only."

"We're not leaving him alone with you," she said.

"Then that puts you in a bit of a predicament, doesn't it?"

The room remained silent for the moments that followed. I felt rather guilty for having thought so unkindly of Julianna, while there she stood protecting me. Of course, it was her job, but she could have just as easily handed me over to Cain in exchange for peace. And after learning that she and my father had nothing between them, my respect for her had gradually returned.

She glanced up at my father in search of some kind of guidance, but he appeared as uncertain and defeated as she did. I knew there was only one thing to do.

"It's all right," I spoke up, stepping forward. "I'll be fine on my own."

"No," my father instantly denied.

"It's okay," I reassured him. I faced Wolf and locked my gaze with his—which was quite difficult, but I managed in spite of myself. "He can't do anything while he's tied up."

Wolf grinned, amused by my bravery.

My father gazed past me, but I could read the look in his eyes: he didn't like it, but leaving me alone with Wolf was the only way to move things along.

He drew himself upright and summoned a deep breath. Then, he marched towards Wolf and bent down at eye-level before him. "If you do anything," he warned darkly, "if you even *try* to do anything, I will make sure you're left here to die."

Wolf's annoying, creepy grin did not waver.

My father rose to his feet and backed away towards the door, and Julianna, David, and Emma followed. Within a moment, the room had cleared and the door closed behind me. I stood only five feet away from the traitor.

I drew in a deep breath and took two nervous steps forward. "So, I'm here," I said. "What's your message?"

He gazed thoughtfully up at me. "You enjoyed that back at the sanctuary, didn't you?"

I glared at him. "What are you talking about?"

"The power of the dragon. I know you felt it."

I lowered my gaze. Was it that obvious? My father knew, and even Wolf knew. Cain must have known, too. I couldn't help the way it made me feel—like Cain had said, it was part of our nature. I was just better at controlling myself than he was.

I shrugged. "So?"

"You don't have to be ashamed," he said. A smile crossed his lips, one of sympathy and intrigue. "It's funny. You remind me a lot of Cain when he was your age."

My stomach turned. "Get to the point, already."

"This *is* the point, Logan," he replied. "What do you plan to do? Do you want to spend the rest of your life hiding away from who you truly are until your heir succeeds you? Or do you want to be free?"

"I plan to do what I'm told," I said, but even to me, it sounded pathetic and stupid.

He shook his head disapprovingly. "To do what you're told," he echoed. "What a good student you are. But I'm afraid that those rules don't apply here. The Order only protects you because it's their job. And you do what they tell you to do because you don't know what else there is."

"It's the right thing to do," I argued.

"Logan, what Cain did wasn't evil or wrong. The Order has feared the power of the dragon because of what *could* happen if she were released. But do you see anything terrible happening?"

"Power in the wrong hands is evil," I corrected him.

"But is it truly in the wrong hands?"

"Cain wants to use the dragon's power to enact his revenge upon the Order for what they did to him and his father," I said. "Is there any way that could possibly be a good thing?"

He nodded. "You're right, but let's go even further back to Ethan Hunter. What had he ever done wrong?"

He'd hit me where it hurt. The same fear I'd been trying to ignore had been brought forth once more.

I had spent the past several days—and what would have been my entire life, if it hadn't been for unfortunate circumstances—trusting that the Order knew what to do and how to do it. I put my faith in Julianna and the others because…well, because I was told to.

Was it possible that Cain was simply the

product of bitterness? Would he have done any of this if he had been given a fair chance from the beginning? Would his father have set him on a self-destructive path if *he* had been given a fair chance from the beginning? Was it possible that none of this was pre-destined, like Julianna and my father seemed to believe?

And if it *was* possible, was Cain truly doing anything wrong?

"Had the Order respected Ethan Hunter," Wolf continued, interrupting my thoughts, "I doubt he would have gone so far as to turn against them almost thirty years ago. But they condemned themselves." He sighed, looking me up and down with sympathetic eyes. "I'd hate to see you do the same to yourself, Logan."

If he kept talking, I might believe him. I needed to end things immediately. "So, what is your message?"

He stared at me for a long, awkward moment. Then, "Not so much a message, but a deal."

I raised my eyebrows. "A deal?"

"Cain would like to make a peace offering," he continued. "You see, he understands the extent of your powers, even though you don't. And he sympathizes with you, knowing that you just found out about all this Dragonlord business a few days ago. He's not blind, Logan. He understands your loyalties to your father. Believe it or not, bloodshed isn't what he is after."

"So, he thinks I'm corruptible."

"Not corruptible," Wolf corrected, "but

open-minded. He could have killed you in the sanctuary if he wanted, but he sees something in you that he's not willing to pass up."

I tried not to ask, but I couldn't help myself. "What is it?" I almost whispered it, as if saying it too loudly might give me away for a crime I hadn't committed.

Wolf locked eyes with me. "Honor."

I had expected him to say something like, "*Ultimate power!*" But honor? What did that even mean by that point?

"You can see what others can't, and you can choose beyond that." He paused. Then, "You're sympathetic towards Cain."

The words felt like a stab in my gut. "I'm not," I denied, but my voice cracked.

"You are. He can see it, and that's why he spared you."

I didn't like how things were going at all. The walls were closing in around me, suffocating me in the room with Wolf and my own convictions. So, what if I felt a little sympathetic towards Cain? What happened to him and his father was unfair. But that didn't mean I approved of what he was doing, or would help him out in any way.

I really, *really* needed to get away from Wolf before he said anything else that might make me question myself.

"So, what is this deal?" I demanded, folding my arms over my chest.

"You want your friends in the Order to live, right?"

I narrowed my eyes. "Of course I do."

"In exchange for my release, Cain has offered to spare their lives. And in addition to that, I will tell you where you can find him."

I scoffed. "Why would you do that?"

"Because he asked me to. The two of you still have much to discuss." Then, he grinned. "And because I'd like to get out of here sooner rather than later."

"Well, that's a great offer," I said. "But I think we can find him on our own. It's kind of hard to miss a giant black dragon flying around the city."

"You plan to rely on your own insights, do you?"

"It seems like a minor risk compared to freeing you."

"And the lives of your friends?"

He knew how to get to me. But I said, "Cain wouldn't keep his word."

"That's where you're wrong. He's an honest person. He has never pretended to be anything he isn't. And if he wanted to destroy the Order, Logan, he could do it at any moment. He's trying to keep the peace."

Peace? By releasing the great dragon, he was trying to *keep* peace?

"The only thing he wants," Wolf said, in answer to my thoughts, "is *you*. The rest doesn't matter. Not even the Order. He can get over his differences with them if he has your compliance."

Unfortunately, Wolf was right. If Cain had wanted to destroy the Order, he could have done it as soon as he'd resurrected Bolla.

I knew what my father would say: the only

life that matters is mine. But even so, I still couldn't bring myself to sacrifice the members of the Order. Cain would murder all of them in an instant if I didn't comply. Sure, it was a great risk to give myself up, but without the Order, I couldn't survive anyway.

This was certainly a terrible idea—there was no denying that. But I thought there might be a way I could twist it to my advantage.

I drew in a slow, deep breath. "You'll spare their lives," I repeated. "No matter what happens?"

"No matter what happens," Wolf agreed. "There is only one condition: you must meet Cain *alone*. If any of your friends accompany you, the deal is off the table."

A chill ran up my spine, but I nodded in spite of myself. "I understand."

Wolf grinned up at me. "So, do we have a deal?"

I tried to shake the nagging feeling in the back of my mind that told me this was a terrible, terrible plan. I would be putting everything that the Order stood for at risk, not to mention my own life.

But in the end, I *was* the only one who could stop Cain. And if I could find a loophole, then by God, I would use it. It would simply take some maneuvering.

I drew in a deep breath. "We have a deal."

"Wonderful," he said. "Now, get me out of these binds."

I glanced around the room. There was a lot of junk lying around, but none of it really looked useful. Scattered throughout the room was a broken lamp, a three-legged nightstand, and a smashed television, but what could I do with any of that?

Something on the floor glittered back at me underneath the sun's rays streaming in through the window. I retrieved the silvery letter opener with the hotel's insignia upon the handle. Bingo.

I positioned myself behind Wolf and stared down at the ropes tied around his wrists, digging into his skin.

What was I doing? I couldn't let Wolf go. This was a terrible idea…

"What are you waiting for, kid?" he said in a hushed voice.

…but it was the only way to face Cain without risking everyone else's lives…

I drew in a deep breath and plunged forward, sawing at the ropes, keeping my focus only upon the task before me.

After some effort, the ropes fell to the floor with a soft thud. Wolf's wrists had been rubbed raw from the splintery binds, but he didn't seem to mind. I stepped back, moving towards the door with the letter opener still in my hand for protection.

Wolf rose to his feet and rolled out the soreness in his wrists. He fixed his gaze upon me and grinned. "You've done well, Logan," he said, "and Cain will uphold his end of the bargain for this."

My grip on the letter opener tightened. "Fine," I said. "Now…now get out of here."

He held out his hand expectantly. "Give that to me," he said, eyeing the letter opener.

I swallowed and placed the letter opener into

his hand, trying not to shake with fear. He tucked it into the pocket of his blazer and smiled. "Now remember what I told you, kid," he said. "You come alone. And don't try to pull the wool over our eyes. If anyone shows up…" He didn't finish. I knew what would happen without him saying it.

"I get it," I said. "Now tell me where to meet Cain."

"The New Point Loma Lighthouse off of Cabrillo Road," he replied. "One hour."

"One hour?" I exclaimed.

He shrugged. "His idea, not mine. Just be there on time. Miss it, and—"

"The deal is off?"

He grinned. "You got it."

"I'll be there."

And so, the conversation came to a close.

Wolf walked towards the broken window behind him and peeked out at the street two stories below. After determining he had a sure escape, he drew back and faced me. "Well, this is where we part ways, kid. But…" He stepped towards me, and I knew something wasn't right. "We don't want them to suspect you had anything to do with my escape, do we?"

I took a nervous step backwards. "No…"

He gestured for me to turn around.

"W-What are you going to do?"

"Just turn around, kid."

I swallowed and slowly turned to face the door, my heart pounding in my chest.

"In advance," he said, approaching me, "I'm sorry for this."

I opened my mouth to reply, but before I could, Wolf wrapped an arm around my throat and pressed my head forward with the other, putting me into a painful chokehold. The oxygen in my lungs immediately began to deplete, and I crumpled to my knees, struggling against his powerful grip.

After a few short moments that felt quite lengthy, I stopped fighting. My vision blackened as he lowered me to the floor, and in the next second, I passed out.

"Logan, wake up!" I heard my father's distant voice calling to me, and I felt someone shaking my shoulder.

I opened my eyes to the sight of my father, Julianna, and David standing over me.

"What happened?" Julianna demanded before I had fully adjusted.

My father helped me sit up, keeping a firm grip on my arm to steady me. "Wolf..." I groaned. "He got away."

"How?"

I would have to make something up—something infallible and convincing. "He had a blade up his sleeve," I lied. "I turned around for a second, and the next thing I knew, he was out of his seat attacking me."

Julianna narrowed her eyes at me. "We didn't hear anything. And we checked him for weapons before tying him up."

I shrugged. "He must've hidden it well. And it only took him one hit to knock me out."

Her suspicious gaze lingered over me, and I could tell she knew I was lying. I cleared my throat to break the silence and rose to my feet, glancing over at the window through which Wolf had fled.

"What was the message he gave you?" my father asked.

"There was no message," I said. "He just wanted to get me alone so he could get away."

My father swore under his breath, and Julianna's eyes narrowed even more—if that was possible. "I'm sorry," I muttered. "I should've known he was going to try something."

My father sighed. "It doesn't matter. We're just glad you're okay."

He had put it off almost immediately, but Julianna hadn't moved. I didn't like the way she was looking at me, deducing things I couldn't even imagine. I feared she could see right through me and my terrible lie. If I didn't get away from her, I would probably crack.

"Guys!" Emma's distant voice called from the first story. "Get down here! Quick!"

Thank God for Emma, once again. My father and David made their way out the door, but Julianna didn't budge until I set forward. I snaked my way past her, but I could still feel her eyes boring into the back of my skull.

We reached the landing of the first floor and found Emma staring at an almost dysfunctional television. How she'd gotten it to work in the midst of all the junk was beyond me, but that thought quickly evaporated when I saw what she was staring at.

"...reports of *dragon* sightings, Steve," the reporter said. She stood on the main street in a red pantsuit, her eyes wide in disbelief and horror. "That's right, a dragon. Frantic calls have been made to the police over the past two hours from people claiming they saw a black dragon flying across the sky. I'm standing outside of the San Diego Convention Center right now, where the most recent reports have claimed another sighting of the dragon only half an hour ago..."

"How bad is this?" I murmured, my eyes fixed upon the screen.

"Bad," Emma replied. "Very bad."

"What's worse, it forces us out into the open," David added. "We obviously can't just sit here and let things go south."

"...that's right, Steve," the reporter continued. "Whether this is an elaborate prank or a sign of an approaching doomsday is unknown. We don't have any other information to give you right now, but stay with Channel 47 for continued coverage of the dragon sighting."

"We've spent the past hundred years keeping the legend of the dragon a secret," my father muttered, "and in one day, everything has changed."

"It doesn't matter," Julianna declared in a voice so firm, we all turned away from the television and faced her. "We'll send her back just as easily as Cain called her out."

"We can't do that without Ascalon," David pointed out.

"No, we can't, but we still have the one

thing that matters." She fixed her eyes upon me. "Our Dragonlord."

"And he doesn't have Ascalon," Emma added.

I had my own plan in mind, so I had to keep Julianna at bay—which wouldn't be easy at all. "Look, you guys," I spoke up. "For whatever reason, Cain hasn't attacked. He could have killed us in the sanctuary, but he let us get away. It's been at least three hours since he freed Bolla, and nothing has happened. He could destroy this city in an instant if he wanted to, but he hasn't yet. Doesn't that mean anything?"

"He's waiting for the opportune moment to strike," my father responded.

"What do you suggest?" Julianna demanded. "That we wait until he makes the first move? No, we can't do that."

"Well, we have no idea where he is," I pointed out. "And even if we happen to catch Bolla flying around, we can't just follow her back to wherever Cain has hidden himself."

Julianna glared at me and folded her arms over her chest. Clearly, she didn't like being upstaged in front of her subordinates. "What exactly are you suggesting, Logan?"

She wouldn't buy it, but I would say it anyway. "That we wait for him to come to us. After all, we're the ones he wants."

She stared at me with fire in her eyes, and I almost buckled. "We wait," she repeated. "We just wait around while Cain destroys all of San Diego."

"He won't," I insisted.

Julianna waved a hand at me. "You're wasting time by arguing with me about this," she said. She faced my father and David, blocking me out. "What do the two of you suggest?"

My faced flushed. Who did she think she was?

I glanced at Emma, who seemed to be just as annoyed with Julianna as I was. "We're part of this, too, you know," she spoke up. "Logan *is* the Dragonlord. You can't just pretend he isn't here."

Julianna whirled around and faced her. "This is between the members of the Order *only*," she snapped. "And you, Miss Kingsley, are not part of the Order. Now, I suggest the two of you wait outside."

Emma started to rise to her, but I pulled her back. Between Julianna and Emma, I wouldn't know who to bet for, and I didn't really want to see the outcome.

Emma huffed and muttered curses under her breath the entire way down the steps and out through the back door. Once outside, we found ourselves in a small, grassy park outside of the hotel. The sun had retreated behind puffy gray clouds, probably as afraid of Bolla as the rest of San Diego was.

Emma groaned. "Who does that woman think she is?"

"I'm with you on that one," I sighed.

"You know what? We should just go—" She cut herself off and darted her eyes to the ground. "Never mind."

"Go where?" I asked. "Go out and find Cain

on our own?"

She glanced up at me with guilty eyes. "Yes," she said. "I mean, no! That would be suicide. It's just...well, I just wish they would treat me like I was part of this, too. You know?"

So, that's what was really bothering her. And I couldn't blame her. She'd lost her dad several days ago, and hadn't even had time to mourn over his passing. She had fled to the only people she thought she could trust, and they had hardly given her the time of day. She deserved more than that.

Another bad idea came over me, but I couldn't help myself. I drew in a deep breath. "Can I tell you something?" I asked. "Something that you can't tell anyone else?"

She raised an eyebrow. "Like a secret?"

I nodded.

"Yeah," she said. "I suppose so..."

I glanced behind her at the door, making sure no one was coming. We were alone in the small grassy area, but even then I didn't feel safe. "Let's take a walk," I suggested.

She chewed on her lip. "They would be mad if we left..."

"Since when do you do what you're told?" I asked. Then, I set forward down the alley leading to the front of the hotel, without waiting for Emma to follow. She hesitated, uncertain about whether or not it was safe to go alone, but she eventually followed after me.

We strolled down the sidewalk past shops and parking lots for about ten minutes until the hotel was no longer in view. We stopped at an empty park and made our way towards the jungle gym. I guessed that everyone had boarded up in their homes to hide from Bolla. Those who had remained outside stood idly on the sidewalks, conversing amongst themselves and training their nervous gazes on the sky in hopes of sighting the dragon.

I climbed through the bottom section of the dome-shaped jungle gym and settled myself on the cold metal bar, staring out at the street before me. Emma stood next to me with her arms folded over her chest. "So, what is this secret?" she asked.

I drew in a deep breath. "I know where Cain is."

Her eyes widened. "Why didn't you say anything?"

"Because," I said, darting my eyes to the ground, "I made a deal with Wolf. And it doesn't involve the Order."

"What did you promise him, Logan?" she demanded.

"Cain wants me. He promises to leave the Order unharmed if I meet him…alone."

Emma groaned and flopped herself down next to me. "That's just what he wants, Logan! Your life—"

"Is the only one that matters," I finished. "I know. My father already made that clear. But I'm not going to risk everyone else's lives for mine. For some reason, Cain trusts me."

She narrowed her eyes at me, and for a second, she looked like Julianna.

"I can reason with him," I insisted. "And if I

can't, well…he has Ascalon. All I have to do is get the lance from him, and I've got the upper hand."

"You say it like it's so easy," she murmured. "So, you've agreed to this, then? You plan to meet with him?"

I nodded.

"You're risking *everything,* Logan," she said. "He's asked you to come alone because no matter what happens, he wins. If you agree to whatever crazy thing he's going to propose, then you'll be at his mercy. And if you oppose him, then he'll kill you right then and there. How is this going to benefit us in any way? Did you even think this through?"

"I did," I replied with a small grin. "He *can't* kill me."

She raised her eyebrows.

I remembered something Wolf had told me at the diner in Redding, the only thing that would work to my advantage. "I'm as invincible today as he is," I explained to her. "It's Saint George's Day, and we're both protected by our powers. Only the dragon can do us harm. Cain himself is nothing to worry about—at least, not until after midnight."

She narrowed her eyes at me again, but she appeared to be thinking over my words. "That's a big gamble to make, Logan."

I nodded. "I know."

"I still don't see why you didn't tell us," she continued. "We could work something out. You're just being ridiculous and irresponsible."

"This is the only hand I can play right now," I replied. "Cain and I are on equal playing grounds for the day, and I have to make a move while I can. And I only have an hour until I have to meet him."

She drew in a silent breath and stared forward at the empty street. "Where are you supposed to meet him?"

I shook my head. "I can't tell you."

She glared at me. "If something happens to you—"

"You're not going to help me, and you're not going to come after me. You'll know my fate by the end of the day."

"You can't fight him and get Ascalon on your own, Logan," she said. "You're walking into a trap empty-handed. Let me help you."

"No," I said, rising to my feet. She stared up at me through desperate eyes, and I sighed. "Look, Emma. I'm thankful for your help. You've saved my life several times in the past few days, and you're a lot braver than I could have thought. But this is something I can't allow you to do. You can't risk your life on me."

She rose to her feet and stood inches away from my face. "That's what the members of the Order do."

I looked down at the ground. "You're not a member of the Order."

The words were bitter on my tongue, but I had to get away from her. She stared at me as her eyes filled with tears. She wouldn't believe me, but it hurt me to say it as much as it hurt her to hear it.

I turned on my heel, heading towards the street and leaving Emma behind—which was a lot more difficult to do than I thought it would be. It didn't help that I had no idea how to get to the Point Loma Lighthouse—I would have to hail a cab.

Then, I heard Emma call, "Stop right there, Dragon Boy!"

I faced her, and saw an arrow aimed straight for me. "W-What are you doing?"

"I can't let you walk away," she said. "Take another step and I'll shoot."

I looked at the gleaming arrowhead, at the way it seemed to be blinking red. It wasn't like the other arrows she'd used before.

"Go ahead," I said.

She pulled the string of the bow even tighter. "I'll do it!"

I locked eyes with her for a long, hesitant moment. Then, I turned on my heel.

Almost immediately, I heard a buzzing noise, and a sharp pain erupted in the back of my right shoulder. I cried out and crumbled to the ground.

I looked down at the front of my right shoulder and saw the arrowhead pointed towards the ground. The arrow had pierced through my entire shoulder.

If there was one thing I'd learned from that incident, it was this: Emma was a girl of her word.

I reached my free hand towards the arrow and gripped the bamboo shaft. Gritting my teeth, I snapped the arrowhead off of the shaft, and a sharp pain raced through my shoulder. I leaned back on my feet and reached my hand behind my back, slowly yanking the rest of the shaft out of my shoulder. The bamboo was caked in the red shine of blood.

I closed my eyes and willed my body to heal. When I looked down at my shoulder, the gaping hole slowly sealed shut. Only a few moments later, the pain was completely gone.

I rose to my feet and faced Emma. She had readied another arrow, but it was lowered in her hands. She stared at me with wide eyes, as if she hadn't believed in my temporary invincibility. Honestly, I hadn't believed it either until I saw it for myself.

I gripped the arrowhead and the broken shaft in my left hand and held them up for her to see. Then, I tossed them down on the ground at my feet.

CHAPTER FOURTEEN

CAIN'S LAST PROPOSITION

So, I had lied to my father when I promised I wouldn't run off again on my own without permission. But this time, things were different.

At least, I hoped so.

Emma was right: this was a big gamble to make. But the fact remained that I was invincible for the next several hours—invincible to anything and everything except the dragon. It was a narrow window that I had to leap through.

"Here we are," the cab driver said, pulling the taxi to a halt. "Cabrillo Road."

I had asked the cabbie to drop me off down the road, just for precaution. The last thing I needed was for him to see Bolla.

"Are you gonna be okay, kid?" he asked. "With all this talk of dragons flying around, don't you think you ought to be at home with your parents?"

"Thanks," I replied. "But I'll be fine."

Although, the guy did have a point. During the drive to the lighthouse, I had counted ten police helicopters and fifteen patrol cars. The city of San Diego was on the edge of panic, and if things weren't contained soon, the entire state of California—or worse—would be, too.

I opened the door to step out, but the cab driver said, "Forgetting something, kid?"

"Right," I said, embarrassed. I fished out the twenty-dollar bills my mother had given me days ago and handed them over to the cabbie. He examined them for a moment—I guess I just had that face of a thirteen-year-old boy who could counterfeit money. Then, he nodded approvingly.

I climbed out of the car, and he sped away immediately, leaving me alone at the bottom of the winding road. With a sigh, I set forward.

It took me about ten minutes to reach the top of the road. I approached the lighthouse property and stared on in horror.

The tall, white lighthouse sat at the far end of the property, surrounded by several red-roofed dormitories. But what caught my attention first was the fires and the smoke. Some of the houses had been destroyed, as if a mortar strike had been called on the property. No doubt, it was Cain's doing. He and Bolla must have scared of the Coast Guard so they could take over.

Lush green grasses blanketed the entire property, along with fifty-foot tall palm trees and a low stone wall. Beyond the wall, narrow cement paths led between the dormitories and the lighthouse. On one of the open grass fields sat a red and white helicopter with the words "United States Coast Guard" scrawled across the cabin doors and the tail boom in black letters.

The entire property sat dangerously close to the cliff's edge. Beyond the lighthouse lay the endless blue sea and the rippling white waves crashing against the shoreline below. It really was a beautiful place, somewhere I hoped to visit again in the future—you know, if I made it out alive.

I had been to the lighthouse before, at that exact time, in my dreams. Dark gray clouds continued to gather overhead, warning of an approaching storm. The incoming storm seemed suitable, given the circumstances, but I hoped it would stay away for the time being.

I drew in a deep breath and set forward on the cement path. I didn't know exactly *where* I was supposed to meet Cain, but I had a feeling he would show up pretty soon.

A door creaked open in the distance and slammed against the wall. Arianne emerged with a rifle at hand from one of the houses north of the lighthouse. I froze in mid-step as she aimed the gun at me. The red laser sight burned over my chest like a bee sting. "You came alone, I hope?" she called across the space between us.

I raised my hands defensively. "Just like Cain demanded."

She stood in place for a long moment with the rifle aimed for my heart. I didn't know why she bothered—Cain must have told her she could do me no harm, anyway.

Finally, she lowered the weapon and gestured for me continue forward. We headed down the main path leading towards the base of the lighthouse, where Ridley stood with his right arm in a sling and his shoulder wrapped in a bloodied bandage. I wanted to ask him, "How's the arm?" but it wasn't the time. In spite of his painful wound, a creepy smile was painted across his face. Apparently, both he and Arianne were under the impression that I was surrendering.

"Good to see you again, Logan," Ridley said. If it was possible, he was even more of a creep than Wolf. Where did Cain find these guys?

He opened the door at the base of the lighthouse and gestured for me to enter. "Cain waits for you at the top," he said. "Good luck."

I glared as I moved past him, and he slammed the door shut behind me.

I stood at the base of a long, spiraling staircase, which made me dizzy just to look at. With a deep breath, I set forward, climbing the stairs two at a time. By the time I reached the top, I was out of breath.

Wolf met me at the landing with a pleased grin. On the opposite side of the lens stood Cain, peering out through the window at the ocean below.

"It really is a great view, isn't it?" he asked dreamily.

I moved around the lens and approached his side. A subtle smile was spread over his face, like he was entranced by the beauty of the sea.

I almost laughed. There stood the man who wanted me dead, the man whom the Order feared, and he was captivated by the spread of the ocean.

He drew back and faced me. "So, you made it."

"Like I said I would," I replied. "Now, what do you want?"

He frowned. "Straight to business, then?"

"Let's not waste time."

"No, certainly not." He turned his attention to Wolf. "Leave us, Marcus."

Wolf nodded, then descended down the spiral staircase, leaving me alone with Cain Hunter.

"So," Cain said, "what now, Logan? With the both of us immortal today, and tomorrow, just two more faces in the crowd, what do we do now?"

I shrugged and faced the window, staring out at the ocean below. "Oh, I don't know. You *could* just hand over Ascalon and be done with it right here and now."

He nodded. "I *could* do that, but what fun would it be for me?"

"You've already had your fun," I growled. "You wanted to resurrect Bolla, and you did. You wanted to claim her power, and you did. You wanted to reveal the legend of the dragon to the world, and you did. I think *I* should be asking *you*, 'What now?'"

He sighed. "You're absolutely right. That *is* the problem. In a matter of hours, I've grown bored. I've spent the past thirteen years trying to accomplish what I've accomplished in a mere several days. There isn't much victory left to be claimed."

"How terrible," I muttered.

"Don't be so condescending," he scolded me. "You know, Logan, I was thinking about something earlier—since all of this began, no one has asked you what it is that *you* want."

I shrugged. "So?"

"So, tell me," he said, "what do you want?"

I faced him and tried to stand as tall as he was, and not as small as I felt. "I want you *gone*."

He drew back in surprise. "After I've already spared both your life and the lives of your friends, *this* is your demand?"

"You spared our lives after you tried to kill us," I returned heatedly. "Don't think yourself to be such a saint."

"I'm no saint, Logan," he replied, shaking his head. "And I've never pretended to be. I know you think me to be a monster, but I'm really not. The members of the Order—*they* are the monsters. Certainly, a part of you must agree with me after what you learned about my father."

I was tired of trying to argue with Cain—he was beyond reason. And after all, that wasn't what I had come for.

"I've heard enough," I muttered. "I'm not here to join you, and I'm not here to listen to you cry about how bad you have it. You've condemned yourself."

He glared at me, and for a second, I wanted to suck the words back into my mouth. But, to my surprise, he remained calm. He looked me up and down, cracking a vague smile. "Why don't you come with me?" he said. "I have something to show you."

He turned without waiting for me to follow, under the assumption that I would obey without question or defiance.

I watched as he made his way towards the exit and disappeared from my sight. For the few moments that followed, I was alone. I could have left if I wanted to, could've probably walked right off the property and gone back to my father and the rest of the Order. I was not as much of a prisoner as I feared I would be.

Knowing this filled me with determination. Maybe Cain underestimated me and didn't think I would try anything. Well, he was wrong.

I drew in a deep breath and followed the path which Cain had taken, making my way down the spiral staircase and returning to the ground level. The clouds outside had thickened, and I heard a distant, subtle roar of thunder.

Cain waited outside the lighthouse for me. Thankfully, Arianne, Ridley, and Wolf were nowhere in sight. If I was going to make a move, it would be easier without them around.

He guided me down one of the paths to the outlying dormitory on the eastern side of the property. My fists remained clenched at my sides during the entire walk, prepared to strike should the occasion call for it. Once we reached the dormitory, Cain opened the door and politely gestured for me to enter. If he wasn't a psychopath, he would have been quite the charming guy.

I glared at him for effect before entering the dorm. Then, he followed after me and sealed the door shut behind him, stepping in pace with me at my side. We made our way down a long, dim hallway towards a steel-framed door blocking our continuing path.

"So tell me, Logan," Cain said, his eyes fixed upon the path before us. "What *did* you come here for, if not to accept my offer?"

"You haven't made an offer," I said.

He smiled. "Not yet. But you haven't answered my question."

I swallowed. "I'm here to stop you."

"And how do you plan to do that?" he asked. "Today belongs to us both, and neither of us can win or lose. We're a special breed, you and I. And I hope you'll lend me your ear before you make a final decision. Because once I kill you, Logan"—he stopped walking and placed a hand on my shoulder, smiling sympathetically—"I can't take it back. Can I?"

I stepped back, shaking his hand off of my shoulder and glaring. "You can kill me," I shot back, "but you'll have to wait until tomorrow."

He narrowed his eyes at me. "Don't forget that you're here—*alive*—under *my* grace. And I'm only willing to be hospitable for so long until you push me past my tolerance level. If I have to, Logan, I *will* kill you." His piercing blue eyes could see right through me. I squeezed my fists even tighter to keep my hands from shaking. I didn't doubt he would kill me if he needed to.

After a moment, he continued walking. "I've asked you to come here for a business proposition," he continued. "The truth is, I care about you."

I released a humorless laugh.

"I told you before: I know what you're going through. It isn't easy to resist the temptations of the great dragons and their captivating power. And you shouldn't have to. You should be free to do as you please. Why have the power of the Dragonlord if you can't even use it?"

"I'm not interested in power."

"I thought you might say that," he said. "But you know that Bolla isn't the last of her kind. You know there are hundreds more—if not thousands—lying asleep across the world, don't you?"

"Yeah. And good luck finding them all."

He scoffed. "It shouldn't be too hard as a Dragonlord, but that's not the point. What do you think we could do with all that power?"

"Terrible things."

"And *wonderful* things, Logan. Tremendous things. We Dragonlords are more than slayers and guardians—we're tamers and rulers, too. We could control the power of the mightiest beast known to man and use it to our advantage."

"You really think a dragon would like being controlled in such a way?" I asked, raising an eyebrow. "You'd be dead before you got that far. Don't forget what they are, Cain."

He rolled his eyes. "Please, Logan. They're muscles and teeth, nothing more. Don't give them more credit than that."

I shook my head. "Keep thinking that way, and you'll see what happens."

"Yes, Logan," he sighed. "Continue to mock me. But I don't think you'll find it so laughable in a moment."

When we reached the end of the hall and approached the steel door, Cain removed a key from around his neck and unlocked it. The room was empty except for a long leather trunk on a wooden display, positioned alongside the back wall.

A faint smile spread across Cain's lips as he approached the trunk, like a grandmother reuniting with her grandchild after a long time. He spread his hands over the surface and faced me. "Which was more captivating: the power of the great dragon, or the power of Ascalon?"

I narrowed my eyes at him. "It's hard to say."

He returned his gaze to the trunk. "I'm showing you this because, despite everything that's happened, I trust you, Logan. You deserve to know what's been hidden from you for so long. You deserve to hold it in your hands and relish in its power, even if only for a moment."

He unfastened the set of locks on the trunk and opened the lid, but his smile instantly disappeared a moment later.

Ascalon wasn't in the trunk.

Cain took a drunk, staggering step backwards with wide, horrified eyes, as if he'd been shot in the chest. Then, he jerked his head towards me. Fire raged across his face. "Where is it?" he demanded in a low, threatening whisper.

I took a step back. "Where is what?"

"ASCALON!" he shouted, jabbing a finger at the trunk. "IT WAS SUPPOSED TO BE HERE!"

"Like I would know?"

He grabbed me by the front of my shirt and shoved me hard. I stumbled backwards and struck my head against the concrete wall, yelping in pain as I sank to my feet.

I tried to crawl away, but Cain wouldn't let me go so easily. He yanked me to my feet again, shoved me against the wall, and pressed an arm against my throat, suffocating me. My fingers clawed at his grip, shriveling pathetically in vain.

Cain leaned in, his face inches away from mine. "Where is it?" he hissed.

"I...don't...know!"

"Don't lie to me, Logan!"

"I swear to you," I gasped. "I don't know!"

He threw me down to the ground. I coughed and sputtered as air surged into my lungs. Cain paced behind me, mad with hatred and rage. He watched me like a lion stalking its prey.

I turned over on my hands and knees and crawled backwards. "You have to believe me, I don't know where it is!" I cried.

He looked at me with wide, dangerous eyes, and I half-expected him to jump on me and rip my throat out with his fingernails. By the grace of God, though, I was interrupted.

A high-pitched ringing noise filled the room. Cain, still heaving, shuffled through the pockets of his blazer and removed his cell phone. His gaze did not waver from me, and I could see the craving for blood in his eyes. He wasn't finished with me.

"What?" he demanded into the phone. He stared at me, listening to the voice on the other end of the receiver. After a long moment, his features softened and relaxed.

At last, he said, "Fine." He ended the call and shoved the phone back into his pocket. Then, he adjusted his jacket and cleared his throat. He ran a hand through his dark hair, smoothing it and flattening it into place. Finally, he smiled with what seemed like relief. "I'm terribly sorry, Logan," he said in a strangely polite voice. "I may have overreacted a bit."

A bit? The cold sting of blood on the back of my skull told me that that episode was anything but "a bit" overreacted.

"I think we ought to return to the others and see just what they've found." He smiled triumphantly at me, and I knew something terrible would soon follow.

He marched his way around me without so much as a glance in my direction and headed down the hallway. I would have remained in that room if my stomach wasn't turning with uncertainty. What could the others have found that would have instantly calmed—or at least soothed—the rage of a madman? Either they had found Ascalon, or they had discovered something that would appease his anger for the time being. Either way, it couldn't be good.

I scrambled to my feet and jogged my way down the hall after Cain, who had already emerged from the dormitory and had left the door wide open.

I froze in my tracks as soon as I stepped outside. Standing encircled by Arianne, Ridley, Wolf, and Cain, was Emma, and in her hands was Ascalon. Her blue eyes were wide with fear and craze, like she couldn't believe herself or what she had done. How had she found me?

Cain turned on his heel and faced me. "I thought I made myself perfectly clear, Logan," he said in an unsteady voice, on the brink of exploding. "YOU WERE SUPPOSED TO COME *ALONE*!"

I stared at Emma, dumbfounded. "I...I did. She must have followed me here!"

"Oh, how convenient," Cain sneered. "And how convenient that she holds Ascalon *in her hands*!"

"I came on my own," Emma declared, her voice shaky. "Logan had nothing to do with it. He didn't even tell me where he was going."

Wolf made his way towards her, reaching inside his coat for what could only be a gun. He froze as Emma faced him and pointed the lance towards his face. "Cain may not be able to die today," she said, "but *you* still can! *Get back!*"

Wolf stared down at the golden spearhead and took a nervous step backwards.

"How dare you?" Cain shouted. "Who do you think you are? You can't wield the power of Ascalon!"

"No, I can't," Emma agreed. "But Logan can. And even if you kill me, *he* will still be here to finish the job."

Cain stared thoughtfully at her as a tiny smile crept over his face. "Kill you," he repeated. "Now, that sounds like a good idea."

It all happened in the blink of an eye: Cain reached into his coat and removed a gun, Emma's eyes grew wide, and the weapon fired.

Then, she fell to the ground screaming, and Ascalon dropped from her hands.

I didn't remember running towards her or coming to her aid—the world had gone black for several seconds. But the next thing I knew, I was on the ground, cradling Emma in my arms. Her beautiful green-blue eyes stared fearfully up at me as she gasped for air.

The bullet had only pierced her shoulder. She would live. But that didn't relieve me—in fact, it enraged me.

"She brought it upon herself, Logan," Cain called to me.

I lowered Emma to the ground and rose to my feet, my chest heaving as I struggled to control myself. "You went back on your end of the deal," I said through clenched teeth.

Cain ran the hem of his shirt over the muzzle of the gun to clean it. Then, he holstered the weapon and shrugged. "She has compromised the deal."

Ascalon lay at my feet. In an instant, I retrieved it and held it before me. Ridley, Arianne, and Wolf reached for their weapons, but Cain put a hand up to stop them, glaring at me. "He can't die. Don't bother."

They hesitated and glanced between each other. Cain sighed and stared down at Emma as she lay on the ground in agony. "She has undoubtedly brought the rest of the Order with her," he muttered. "We need to get out of here immediately before they reach us. Get the chopper ready."

"What about the kid?" Wolf asked.

Cain narrowed his eyes at me. "I'll take care of our little Dragonlord."

Wolf glanced at me. For a moment, he almost looked guilty, like he felt sorry for me. Maybe he knew how much trouble I was in—unlike my previous confrontations with Cain, he would hold nothing back.

I stood protectively before Emma and aimed the spearhead towards Cain's buddies as they made their way past me. They glanced nervously at the tip of the glowing spearhead as they passed by. They wouldn't dare attack her with me standing before her and Ascalon in my hands.

Emma gripped her wounded shoulder, groaning in pain as she tried to drag herself away from the scene of the crime. Cain glared at me, his mouth set in a firm grimace. "What exactly do you think you're going to do with that, Logan? Have you forgotten that I'm as invulnerable to death today as you are?"

During my short-lived victory of acquiring Ascalon, I had forgotten about that one important fact. I hesitated, my fingers tightening around the shaft of the weapon. He would be able to heal himself, no doubt, but he would still be susceptible to injury, and that injury could take him out of the fight long enough for me and Emma to get out of there.

I lowered the lance, exhaling in pretend defeat. "You're right."

I paused. Then, with a battle cry, I lunged forward and stabbed Ascalon deep into his chest.

Cain choked on a gasp, and his eyes widened until I thought they might pop out of his head. He grunted as blood poured from the wound. I shoved the spearhead as hard as I could, forcing him backwards and away from Emma. When he was a safe distance away from her, I yanked Ascalon out of his chest, preparing to make a run for our escape.

But he wouldn't let me go so easily. Cain grabbed the shaft of Ascalon before I could remove the spearhead from his chest. "Did you think this would stop me?" he asked in a chillingly calm voice. Blood oozed from the corners of his mouth. He gripped the lance with both hands and pulled it out of his chest, wincing and groaning as the sharp blade retracted. I stood frozen in place with wide, disbelieving eyes.

With one quick movement, he yanked the weapon out of my hands and swung the shaft at my head. My vision blackened, and I crumpled to the ground at his feet.

"Really, Logan," he sighed, adjusting the weapon in his hands. "By this point, I would have thought you'd learned."

My vision began to adjust, but I couldn't bring myself to rise and face the consequences of my actions. Once again, my brilliant escape plan had done nothing but return Ascalon to Cain, obliterating my only chance to defeat him and Bolla.

"Well, little cousin," Cain sneered, "it seems as though there will be no convincing you to join me in my efforts. That leaves just one option, and as much as I would love to watch this next part unfold, I have some very important business to tend to."

Thunder crashed and lightning stretched overhead, an appropriate backdrop for my villainous cousin. He turned around and stretched his arms out. Ascalon glowed in his right hand, submissive beneath his control. "O, GREAT DRAGON!" he shouted to the stormy skies above. "SERVE ME! DESTROY THE DRAGONLORD!"

My stomach dropped, and I knew what was coming.

Bolla rose from over the cliff's edge—seemingly out of nowhere—and hovered in the sky, roaring and breathing a funnel of fire into the air. Her wings flapped steadily, sending currents of air away from her monstrous body.

Cain turned and faced me with a delighted grin. "Well, Logan," he said, "if you want Ascalon so badly, I suppose you can have it."

He held the spear laterally before him. Then, he raised his knee and snapped the lance in two pieces across his leg.

"No," I whispered. My heart stopped beating for the briefest moment.

Cain tossed the broken lance down on the ground before him and backed away with a helpless shrug. "Sorry, Logan!" he shouted over the rolling thunder. "It seems you'll have to think outside of the box for this one!"

The helicopter on the grassy patch in the distance fired up. Cain climbed into the cabin alongside Ridley and Wolf, and the helicopter lifted off the ground under Arianne's control. "So long, Dragonlord!" he shouted, mock-saluting me as they ascended. "And don't worry about Bolla! I can always find another to replace her!"

The last I saw of Cain Hunter was his devilish grin, then the helicopter disappeared.

CHAPTER FIFTEEN

THE DRAGONLORD'S BANE

I didn't have time to think about anything but Bolla hovering over me.

I scrambled for Ascalon lying at my feet and snatched it up as Bolla breathed a pillar of fire at me. I dived out of the way just in time and ducked behind one of the dormitories, crouching down beside Emma. Bolla's wings flapped in the distance as she sought me out.

I fumbled with the broken pieces of Ascalon, hoping I could simply wish them back together. I cursed under my breath when it didn't happen. "What are we supposed to do? Ascalon is useless!"

"No," Emma grunted, gripping her wounded shoulder. "It should still have power. You can use the spearhead."

I stared down at the broken shaft in my left hand and the spearhead in my right. The pieces were still gold and glowing, but the color was fading. When the color finally disappeared, I doubted it would ever be useful again. I needed to move fast, before the power of Ascalon faded completely.

But what was I supposed to do? I needed to get directly underneath her and stab Bolla in the heart, something that I knew I couldn't do without being scorched to death.

"Logan!" a voice shouted across the way.

I poked my head out from the side of the dorm and saw my father, David, and Julianna crouched behind another dormitory fifty feet across from me. Bolla must have seen them, too—she curiously floated her way towards my father's voice and away from us.

"Logan, stay there!" my father shouted. "I'm coming over to you! Julianna is going to buy us some time!"

I nodded and crouched low to the ground at Emma's side while my father returned to David and Julianna, discussing a plan of attack with them.

I turned my attention towards Emma and away from the dragon lurking nearby. I hoped that the others would be able to keep Bolla away long enough for Emma to escape.

She grimaced in pain—her skin had become pale and sweaty. I planted myself at her side and reached a hand around her shoulders to help her sit up. "How badly does it hurt?" I asked.

"A lot more than I ever imagined it would," she replied with a strained chuckle. "The movies don't make it look *this* bad."

"I'm just glad he missed."

"That makes two of us."

I stared thoughtfully up at the gray storm clouds above. "How did you find me?"

"The arrow I shot you with had a tracker embedded inside of it," she replied. "The arrowhead released a tiny bug into your blood stream."

I glared at her. "So, I'm like a walking cell phone now?"

She grinned. "Only to me. The government can't trace you or anything. Don't worry. And it was designed to dissolve into your blood stream after twenty-four hours. Think of it as a biological global positioning system."

My head was spinning. "Where did you get technology like *that*?"

"My father made it for me."

"He must've been a genius."

"He was," she replied with a faint smile. "After all, that's how he met your father."

"I thought he was some kind of historian."

"He was some kind of everything," she said. "To the average eye, he was a weapons manufacturer for the U.S. military. He designed prototypes for revolutionary weapons—some, the military used. Others, they tossed out—like the arrowhead I shot you with. They didn't think it was ethical, thought it might be an invasion of privacy or something. But my father was incredibly smart. And beneath all of that, he was a superhero."

I smiled at her. "I wish I could have met him."

Her smile faded, and she lowered her head. "Anyway. After I shot you with that arrow, I was able to follow your footsteps. I told the Order all about your plan of escape, and we set out after you."

"Thanks for keeping my secret," I murmured.

She frowned. "Come on, Logan. You didn't think I'd just leave you on your own, did you? Our job is to protect you. Especially when you make stupid decisions."

I rolled my eyes and rose to my feet. "Well, I'm going to make another stupid one in about five seconds."

She raised her eyebrows. "What are you planning?"

I turned and looked across the way at my father. "You'll find out in a minute."

My father turned his attention back to me. Bolla hovered over the dormitory that they were hidden behind, roaring and clawing at the roofs, in an effort to expose them. Then, Julianna darted inside of the dormitory, disappearing for an incredibly long five seconds. When she emerged, she had a red gasoline can in her hands. She moved to the side of the house and ascended the ladder.

David stepped out of hiding and whistled a loud, high-pitched whistle. Bolla turned her attention towards him, and he waved his arms at her. "Over here, ugly!" he called.

Julianna raced up the ladder and climbed onto the roof. With Bolla preoccupied with David, she quickly dumped all of the gasoline onto the roof of the house. Bolla dipped towards David, trying to pluck him up with her claws. He took off running away from the others to lure her away. Fortunately, it worked.

Julianna clambered halfway down the ladder and reached into her pocket. A shiny metal object flickered in her hand, then a flame appeared. She whistled at the dragon, and Bolla stopped pursuing David and turned her attention towards Julianna. Her red eyes raged with anger, and she released a mighty roar.

Bolla swept towards Julianna, gliding across the sky. Julianna waited until she was directly over the house. Then, she tossed the lighter over her head onto the roof, and the building ignited in flames. Bolla screamed in pain as the hot fire scorched her belly and feet.

My father and David took advantage of the moment and sprinted towards us. They ducked behind the dorm, crouching beside us.

"I have an idea," I said. It was probably the worst one I'd had yet—and if you remember, I'd had quite a few terrible ideas as of late—but it was possibly the only way I could defeat Bolla.

I poked my head around the corner and glanced at the lighthouse in the distance. "I need to reach the lighthouse," I said. "Do you think you can keep Bolla distracted?"

"Of course," my father replied. "What are you planning?"

"You'll just have to see," I said. "Just keep her preoccupied until I'm ready for her to come my way."

"And when will that be?"

"When I get her attention. Until then, keep her busy." I turned towards David. "Can you get Emma out of here?"

He glanced at her, noticing the bullet wound in her shoulder for the first time. "Yes," he said with a nod. "We'll sneak out through the side and head down the road."

"Good," I said. I made eye contact with her, trying to communicate telepathically with her: *Be safe.* She must have understood—she nodded and set her mouth in a tight, determined grimace. She would be okay. At least that was one less thing to worry about.

"All right," I said, drawing in a deep breath. "Let's do this."

I rose to take off, but my father gripped me by the arm and held me down. He locked his blue eyes with mine. "Be careful."

I nodded. "I promise. Just trust me. I know what I'm doing."

He stared longingly at me before releasing his grip on my arm. David helped Emma to her feet and wrapped an arm around her to guide her. "Good luck, Dragonlord," he said, winking at me. Then, he sneaked his way around the back of the dormitory and disappeared towards the road with Emma at his side.

I drew in a deep breath and bolted out of hiding. Bolla was still screeching in pain from being burned. She had escaped the clutches of the dancing flames, but she was in terrible pain and she was furious. Julianna might have inadvertently made things worse.

I sprinted towards the lighthouse in the distance, blocking out all other thoughts from my mind. I hoped I could reach it before any distractions occurred, but I knew better than to wish for something like that.

My feet pounded on the grass, and the cold wind rushed past me, stinging my face. The lighthouse felt farther with each step I took, but I didn't slow my pace. Bolla screeched behind me, and my heart skipped a beat with fear. *Run,* I told myself. *Run, run, run.*

But no matter how hard I ran, no matter how fast I moved, Bolla still managed to get the upper hand—or, upper claw. A sharp, burning sting reached across my back as she sank her talons into my left shoulder and swept me off the ground.

There I was, dangling in her clutches, soaring two hundred feet above the ground. Her claws dug so deeply into my skin that I thought my arm would rip off. I screamed and wriggled against her restraint, but it was all to no avail. She released a victorious roar and soared into the distance, making her way across the lighthouse property. My father shouted my name somewhere down below.

Luckily, my right arm was free and unscathed. I did the only thing I thought might work: I waved the spearhead towards her, slicing across the air in an effort to pierce her in any way possible. She dipped and swerved across the sky, sensing my intentions. My arm continued to flail as I repeatedly slashed at the air, attempting to make even the slightest dent so she would release me. The shooting, burning pain was unbearable.

Bolla dipped down towards the earth, and I swung my arm again. Finally, I made contact. The spearhead slashed across her front leg, and she screeched so loudly that I thought my eardrums would burst. Fortunately, my plan worked, and she released her painful grip.

The bad part of my plan, though, was that the ground was several hundred feet below me.

I fell through open air towards the roof of one of the dormitories that hadn't yet been destroyed, swinging my arms and screaming. I crashed through the roof and landed in a heap of mess inside the building.

My entire body ached and throbbed with terrible pain, and my shoulder screamed in agony. I craned my neck and observed the wound that would inevitably become a scar, coming face-to-face with a gaping, bloody hole. Thick globs of black blood soaked through my sweater, and my stomach turned.

But it wasn't time to rest yet. With great struggle and determination, I pushed myself up from the debris and stumbled my way through the dormitory and back outside. Bolla was still in the air, but she was coming in for a crash landing. She swept in loopy circles across the sky, screeching in pain. Then, she plummeted towards the earth below, forming a crater in the middle of the lighthouse property.

She sat up, favoring her wounded leg. The slash I had made with the spearhead was illuminated with a silver-white light, oozing silver globs of blood. She tried to stand on all four legs, but when she found the effort to be too much, she crumpled forward.

It was my chance. I drew in a deep breath and charged towards her with my arm drawn back, ready to shove the spearhead into her chest. But as soon as I drew near, she sprang onto her three good legs and breathed a funnel of fire at me. I managed to avoid being barbecued and stumbled backwards onto the ground.

Good bluff, Bolla.

She soared into the sky once more, taunting me with another challenging roar. I returned my attention to the lighthouse in the distance. Thanks to Bolla, I had been set back by about fifty feet. I drew in another deep breath and charged towards the lighthouse yet again, ignoring the tremendous pain in my shoulder.

Bolla bulleted into the sky and circled above me, like a looming cloud of death waiting to unleash a lightning storm upon me. The lighthouse was only about a hundred feet away from me, but at that point, it seemed like a million miles.

Bolla descended in one swift drop until she was right over my head. Her talons grasped for me like a bird hunting rodents. Fortunately, the wound on her leg gave me an advantage—I wasn't about to be plucked up from the ground a second time. I ducked my head and swung the spearhead blindly, and she ascended once more. She continued to dip and swipe at me, drawing so close that I could feel gusts of air tickling the back of my neck. I was a field mouse, and Bolla was the vulture. She was toying with me.

"HEY!" a voice screamed in the distance. Bolla snaked her long neck backwards and searched for the source of the noise. I reached the base of the lighthouse and looked up to see my father standing on the roof of one of the dormitories, waving the broken, golden shaft of Ascalon in his hands.

She roared angrily and changed direction, determined to destroy my father and the threatening weapon in his hands. She rocketed towards him, grasping for him with her talons as she neared the roof. He ducked just as she approached and leapt to the ground, out of my sight. I hoped he would be all right, but I didn't have time to ponder it.

I threw the door of the lighthouse open and climbed the stairs two at a time. My chest ached by the time I reached the landing.

The lens was already active, rotating every fifteen seconds and blinding me with its bright light. I climbed onto the balcony and peered over the edge. Bolla was still preoccupied with my father and Ascalon.

"HEY!" I screamed. "HEY, YOU STUPID DRAGON! OVER HERE!"

She hovered over the building and turned her attention to me. With a mighty roar, she shot across the sky in my direction, no longer concerned with my father.

I tightened my grip on the spearhead and carefully climbed onto the railing of the balcony, balancing myself on the slippery metal fence. Bolla soared towards me, determined to destroy me.

This is it, I thought. *This is it, Bolla.*

She was almost to me when I heard a rocket fire behind me.

Wait a minute—a *rocket*?

I nearly slipped off the railing and fell towards the earth below—although it wouldn't have mattered anyway, since I was invincible. I climbed down and turned to face three F-35 Lightning jets hovering over the ocean. On their sides, three more jets raced across the sky, circling high above the lighthouse property.

The missile impaled Bolla in her chest and exploded, launching her backwards. But I knew that even military weapons couldn't keep the beast at bay. The only thing that could defeat her was the spearhead, and the only person who could defeat her was me.

Helicopters whirred in the distance, and within seconds, they were hovering over the lighthouse property. "Evacuate the lighthouse, or we will fire!" a voice boomed from the helicopter's speaker.

Great. I had become the target. If only they knew I was on their side.

But I didn't have time to obey. I returned to the railing and crouched, staring forward at Bolla as she recovered from the rocket's explosion. She roared angrily, and, to my dismay, turned her attention to the jets hovering in the distance.

I stood up so quickly that I almost plummeted to the ground seventy feet below. "THIS WAY, BOLLA! OVER HERE!" I waved my arms like a madman.

She hesitated in mid-flight, trying to decide who would make a better snack between me and the jets. I thought, surely they wouldn't destroy the lighthouse just to get rid of me. Surely, they knew how dangerous that would be…

But then, I heard the hiss and screech of a missile being fired. Time stood still as a silver bullet rocketed towards me. I only had a mere second to think.

They couldn't kill me, of course, but I doubted getting hit by a missile would feel any less painful than falling ten stories from the top of a lighthouse. I turned my head and glimpsed Bolla soaring towards me in what felt like slow-motion. She was fifty feet away. Then, forty…thirty…twenty…

I threw myself forward from the edge of the railing and soared towards the massive beast coming my way. Behind me, the missile collided with the lighthouse, and an explosion followed, so loud that I thought I would be deaf if I survived the day.

I plummeted towards Bolla like a cannon, spreading my arms wide and gripping the spearhead in my hand. I collided with her and flung my arms, searching for something to grasp. My hands scraped against the rough scales of her body, but before I could lose my grip and suffer a fifty-foot plunge, I found my grip around her neck.

Bolla would have thrashed me from side to side until I released my grasp around her, but the exploding lighthouse distracted her and sent her flying across the sky once more until she was hovering over the open sea below. That's not to say it wasn't difficult to keep my grip on her—try to imagine clinging to a massive tree trunk in the middle of a tornado. *That's* what I was doing.

As Bolla performed a series of barrel rolls, my heart thundered in my chest. I feared I would slip at any moment. Eventually, she straightened out her flight pattern and regained her balance, but she was ten times angrier than she had been, and she finally noticed that I was hanging around her neck.

This is it! I thought. My plan was a crazy one, but it was the only plan that might work.

I released my grip on Bolla with one hand, still clasping the spearhead and favoring my injured shoulder. My grip was slipping, though, and I knew I needed to act quickly.

Bolla roared and started thrashing, just as I had predicted. I forced my hand upwards towards her chest and shoved the spearhead between two of her iron-like scales.

I hadn't expected that it would hurt me as much as it hurt her.

As soon as the dagger pierced her heart, a blinding white light burst forth from where the weapon met her body. A sharp, terrifying pain ripped through my chest, so strong that I cried out in unison with Bolla's painful screeches.

She shriveled and shuddered, giving in to death's grasp. In the midst of my suffering, I released my grip around her neck and soared through the empty space towards the ocean below.

Was I dying, too? Had there been some kind of fine print that I had missed? Had the others known and refused to tell me to spare me the torment? Had my father known?

I clung to the spearhead, the only life force that I knew at the moment. I pressed it to my chest and closed my eyes as I fell towards the sea. Above me, Bolla began to disappear into a cloud of dust. Her entire being swept away along a current of wind. Her red eyes sought me out, raging with sheer hatred, but she knew she had been conquered. One last roar echoed, dissolving like a stifled cry for help. The great dragon disappeared as if she had been a mere hologram, unreal and imaginary.

I had defeated her, but the victory might have cost my life.

I collided against the hard surface of the ocean, and each of my limbs shuddered with pain. My body began to sink through the cold water. The chill was so sharp that I couldn't think straight, and at that moment, I didn't care to.

I was dying. I had to be. The pain that coursed through me was so intense that I couldn't feel it, which had to mean *something*.

I opened my eyes despite the stinging of the salt water and stared up at the ocean's surface above me. The light began to dissolve as the darkness of the ocean enshrouded me, wrapping me in death's embrace. Thick streams of dark blood oozed from the hole in my shoulder and drifted towards the surface, leaving a trail for any hungry sea creature to find me.

Then, I felt a ripple of water stir against my skin. I turned my head just enough to see a sea serpent slithering by.

A sea serpent?

That was enough to keep me from giving in to death just yet. I struggled against my pain and reached a limp hand towards the creature. It circled around me, its neon green eyes fixed upon me with curiosity. I considered that it might try to eat me, but it seemed more intrigued than hostile.

It looked like an eel, about fifteen feet in length, but it had several small fins protruding from its belly and it was covered in shiny green and blue scales. One long, transparent dorsal fin stretched from the end of its tail towards its head, which was long and narrow like a snake's. It even had a darting pink tongue.

From the darkness of the ocean, another sea serpent appeared. Together, they continued to encircle and observe me. Then, three more emerged from the depths. And then another two. Within a minute, there were ten sea serpents circling me.

I suppose I should have been afraid, but I was already prepared to give in to death. So, I watched as the curious sea serpents continued to circle me. Their speed increased to the point where I was drifting in the whirlpool they had created.

For a moment, I was floating. It was a peaceful way to go, I thought. I closed my eyes, allowing my body to relax.

Then, just when I'd gotten comfortable, the sea serpents dispersed.

Wait… I tried to call to them. *Don't go…*

I reached a hand towards them, but my fingertips collided with some invisible force preventing me from moving forward.

I looked down, and a sphere of golden energy had encompassed me. The sea serpents had trapped me in a bubble of water, so that I would suffocate rather than die by sharing Bolla's fate.

But before I could panic, I realized I wasn't in a bubble of water—I was actually in a bubble of *air*. The sea serpents had saved my life.

I gave in to my fatigue and passed out in the safety of my bubble of air.

CHAPTER SIXTEEN

THE VISION

For the first time in my life, I felt like a ghost.

I wasn't quite sure where I was. I felt like I was in between death and a dream. I knew I hadn't died, but I didn't quite feel alive.

Something inside of me had been sucked dry, had evaporated and dissolved completely, leaving me as an empty husk yearning for something fulfilling. A piece of my heart had been ripped out of my chest. I felt incomplete and empty.

When Bolla had died, something inside of me had died as well. Cain had once told me that I was connected to the great dragons, and that I could therefore share in their agony—then, I thought, he must have felt it, too. He had to know Bolla had been defeated.

He's alive... I heard a desperate, manly voice say. *He's barely breathing...*

It was my father. I had never heard him sound so panicked, so terrified.

I still couldn't see anything, but I couldn't have been asleep—the world around me was white, and not dark like it should have been if I were unconscious.

Come on, Logan, wake up...

It was a girl's voice this time, filled with concern, possibly even tears. Was that Emma?

We need you, Logan...

I tried to open my eyes, to see the people around me and assure them that I was all right. But despite my efforts, I couldn't move. I couldn't speak.

"It's not the end yet, Dragonlord," I heard a smooth, quiet voice say.

Then, things began to appear to me. Blurs of color emerged on the white canvas of my vision, coming into focus. I could barely make out my surroundings or see where I was. Then, my stomach dropped in horror.

I was in the sanctuary again, standing outside of Bolla's pit.

Had I defeated her, or had everything been a dream?

"You didn't think it would be that easy, did you?"

In a cloud of shadows, Cain materialized before my eyes, standing on the opposite side of the pit. This time, though, he looked different. His skin was a pale, sickly color. Dark circles had formed underneath his eyes, which had dimmed considerably, tinted gray with despair. Shadows swirled around him, as if he was on the verge of disintegrating.

Logan, please wake up! Emma's voice echoed across the dome, sending a mind-numbing ache across my brain.

"Don't worry," Cain said. "You're not dead. Not yet."

Then where am I? I tried to ask him, but I couldn't speak.

He peered down at the dark pit of Bolla's tomb, and his mouth twitched into a relaxed grin. Then, he looked straight through me with those haunted gray eyes. A shudder ran down my spine.

"You'll see me again soon, Dragonlord," he said. "Although, there is one way out. And I think you know what it is." He pointed into the pit and stared at it once more, releasing a low, evil chuckle.

Then, the colors of my dream swirled together, dissolving into a messy mix of watercolor paint. Cain's chuckle faded with the dream, and darkness followed.

CHAPTER SEVENTEEN

SAYING GOODBYE

When I awakened, I found myself tucked underneath warm blankets and lying across my bed.

My bed.

I sat up and gasped, finding myself in the evening's darkness. The bright moon hung low outside my window, watching me protectively. The computer screen hummed quietly in the corner of my room. Faint voices echoed beyond the closed door of my room, coming from downstairs.

I threw my blankets aside and climbed to my feet, collecting my bearings. Dizzy and lightheaded, I stumbled towards the window. I had to see this for myself.

I peered outside at our backyard, at the patio bench and my mother's flowerpots. Everything was there, just like I remembered it. As if I had never left Ashland in the first place.

I was getting really tired of wondering if everything had been a dream.

Sighing, I turned around and leaned against the wall. My stomach dropped through the floor, though, when I glimpsed Cain's face glaring back at me through the mirror hanging on the back of my door. I cried out and covered my face, stumbling to the side and tripping over a pile of dirty laundry.

I scrambled to my feet and dared to look in the mirror once more, but he was gone. I only saw my own eyes looking back at me.

Relief flooded over me, but my heart hadn't stopped pounding. *Calm down, Logan,* I told myself. *You're imagining things. That's all.*

A round of thundering footsteps sounded outside of my room as someone plowed up the stairs. My father threw open the door to my room and searched in every direction, looking for a dragon or Cain himself. He exhaled when he saw me standing safely in the corner—although I don't know how he could have been relieved, since I probably looked like I had seen a ghost. And in a way, I suppose I had.

"Is everything okay?" he asked.

I nodded. "Sorry." He must've heard me fall from downstairs. "I just, uh…tripped."

He forced a tiny smile. "No worries." Then, he pulled himself into the doorway and folded his arms over his chest. "How do you feel?"

I shrugged. "I feel…fine, actually. How *should* I feel?"

"Well, you've been out for three days."

My eyes widened. "*Three days?*"

He sighed and approached me, squeezing my good shoulder. My wounded shoulder had been wrapped in white gauze beneath my thin long-sleeved shirt, but I could still see the blood that had soaked through both the wrap and my shirt. I turned my head away. "It's a long story, son," he said. "Why don't you come downstairs so we can talk? Everyone else would like to see you, especially your mother."

My heart skipped a beat. "Mom? She's here?"

He chuckled. "Of course she's here. It *is* her house, after all."

When had I last seen my mother? It must have been at least a week—or maybe it just felt that way. The past several days had blurred together.

My father filed out the doorway with me tagging along behind, but I stopped at the threshold and glanced at my door. I wondered if Cain's face was still hanging in the mirror, waiting for me to return so he could watch me.

Calm down, man, I told myself again. *Cain isn't here. Relax.*

I drew in a deep breath and descended the stairs with my father, forcing all thoughts of Cain and the dragon out of my mind.

The living room was fully occupied by Julianna, David, Emma, and my mother, who sat on the couches with mugs of coffee like a couple of friends socializing after dinner. The sight was so shocking, I stopped at the base of the stairs and stared at them with confused eyes.

My mother was the first on her feet, her eyes wide with relief. She placed her mug on the nearby coffee table and jogged towards me, throwing her arms around me into a suffocating embrace.

"Logan," she whispered. "You're okay, you're okay, you're okay."

As if she hadn't believed it until she saw me up and moving around. I suppose I couldn't blame her, though—if I really had been passed out for three days, everyone probably thought I *was* dead.

I returned the bear-hug and inhaled the scent of my mom's strawberry shampoo. My heart filled with warmth over the familiar aroma, and I felt guilty for ever wishing that things would be different, for ever thinking that my mother alone was not good enough.

My mother, though, didn't even try to be modest. She pulled away from me and grasped my hand, smiling wide with glistening eyes. How had I ever thought Julianna could even come close to being as beautiful as my mother?

I squeezed her hand. "I've missed you, Mom."

She choked on something between a laugh and a sob. "The house has been so empty without you, Logan," she said. "When your father told me what happened, I thought…well, I didn't know what to do if…" She sighed and shook her head to clear her thoughts. "I'm just glad you're safe."

I smiled and squeezed her hand again. Then, I surveyed the faces of my allies standing in the living room, beaming at me with proud grins. I descended the stairs and entered the living room. Their eyes trailed me like I might do a back-flip at any moment.

Emma was the first to act. She threw her good arm around me and gave me a bone-crunching hug stronger than my mother's had been. Her injured arm hung awkwardly at her side in a sling, but it seemed she had recovered from the bullet wound for the most part.

Even though it wasn't the first time she had surprised me with her sudden affections, my heart still fluttered. "We thought we'd lost you," she muttered into my chest. "We thought you were gone for good."

I chuckled and returned the embrace. "Way to stay positive, guys."

Emma released me and stepped back, smiling up at me with sparkling aqua-green eyes. David and Julianna were much more modest than my mother and Emma had been, the former clapping me on the shoulder and the latter squeezing my arm.

"We owe you our lives, Logan," Julianna said, smiling at me with her sharp blue eyes.

"You fought like a real Dragonlord out there," David added.

I raised my eyebrows. "Are you saying you had doubts?"

He grinned and winked.

"But," Julianna interrupted in a loud, authoritative voice, "we still have a lot to discuss before we can relax."

I could feel the collective suppression of groans—from everyone including David and my father—but no one said anything or made a noise. We filed onto the couches like children ready for their bed-time story.

Julianna stood before us with her arms folded over her chest, glaring down at the carpet. She drew in a deep breath and stared past us at the opposite wall. "Cain is still alive."

We all knew that.

"And just because he succeeded in resurrecting Bolla doesn't mean he's satisfied."

We knew that, too.

"And there's also the question of Ascalon." She began to pace in a small circle. "It's been severely damaged, possibly to the point of being useless. I don't know how we'd even begin to repair it."

"Well, if Ascalon is useless," Emma chipped in, "then that means Cain can't use it. And then we don't have anything to worry about. Right?"

"Not exactly," Julianna answered.

"Not to mention," I spoke up, "the fact that just before he took off, he didn't seem too worried about me defeating Bolla. He's definitely got something else up his sleeve."

Julianna narrowed her eyes. "Such as?"

"Bolla wasn't the last," I explained. "He may not have Ascalon, but he'll find a way to get what he wants. I don't think Cain Hunter would have spent the past thirteen years on something like this, just to have it fall apart in seconds. He's got a back-up plan."

"Well," Julianna sighed. "We can at least be thankful that he didn't get *everything* he wanted." She focused her eyes on my father and David, and a little bit on me. Apparently, defeating a dragon and almost dying by it hadn't yet earned me recognition in the Order. "He still wants us. He wants to destroy the Order. And he's going to keep trying until that happens. It might not be next Saint George's Day, and it might not even be the one after that. But it *will* happen at some point."

"I'm not so sure about that," I interrupted, much to Julianna's annoyance. "He had plenty of chances to destroy the Order, and he didn't seem to care. Sure, he hates all of us, but he was preoccupied with other things."

She narrowed her eyes. "Other things?"

"Like convincing me to join in his efforts." My mother gasped, but everyone else seemed like they already knew that or had already guessed it. "He even said it himself: he doesn't care about what happens to you guys, so long as he had me on his side. All he wants is power, and he'll do whatever he needs to get it."

"So, what do you suggest, Logan?" Julianna asked in that bitterly polite tone, as if she thought I was a complete idiot.

I lowered my gaze, embarrassed. "Well, there isn't anything we *can* do."

She rolled her eyes. "*Suggestions* would be nice."

I shrugged. "What do you want me to say? I have no idea how we could—" I stopped mid-sentence, my eyes growing wide as one thought filled my mind.

I remembered my most recent dream—if it could even be called that—and I explained it to the others.

When I finished, Julianna was staring at me in that familiar convicting way of hers that made me feel like I had done something wrong. At least I knew I had hit a soft spot.

"What does it mean?" I asked. "It wasn't a dream. I know that much."

"You and Cain have a connection with each other," my father spoke up, and all heads turned towards him. He did not meet anyone's gaze.

I frowned. "What do you mean? How do you know that?"

My father sighed and leaned against the wall, crossing his arms. "Because I felt it with Ethan."

I glanced at Julianna, who, for once, didn't have that "I know everything" look on her face—even *she* seemed surprised by my father's revelation.

"Logan," my father said in a hollow, dismayed voice, "you weren't supposed to be born."

Ouch. Coming from anyone else, it might have been annoying—coming from my own father, it was like being punched in the face. I tried to force back the tears welling in my eyes. "Um…thanks," I muttered.

He shook his head and rose to full height. "Let me explain," he said. "The Dragonlord was sworn to only have one heir, to avoid the…*situation*…I was in with Ethan, and the situation you are in with Cain. But my parents were careless, and ended up having me a few years after my brother had been born. My father thought that somehow, Ethan and I could grow up and live together in peace. But…things changed." He glanced away for a moment before returning his attention to me. "Given our unusual circumstances, I would have been aware of Cain's birth immediately, and thereafter would have been forbidden to have a child. But since Ethan disappeared, we had no way of knowing if he'd had his own child."

"Well, it sounds like you were a little careless yourself, then," I fired at him. He hadn't meant to hurt my feelings by telling me these things—he was only offering the truth. But all the same, I wanted him to feel as empty as I did.

He shook his head again. "What were your mother and I to do, Logan? Wait our entire lives, hoping and praying that Ethan had never had his own child? That was too much of a gamble to make—the Dragonlord *must* have an heir."

That didn't really make things better. "So, I was just born to relieve you of your duties? Is that it?"

He drew in a silent breath, evidently struggling to be patient with me. I knew I was being difficult, but each word he spoke felt like a stab in the gut.

"That's not what I meant," my father muttered.

I sighed and collapsed into the loveseat, staring forward at the empty wall across from me. "So, about this connection," I muttered. "Explain it to me."

I could feel him gazing at me, wondering if I would be all right or if I would continue to pout and be angry—I *did* have a right to feel that way, after all—but after a hesitant moment, he continued. "Because there are two Dragonlords, you two are connected to each other. You can communicate with each other in a particularly *special* way."

"Does he know about this?" I asked.

"Only if Ethan made him aware of it, although I doubt he did. But we'll have to play it safe and assume that Cain knows."

"And if he does?"

"He can manipulate the visions you have," my father responded. "He can show you something that isn't there, or worse, draw you out by tempting you with something that *is* there."

I returned to my feet. "I don't care about that. I'm not afraid of him. If we can use it against him, we will."

"No, Logan," Julianna spoke up.

I faced her, confused. "What are you *talking* about? You're the one insisting that we figure out what to do—"

She held up a hand to stop me and shook her head. "That was before *this*. It's a big risk to use you this way."

"*This* way?" I scoffed. "But any other way would be okay, right?"

She glared at me. "It's out of the question."

I threw my hands up in surrender. "Fine. But I can't stop myself from having these visions. It's not something I can help."

"We understand," Julianna said. "But for now, it's okay to wait."

She was up to something. There she sat, insisting that we find a way to hunt Cain down and stop him, and in the next moment, she swore it was nothing to worry about. I knew it had nothing to do with her alleged sympathy.

But whatever she was up to, I would never know. Or at least, I wouldn't know for a while.

I flopped onto the couch once more and rubbed my eyes. For having been asleep for three days, I felt like I had only slept for a few hours.

Finally, my mother rose to her feet. "I think this conversation is over," she said in that soft tone of hers that still managed to be commanding. "Logan needs to rest. He defeated Bolla, like you asked him to do, and Cain isn't going to make another move for a while. He *deserves* to rest."

Thank you, Mom. She was the only person on my side at the moment—not even my father seemed concerned.

Truthfully, I was scared. I didn't mean to come across so angry and resentful, but I felt like the world was caving in around me, suffocating me with all of these horrifying revelations. As if defeating Bolla and stalling Cain hadn't been enough, finding out I shouldn't have been born and that I had a connection to my psychotic cousin only added to the situation.

Julianna stared at my mother with her convicting, calculating gaze for a long time, which made me angry. She was in *our* house—who did she think she was?

Finally, she forced a sympathetic smile. "You're absolutely right, Laura."

My mother wrapped a protective arm around me and smiled bitterly at Julianna.

"Well," Julianna sighed, "it seems we've overstayed our welcome, and we all have quite a lengthy drive back to our own homes." She retrieved her long black coat from the coat rack near the door and pulled it over her shoulders. Then, she approached my mother and extended her hand, smiling. "Thank you for your hospitality for the past three days."

My mother shook her hand and returned the smile. "Of course. The Order is always welcome here."

Julianna held her deceitfully sweet smile for several moments, then faced the others. "Take your time," she told them. "I'll meet you out in the car." Then, she turned and exited through the front door into the chilly spring evening.

I smiled inside. My mom was perhaps the only woman on the planet who could hold a candle to Julianna Thorne. How had I ever been worried about my father choosing the head of the Order over my own mother?

David and Emma donned their coats next, preparing to brave the cold weather outside. Surprisingly enough, though, my father remained standing near the wall by the stairs. I had expected he would leave with the others, would return to Ontario and disappear for another thirteen years. Was it possible that he meant to stay with us?

David approached me with a grin and clapped me on the shoulder. "You're a brave one," he said. He nodded towards my dad. "Just like your father over there. I'm proud to serve you, Dragonlord."

I couldn't help smiling.

David grinned at my mother and nodded. "Good to see you again, Laura," he said. Then, he offered me a two-finger salute and headed out the door. I wouldn't miss Julianna, but David had been decent company during my wild adventure. I would miss him.

I was eager to hear Emma's goodbye, and hadn't realized until everyone was heading for the door that I would actually miss her the most. Sure, she had been rather temperamental and difficult at the beginning, but in all honesty, she was probably the closest friend I had. I didn't want her to leave.

But my heart sank when the only dismissal I received was a tiny smile. Then, she headed for the door, following after David and leaving me alone with my mother and father.

The evening had been nothing but an unending series of slaps in the face.

I wasn't going to let her go that easily. The door had almost closed when I flung myself after her and threw it open, stepping out into the cold spring night in nothing but my flannel pajama pants, a long-sleeved shirt, and socks with holes forming in the toes and heels. "Emma!" I cried.

She had just reached the side door of the van—a *different* van, which I guessed Julianna had found the time to get a hold of in the past three days I'd been out. She turned and faced me, frowning.

I raised my arms into a baffled shrug and slapped them down at my sides.

"Logan, what are you doing?" she called. "It's freezing out here. Go inside!"

"What the heck was that all about?" I demanded. "Don't I get a goodbye from you, too?"

She sighed and closed her eyes. Perhaps she was angry with herself for not escaping before I made it out the door.

David and Julianna peered through the passenger side window at me and Emma. "I'll be back in a minute," she muttered to them. Then, she slid the door of the van closed and crunched across the icy path to our front door.

"Are you crazy?" she asked, climbing the steps. "You're going to catch pneumonia out here if you don't—"

"What am I now, chopped liver?" I cut her off. "I mean, after everything that's happened over the past few days, after fighting Cain and killing Bolla, after you got shot in the arm, after you saved my life who-knows-how-many-times, after—"

She put a finger to my lips and shook her head, but there was a tiny smile on her face. "Logan, stop." She pulled her arm back and drew in a deep breath.

I stared at her, waiting for some kind of explanation that would justify her leaving without saying goodbye.

Finally, she met my gaze. Her mouth was set in a firm grimace and all traces of her sweet smile were gone. "Look," she began, "I hate goodbyes. And I know I'm not going to see you anytime soon, which…sucks."

Sucks. There wasn't really a better way to put it.

"To be honest, you've been one of the best friends I've ever had," she continued. "I mean, I know we've only known each other for a few days, but it's been a nice few days. And I'm sorry I have to leave."

A lump had formed in my throat, and I was certain I was blushing. "Well, where will you go?"

She sighed. "I *should* go back to my aunt's house and live there, but Julianna insists it's not safe for me to be so far away from the Order with Cain still at large."

"You and Julianna?" I asked, trying to hide my surprise. "One of you is going to end up killing the other."

She rolled her eyes. "Don't be ridiculous. I can handle a woman like Julianna Thorne. We'll just have to see if she can handle *me*."

That was a good point. Julianna and Emma were like a volcano and a tornado. I would be eager to hear about Emma's adventures in Tahoe the next time I saw her.

"And that's not all," she said as a smile spread across her lips. "Julianna has appointed me into the Order. Can you believe it? After all this time, after everything that's happened, I'm officially going to be part of the Order!"

I drew back, my face displaying my evident surprise. "Seriously?" I asked, open-mouthed. "You get to join the Order?"

She smiled and nodded. "Julianna was so impressed with me, she appointed me into the Order without even asking David or your father, or even you."

"That's great, Emma! If anyone deserves it, you do."

Emma grinned. "So, it looks like I'll be saving your life a lot more times than I already have, now that you've got me officially watching your back year-round."

I scowled. "Hey, now. I survived for the past thirteen years without you and the rest of the Order. I think I'll be okay."

She raised her eyebrows and gave me a disbelieving look. "We'll see how that goes."

I sighed in defeat. Emma would never change, but I was grateful. In all truth, if it hadn't been for her, I *would* have been killed about ten different times in the past few days.

Then, Emma looked up at me again, and her eyes filled with tears. She smiled sadly at me. "I'm living my father's dream."

I placed a comforting hand on her good shoulder. "He would be proud of you, Emma. After all, this was what he wanted for you all along."

She nodded, and a tear trickled down her cheek. "It's funny, actually. I hadn't really thought about it that night when Arianne killed him, but when I set out to find your father and to protect you, I went into it thinking I wouldn't make it out alive. I hadn't planned what would happen after all of this. And now, well…" She glanced back at the van again and faced me with another smile. "It looks like I've gotten more than I bargained for."

I smiled, genuinely happy for her. After all she had gone through, she deserved to be a part of the Order, at the very least.

"I haven't really had time to think about him," she said, "but once I get home, I'm going to bawl my eyes out." She laughed at herself, but I didn't think it was very funny.

"Well, hey," I said. "If you need a friend to talk to, you've got one." I pointed at myself and grinned. "Call me or write me anytime."

She rolled her eyes and grinned. "I'll definitely be in touch. I don't have much of a choice, do I?"

I scoffed, but I managed a smile in spite of myself. "I guess not."

"Well…" she sighed. "I guess…I guess this is it, then." She reached her hand forward and smiled at me. "It's been fun, Dragon Boy."

I shook her hand, regretting that I hadn't gotten to know her better over the past few days.

Then, she released my hand and gripped me by the shoulders, pulling herself into me and kissing me on the cheek. She drew back and smiled. Her warm fingertips burned through my thin shirt. My face flushed, but if she noticed, she didn't say anything.

She released me and headed down the porch stairs, turning over her shoulder and waving. "See you next Saint George's Day," she called with a grin. Then, she rushed towards the van, threw the door open, and climbed inside.

Almost immediately, the van rumbled to life, crawling down the wet street and out of my range of vision. I touched the soft spot on my cheek where Emma had kissed me, and I blushed again. I was so warmed by the simple gesture that I didn't even notice myself shivering from head to toe in my thin pajamas, standing outside on the porch.

Between you and me, I had never had a girlfriend—that was the closest thing to it. But in spite of that fact, in spite of finding Emma to be the most beautiful girl I'd ever met with a personality that could start a fire, I would miss her friendship. I hoped that I wouldn't have to wait until Saint George's Day to see her again.

When I went back inside, it barely occurred to me that the van had left *without* my father. My heart skipped a beat when I saw him conversing with my mother, seated at the table while she hustled through the kitchen to prepare what I guessed to be—by the smell of it—beef stew with potatoes, carrots, and onions.

I stopped near the doorway and watched them interact, something that I had never been able to do before. They talked as if they had never lost a day between them, as if my father lived here and we were a happy family of three.

It was strange, almost uncomfortably so. I had spent my entire life wishing for my father, and there he was, yet all I could think about was how awkward the picture seemed to be. Surely, I had entered another dimension where my father and mother had been together their entire lives, where such a scene was perfectly normal.

My father glanced at me from across the dining room and rose to his feet. "You look like you're freezing," he said.

"I'm okay," I returned. I jabbed my thumb behind me, pointing to where the van should have been outside. "They left, you know."

He nodded. "I know."

"Aren't you…aren't you going with them?"

My mother rose from her bent-over position near one of the lower cabinets, clutching several bowls in her hand and smiling. "He's staying for dinner, honey," she said.

I must have looked either shocked or displeased—my father cleared his throat, and my mother frowned. "Is that okay?" she asked.

I nodded like a bobble-head doll. "O-Of course!" I insisted, my voice a high squeak. "I just didn't know he was staying…"

"Well, someone needs to watch after you," he said. "The rest of the Order lives too far away, and I…"

Wait a minute—was he going to *live* with us?

He frowned. "I can leave, if you want me to."

I shook my head at lightning-speed again. "No, it's not that," I assured him. "This is all just a bit of a surprise to me. I hadn't expected it, I guess." Then, I quickly added, "Not in a bad way, though! But a surprise, nonetheless."

He studied me for a long moment, eventually lowering himself into the seat once more. My mother returned to her task of making dinner.

I seated myself at the table with my father, realizing for the first time since meeting him that things were…well, awkward. The elephant in the room couldn't get much bigger.

For the past few days, we had only spoken about matters of Cain and Bolla, and anything else related to those subjects. While casually seated at the table for dinner, I had no idea what to say.

I cleared my throat and leaned forward on the table with my elbows. "So…what happened exactly? I remember stabbing Bolla, and then it felt like I was dying along with her."

"You fell into the ocean," my father explained. "I thought…I thought you had been…" He couldn't say it, so he cleared his throat instead. "Well, anyway. We made it off the lighthouse property before anyone could catch us. It pays to be sneaky sometimes."

"And after that?"

"We went down to the shore and searched for you for almost an hour. But we didn't find anything." He paused. "And then out of nowhere, you turned up, floating across the ocean like a beach ball."

I scrunched my forehead in thought. "You know, I remember something else, actually. After I fell into the ocean, there were a bunch of *sea serpents*"—I said it carefully, unsure of whether or not it had actually happened—"that saved my life."

My father stared thoughtfully at me. "It doesn't surprise me. You are the Dragonlord, after all, and sea serpents are like the distant cousins of the dragon. They knew who you were."

I straightened up with an excited grin. "So, are you saying that not all dragons are evil?"

He stared down at the table. "I hadn't thought about it that way, Logan. But I don't know if it would be wise to push your luck."

I waved a hand. "I wasn't planning on going up to them and asking. I was just wondering. If it were possible, it would definitely be a game-changer for the Dragonlord, though. Wouldn't it?"

My father nodded. "And for Cain, too."

Well, I hadn't thought about that. "You're right," I said with a frown.

"Enough talk about dragons and *that man*," my mother interrupted, entering the dining room with her crock-pot. She placed it right in the middle of the table. Then, she returned to the kitchen to retrieve bowls, spoons, and napkins, handing a set to each of us. "We're going to have a nice dinner without another mention of anything Dragonlord- or Order-related. Got it?"

My father and I nodded in unison.

My mother clasped her hands together with a pleased sigh. "All right, you two," she said, seating herself beside my father with a proud, beaming smile. "Dig in."

And we did, forgetting all thoughts of dragons, Cain Hunter, and the Order.

I didn't know what would happen the next day. I didn't know if my father would live with us, or go back to his home in Ontario. But at that moment, I didn't care. Having my mother and father together—even if it was just for dinner—was enough.

I poured myself a bowl of stew and dug into it like I hadn't eaten in days. I thought humorously of how it may have taken a dragon and my psychotic cousin to bring us together, but after thirteen years, my hopeless wish had finally come true.

ABOUT THE AUTHOR

CHRISTINA KENWAY is an author, a gamer, and a cosplayer. When she isn't working or writing, she spends her free hours creating costumes for conventions and adoring Batman. *The Dragonlord's Heir* is her first novel, and the first book in the Ascalon Trilogy.

Christina lives in California with her dog, Lucy, and her cat, Jayda.

Made in the USA
Charleston, SC
14 June 2014